The Time Bomb in The Cupboard and Other Adventures of Harry and Paul

Paul John Hausleben

ISBN: 978-0-9886336-0-5

DEDICATIONS

The Time Bomb in the Cupboard

To Ronzo, the entire gang, and all those who understand what Christmas cheer really is.

Harry's Resort

To all the folks on John Street then and now.

The Eye of the Tiger

To Harry and his awesome and wonderful 1975 Sonicmobile. I hope it is still rolling off in the night somewhere, the windows open, and the music blasting from its tape deck.

CONTENTS

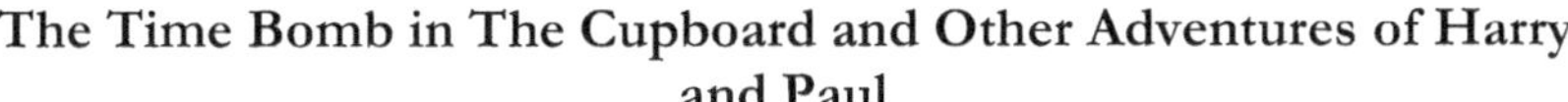

"I think that was part of the magic of this era of the 1970s. It was a time when simple things and events provided joy, and they did not cost a lot of money, or were very complicated. Oftentimes in our lives, it is the simple things that mean so very much."

Paul John Hausleben August 2012

ACKNOWLEDGMENTS

I would like to thank my friends and family and the many others who all supported my efforts in writing down these stories. Thank you, to Harry M. Rogers Junior. I also would like to thank Ms. Vivien Briar for her advice on creative writing. It turned out rather well. Thank you.

The Time Bomb in The Cupboard and Other Adventures of Harry and Paul

Preface

I enjoy looking back in time. I do it often, and I am not ashamed to admit that for the most part, I look back fondly on past times. I decided to create these simple stories about what I feel was a simpler and wonderful time. I included two central characters that become boyhood friends and form a bond that lasts a lifetime.

This book is a compilation of three stories that mark the beginning of when one of the friends decides to narrate his adventures in a memoir type format. The character provides his thoughts from a stream of consciousness, which is almost as though he is speaking to the reader in person with his New Jersey accent and authentic New Jersey, "speak." It is a simple theme, and one that carries the reader from their youth, all the way into later books, when they become grown men. These two friends support each other through thick and thin, and the bond they enjoy is really a once in a lifetime experience. The adventures take place in that weird and strange place known as northern New Jersey. For those who also grew up there, as I did, then I will not have to expand upon it. For others, it remains the strange, weird, and wacky place that it is.

I feel that the human element of life in the 1970s was so much more involved in our everyday lives.

It was my intention to capture a piece of that element, with these stories that poke fun at life, have a good touch of humor in them, as well as some heartfelt influences. They are really about some very special people who shared an awful lot together, changed, and shaped each other's lives through simple everyday events.

I would be remiss to pass this all off as total fiction as there really is some element of truth to these stories and characters. I can easily leave it up to the reader to decide exactly how much of the content actually is nonfiction. That may be part of the fun here!

I hope you enjoy the nostalgia, a look back at these simpler times, and enjoy reading these tales as much as I enjoyed writing them.

Paul John Hausleben

August 2012

A story for the Christmas season

The Time Bomb in The Cupboard

A story for the summer

Harry's Resort

A story for any season

The Eye of the Tiger

Prologue

Memories in time only pass if you allow them to. If you set your mind to it, then they remain with you forever.

I am Paul John Henson, and I can say that memories to me in my life, well, they are a friend, a constant companion to remind me of good times and of bad.

I feel that only you can decide which ones to recall or which ones to forget. Inside of all of us, when you try really hard, you can find there is a special capability to remember all the adventures of our lives.

Sitting around one day, I suddenly decided to begin to write down some of my life's adventures. It seemed to be time, a release of some sort for my soul. It was as if they just had to come out of me, for reasons that I could not really understand.

I just had to do it, so I picked up a pen, grabbed some paper, and started to write them all down.

"Oh, c'mon, Paul! For the love of Pete! Can you stop being an old lady and listen to me for just a minute or two!" Harry M. Redmond Jr. shouted at me. When I tried to interject some logic to my best friend into the current situation, we were about to get ourselves embroiled into this go around.

"Well, Harry, it is just that I think we should. . .."

"Oh, geezzzz . . . stop," Harry said as he walked over to me, put his big arm around me, and squeezed me as only he could.

He waved his hand in the air in front of us and said, "Oh, stop being such an old lady, will you, Paul! You of all people know that for Harry and Paul, it is one adventure after another, so come along for the ride and see where it all takes us."

The Time Bomb in the Cupboard

Chapter One

The Redmond Family

My best buddy growing up was Harry M. Redmond Junior. Even as a little kid and as a teenager, he was loud, bombastic, friendly, and outgoing. He had a mischievous side, but for the most part, he stayed out of trouble. He was a great friend to hang with; no one was more fun. Harry and all of his family were the same. They all were happy, gregarious, and over the top in everything, they did. There was no middle road with any of the Redmonds. There was nothing on Earth that he and his family liked better than a party, a holiday, or any kind of big shindig that you could ever imagine. The Redmond family was the happiest, most carefree bunch of people that I had ever encountered.

Harry and I were best buddies and we would hang around with our mutual friend, Jeff. All of us grew up within a few city blocks of one another, in a hard-core, old, gritty northern New Jersey town right outside the big city of Paterson. Harry and his family were unique in many ways, but one of the aspects of the entire gang that I remember the most was that they worked hard, really hard. In fact, they worked tremendously long hours during the week, from sunrise to sundown. Then, as hard as they worked, they also partied just as hard.

Harry's mother had passed away when he was young and shortly thereafter, Harry's father had then asked his oldest daughter, Linda Boatmann to move into the family home, along with her own family, to help take care of the house as well as Harry and his dad.

Linda was Harry's oldest sister, and she returned to the house which she had grown up in, along with her two children and her husband Ronnie. That was just some of the family, because, along with the humans, the house also had a menagerie of animals.

There was Cocoa, the world's smartest dog; there was Marshmallow, a tiny, miniature poodle, there also were rabbits, and birds, hamsters, fish tanks, turtles, and even at one time; a ferret named Finky! Everyone and everything crammed into this little; typical northern New Jersey Cape Cod house, and somehow, they made it all work. At times, it was a wild scene, with dogs running around barking, big and little kids screaming and yelling, and people laughing and carrying on in an almost constant environment of fun and excitement.

The most important thing was that everyone was happy.

Another detail about the Redmond family was that they were all big. When I mean big, I mean big all over. They were all big in size, voices, personality, and in life.

Harry's father, Mr. Harry M. Redmond Sr., was a large, round, jolly chap with a big belly, bouncing cheeks, a big deep voice, and a heart of gold. He was tall and had a thick shock of pure white hair that he swirled over to the side of his head. He laughed and smiled easily, loved his family and his work, as every man should, or at least, wished that he could.

Mr. Redmond always told us to look upon every day as an opportunity. It was good advice to us kids, in fact, good advice to anyone. He was the supervisor of a sheet metal shop where Harry became an apprentice when he was old enough to begin to work. Mr. Redmond ran the entire shop, as well as the work crews. Mr. Redmond left for work early in the morning, usually around four in the morning, and he did not ever return earlier than seven in the evening.

Ronnie Boatmann was Mr. Redmond's son-in-law. They got along wonderfully, almost like a son, and a father would. Ronnie was a heavyset guy, with a big, round head along with a thin, wispy beard that he trimmed close to his face.

Ronnie was also tall, and he had clear blue eyes and very light blonde thinning hair, and even though he was a heavyset guy, he was quite the handsome man. He would tell all the young neighborhood guys stories of how in his younger days, the young women would chase him all over town! It appeared that he also allowed a few of them to catch him here and there.

Ronnie had served in combat in Vietnam and he had experienced a difficult time over there. He never really spoke of Vietnam very much, just every once in a while. Ronnie was a maintenance electrician in a large building in downtown Paterson, and he too worked from sunup to sundown. People often referred to and spoke to Ronnie by his nickname, which was "Ronzo." In fact, he seemed very often to prefer that name, and he would actually use it to refer to himself in conversation. Ronzo was very smart, and he could engage in a conversation on almost any subject, from politics to history. He also was a happy, go lucky, type of guy. He was always good for a joke or two, and some of them that he had told us now that we were teenagers, I was very careful not to repeat to my parents!

Harry's sister Linda was also quite big; she was round and jolly like her father. Linda was always laughing and smiling, and she was very charismatic and pretty, with short brown hair and a big smile.

Wonderful people were the Redmond family; there was not a sad sack or nasty person amongst them.

The entire neighborhood would always come over to their house for these fantastic outdoor picnics in the summer, with weekend parties and shindigs that lasted from Friday night, all the way until late on Sunday night.

Holidays were extra special celebrations, with huge, wild, all out parties for the Fourth of July, Labor Day, Halloween and every holiday in between.

The Redmond's Labor Day picnics were legendary, and still spoken of in the neighborhood to this day, as often they were theme type picnics. Folks dressed up like cowboys for a western theme one year, the next year they held a Hawaiian Luau, and then the next year, it was a merry old England! The food, beer, wine, and fun never ended during these parties, and they provided lifetime memories of good times. The Redmond gang certainly was the hit of the neighborhood, and they loved every minute of it. It often seemed as if every person from the entire neighborhood would congregate there, and you never knew what kind of fun and excitement the Redmonds would come up with for the next holiday.

The masterminds of all of this holiday planning and merriment were clearly Linda and her younger sister, Patty. Patty was in age right between Harry and Linda and she was just as big, just as jolly, and just as much fun as the rest of the gang. Patty was married to George Pinia, who people knew by his nickname, which was, "The Big Spike." George had been the only person in our entire neighborhood that we knew of who went to college. He had been a power volleyball player in college; he stood about six feet seven inches and weighed about two hundred and fifty pounds.

George was one big man!

In college, George was a legendary and devastating player, who, because of his height and ability, would spike the volleyball down upon his victims, and inflict pain and torture on the opposition team. He earned the nickname and had the trophies on his shelf to prove it. While they did not live at the Redmond's house, George and Patty were always over at the house, and Patty worked with her sister to plan all the fun and activities.

Mr. Redmond always stood on the sidelines, smiling and funding these activities; he was the First National Bank of Redmond. The two sisters combined their innovative talents for parties along with the next-door neighbors, who were the Porters. The Porters were our other friend Jeff's parents, who were famous for always being the hit of the parties with their incredible creativity. One year, for the big Fourth of July party, Mr. Porter attended the party, dressed like Uncle Sam and Mrs. Porter attended, dressed as the Statue of Liberty. These outings led to some fantastic memories and fun. The famous Hawaiian Luau featured Mr. Redmond, Ronnie, and Mr. Porter dressed as hula girls. Now that was some sight to see!

However, no holiday, not the Fourth of July, not Thanksgiving, not Labor Day, not New Year's Day. None of them exceeded the all-out celebrations that went on for a Redmond family Christmas.

Nothing beat Christmas for the Redmond family.

Right after Thanksgiving, the Redmond family transformed their house into a winter wonderland right in the middle of urban New Jersey. They had lights all around the house, inside and outside, lights across the yard, and on top of the pool deck. They had wreaths on all the doors, and mounted on the outside of all the windows, plastic Santa Claus, and reindeer on the porch rooftop, and plastic snowmen, and elves all over the front yard.

Extension cords crisscrossed the paths, illuminating a waving and animated ground-mounted Santa Claus, along with lighted nativity scenes, candles illuminated the inside of all the windows, and candy canes lined all the sidewalk paths. It was a fantastic Christmas wonderland! A large-scale outdoor Christmas electric train chugged around the small front yard in a little circle. It would blow a whistle as it carried waving elves and wrapped gifts in the train cars, driven by a grinning, miniature Santa Claus who was leaning out the locomotive window.

There was a plastic, waving Santa strapped to the chimney on top of the housetop. His sled and reindeer were also up there, but since the house was small, there was not enough room for all of them to fit on the rooftop. Therefore, Ronzo scattered them here and there along the roof and fit them the best that he could. It looked like a haphazard landing for Santa on this rooftop!

They had twenty-four hours, seven days a week, Christmas music playing in a looping tape that Ronzo had rigged up, and piped to outside speaker systems mounted at the front porch, and in the backyard. In between the music, at the top of the hour, you were treated to a loud, "HO, HO, HO, HO, MERRY CHRISTMAS," which bellowed from the speakers to remind everyone in the neighborhood that Santa lived here, along with everyone else in the Redmond household.

Ronnie often utilized his talents with electricity and electronics and at Christmas time, his talents were particularly evident. Ronzo worked into his system that the "ho, ho, ho, Santa" was even triggered by motion sensors when someone came close to the house and set off the light beam to begin the bellowing Santa.

My personal favorite of all the Christmas decorations and animation was the front door bell for the Redmonds. Ronnie had rigged it up with an electronic chime that played "Jingle Bells" when you rang it.

They had everything!

The inside of the house was like Crumbley's Department Store during the holidays. Crumbley's was the largest store in downtown Paterson, and it was where we all shopped. Crumbley's store at Christmas was overwhelming with all the decorations. You could hardly move inside without bumping into a tree, wreath, or a plastic, grinning Santa Claus. The Redmond family would give Crumbley's a run for it, in the old decoration competition, that was for sure. They had almost as much in the way of decorations inside the home as they did outside. It was hard enough to move inside of the undecorated house with all the activity and people who lived there, but it was even worse during the Christmas season. Lights were all over the house, blinking and flashing in your eyes. Music was playing twenty-four hours a day, Santa Claus, reindeer and snowmen blew up balloons floated in the air.

Christmas, Christmas, Christmas, all over the place, wherever you looked, it was an extravagant Christmas celebration. It was fascinating.

The only item missing from the Redmond family Christmas at this time of year was the actual Christmas tree. The Redmonds believed that the tree only went up, and the family decorated the tree together on Christmas Eve after midnight mass at the local Catholic Church. This was a new notion to me, as my old man insisted that the tree went up two weeks before Christmas and we always had an artificial tree. The Redmonds could only have a real tree, and despite the fact that they decorated the entire house from top to bottom, they left the tree for last.

I was about to find out just how important a piece of the giant Redmond Christmas celebration that real tree was.

Actually, the tree was important, but this particular year, as the big holiday approached, there was one other item that I was also going to discover. That one mysterious item turned out to be even more important than the beloved Christmas tree, at least to some of them it was.

This one mysterious Christmas item caused an incident to occur in our neighborhood that continued to be the topic of discussions for years and years. In fact, there are still some folks who were involved, or knew of the incident that even now, gather here and there, and over tea, coffee, or their other favorite beverages, still tell the story of that Christmas long ago.

Chapter Two

Be Careful in the Cupboard!

I was always over the Redmond's house after school and on the weekends, hanging around with Harry, and having a great time doing all the things that a bunch of dopey teenagers would do. Jeff Porter would also come over on occasion after we all finished our homework. We were in a trade school now; all three of us attended a vocational school for our high school education.

We were around fifteen years old or so, early teenagers that were just getting ready for good times and constant fun.

It was right after Thanksgiving, in or around 1973, and on this particular day, I went over to the Redmond's house right after school. It was the time of the year that it became dark relatively early, so there was not too much time after school to do many outdoor activities. Harry had a big driveway with an outside spotlight, so we would go over to his house to shoot our street hockey pucks around in his driveway until it became too dark for us to continue.

Harry, Jeff, and I were shooting around in his yard this one night when we heard the big roar of the engine of Ronnie's sports car pull into the front of the driveway. Ronnie and Mr. Redmond always arrived home very late from work, so when they did get home, they were hungry, and the dinner hour was really becoming late. We went inside to say hello to everyone, and the Redmond family gathered around the kitchen table, getting ready for a big meal that Linda had prepared. Mr. Redmond came in and slapped us all on the back and he sat down, along with Ronnie, at the table.

Cocoa and Marshmallow were running around barking, Harry's little nieces and nephews were screaming and hollering, and there was a Christmas record that was playing on the record player; in other words, all was normal at the Redmond's house.

The transformation into Christmas madness mode had begun.

Patty and the Big Spike came by and Linda invited me to stay for dinner. It was beginning to turn into a typical gathering over at the Redmond's house, and as usual, it was full of laughter and fun. I called my parents and told them I would be eating over at Harry's and they were fine with that.

Linda went into the fridge to get her father and Ronnie some beers and she opened the door, reached in and asked her father, "Dad, do you want a Dingleberry or a Big Boulder beer?"

"Big Boulder, please Linda, those Dingleberries are way too sweet."

Ronzo piped in, "Honey, please, let me have a Dingleberry, would you?" Linda grabbed the beers and gave them to her father and her husband.

I was standing next to Ronnie by the side of the kitchen table, when Ronnie turned to me and asked, "Hey Paul, can you turn around there and reach up into the top of the cupboard and get my special, commemorative, Dingleberry beer mug? But when you reach up there, please be very careful of the Boryeungous!"

Ronnie was up out of his chair now, his voice becoming louder and he had a very serious look on his face. I looked at him, not quite understanding what he had said, but Ronnie was waving and motioning to me towards the top left-hand corner of the kitchen cupboards.

I opened the cupboard and asked Ronnie, "Which one of these is your special mug?"

Ronnie stood up a little from his chair, pointed into the deep recess on the cupboard to a large clear beer mug, and said, "That mug there. But, be careful of that big glass jar in there, in that dark, back, corner of the cupboard, and be sure not to knock it or disturb it! Close the door as soon as you can. I cannot get too much light in there, as it could spoil the mixture."

I quickly grabbed the mug and closed the door to the cupboard. By his intense reaction, I was afraid that some horrible penalty or punishment would come upon me if I had not complied with his instructions. I had to admit, it was now very intriguing as to what Ronnie had hid in the dark recess of the back of this kitchen cupboard.

"Oh, be careful, Paul. You do not want to go anywhere near his precious Boryeungous," Linda cautioned me.

As I handed Ronnie his beer mug, I asked him, "What is up there in the cupboard, booey, what was it?"

"Boryeungous," Ronnie answered without hesitation while taking a long, deep sip of beer.

"That is my special mixture. On New Year's Day, every year, I get out a large, special glass jar that came over with my family years ago, from Holland. It has been in my family for years and years," Ronnie explained between sips. "I then get raisins, dates, figs, apricots, and other little fruits, along with some very high proof whiskey and rum. My father had this special recipe of fruit and booze that he wrote down for my brothers and me to follow every year as a family tradition. I then mix it all together in the jar and heat it up very gently over a low flame on the stove, being very careful not to allow it to become too hot. You do not want too much heat to boil away the alcohol."

Ronnie became very animated in his explanation, and I could see how much of an intricate process this recipe really was.

Everyone was listening and studying his face as he reenacted the cooking process to prepare his special mixture.

"While the mixture is still hot, I seal it off on the top with a special cap and let it cool down. I then put it up in the dark corner of the top of that cupboard and leave it alone. I never even consider touching or disturbing it for almost a year until it is time for the family outing to get our Christmas tree. You see, if you break the seal early, then the mixture is ruined. That is why you have to be so careful!"

Linda then piped in and explained that Ronnie had been doing this every year from when they were first married and she added, "He guards it like a bulldog."

I was now very curious, as I had never heard of such a thing, and perhaps I may have overstepped my invitation a little, because I mustered up enough courage to ask Ronnie if I could look at it.

Ronnie looked at me suspiciously out of the corner of his eye and then he said, "Sure, go ahead, just open the cupboard door a little bit, and take a quick look so the light does not get in there. It has been fermenting for almost a year and light is the enemy of the mixture."

I opened the door to the cupboard just a crack and stuck my head in to take a look. All the while Ronzo kept a watchful eye on me to make sure I did not touch or disturb it. I could see that Ronnie moved the top shelf of the cupboard down in order to make room for the glass jar, which was about eighteen to twenty inches high and about eight or ten inches wide.

It was indeed a big jar!

All I could see was a bunch of raisins, dates, and fruit floating around in a dark mixture. In reality, there was not too much to see. I closed the door and looked over at Ronnie, who was smiling at me and nodding his head.

"This Saturday is the big day, Paul," Ronzo said with a coy smile. I was a bit puzzled as to why this Saturday was so special.

Ronnie explained, "We all head up to the country and pick out and cut down a real Christmas tree and that is when we open up and test the Boryeungous."

I could see the happy anticipation in Ronnie's eyes; it was truly a Christmas spirit to him.

Mr. Redmond then piped in, "You know, we are going to bring the big truck home from the shop on Saturday, because the entire neighborhood rides along with us and we need the truck to haul all the trees." With that classic big smile and twinkling eyes, Mr. Redmond continued with an invitation, "We have been doing this for years and years, and you and your family are invited."

Occasionally, I had seen the big truck in front of the Redmond's house and it was not a pretty sight. The big truck from the shop where Mr. Redmond worked was a huge old bomb of a truck that they used to haul around the giant, stainless steel counters that they made. The company that he worked for made stainless steel counters for the diners that were on every street corner in all of New York, New Jersey, and Connecticut.

The last time the big truck was in our neighborhood, a neighbor called the fire department because of the huge smoke bombs that came out of it. The poor folks were certain that one of the old abandoned factories that were quite abundant within our city blocks was on fire.

Now, my old man was a fake Christmas tree guy; not artificial, not plastic, he called it as it really was.

It was a fake tree.

I knew my parents would not be too keen on an excursion to cut down a tree, or freezing half to death walking around some woods, somewhere, to watch others pick out a tree. Yet this Redmond family adventure sure sounded intriguing to me!

"Where do you go to cut down your own Christmas tree, Mr. Redmond?" I asked, as now my curiosity had picked up considerably.

Harry jumped into the conversation as he sensed my excitement at the prospect of going along. Harry continued with some advertising for the event.

"We go way out in the country, Paul. Way out on this giant mountain, called Christmas Tree Mountain. Our family has been going to the same place for years," Harry explained as he moved closer to me from the other side of the room to push his sales pitch in person. "The guy, and his family that owns the mountain, knows us really well, and they give us special treatment. Everyone from the neighborhood is going this Saturday, and we all ride all the way out there. We set up a base camp with food and music. It is unbelievable! We climb to the top of the mountain, pick out and cut down trees, haul them down, and load them on the big truck from the shop. You have to go. It is a fantastic time!"

Linda, Ronnie, Mr. Redmond, and the rest of the gang nodded their heads and all encouraged me to come with them and the rest of the group. Jeff chimed in now and told me that he and his parents always go, and he testified as to what a great time it was.

For a kid like me, who had grown up in this urban asphalt and cement city, a trip out to the middle of nowhere to cut down a real tree seemed like a cool adventure. After all, we hardly even had trees in our neighborhood, let alone Christmas trees, so this sounded like a holiday scene that I had only ever seen on the front cover of a Christmas card. I promised the Redmond family that I would ask my parents, even though I knew they would not want a tree, but I sure would like to come along.

"Yeah, yeah, yeah, please ask your old man," Mr. Redmond answered. "Everyone in the entire John Street neighborhood is coming along."

After we finished eating, I went home and told my parents all about the big event planned for the weekend.

"No kidding." my father was clearly amazed at the description of the latest Redmond adventure. "How many people do you think are going?"

"Well," I started to count on my fingers. "Let me see, we have the Porters, all the Redmonds, Patty and the Big Spike, the Clipclocks, Joe Hinky Doo and his father, Billy Healy," and on and on I went, as my parents just sat there amazed at the size of this particular Redmond exploit.

As I had expected, my parents, after a few questions, gracefully bowed out of attending, but they gave me permission to go. I was fifteen years old or thereabouts at the time, and they knew that Mr. Redmond and Mr. Porter would be there, so we could not get ourselves into too much trouble.

Harry, Jeff, and I talked it up all week at school, with Harry constantly promoting the weekend. He was quite the salesman, and he had me whipped up into a Christmas tree frenzy.

"You know, there will be snow on the ground way up there on top of the mountain," Harry reported as we walked home from school. "It is all the way up near Pennsylvania."

"Wow," I said, "all the way out to Pennsylvania!"

I had never been that far out west before. The best our family would do was a trip into New York City to see a baseball game at Bugs Stadium or a trip in our 1964 Putter Classic model 200 to the New Jersey shore. As far as a trip on my own, it was unheard of. I never had an opportunity or an offer to go on an adventure such as this one before.

All during the rest of the week, all we talked about amongst ourselves was the upcoming trip. I am quite sure that I drove my parents and my sister crazy, going on and on over the dinner table about the pending excitement.

Just to add even more to the Christmas season feeling, on Friday during the day, it started to snow rather heavily. The storm left a crusty accumulation, along with an intense cold front that settled in for the end of the week. By nighttime on Friday, the snow had ended, and the day seemed to be breaking with very cold, but clear weather. I spoke to Harry one last time on Friday night, and he told me to make sure that I arrived over at his house very early.

Mr. Redmond would be driving the big truck back from the shop early in the morning, so I needed to be over there as soon as I could in the morning.

It would be a restless night for me as the excitement and anticipation were really growing in intensity now.

Chapter Three

The Trip Begins

Overnight, snowplows had cleared the roads, and they removed most of the snow accumulation from the roadways. I woke up very early to the sound of my old man pushing his snow shovel around in the driveway right outside my window. I lifted the shade and looked out my bedroom window to see just the very beginning of a red and yellow sunrise poking over the city skyline. It looked as if it was going to be sunny and very cold. The old steam radiator in my bedroom percolated little puffs of steam, while it creaked and cracked, in an effort to squeeze out a little heat into my room.

I jumped out of bed, grabbed the clothes that I had laid out the night before, and dressed as quickly as I could. My mum had insisted that I dress warmly, and she had laid out all types of cold weather gear for the trip up the mountain. It was just going to be me on my own without my family, one of my first excursions without them into the great unknown! This was a big deal for a kid from my neighborhood; you just never had a chance to escape that often. Little did I know that in a few short years, many more adventures out on my own awaited me, but that was still hanging out there on my horizon.

Right now, for me on this day, it was a Christmas adventure. Along with the entire neighborhood, we would all be heading up to Christmas Tree Mountain.

Mum had cooked up a hearty breakfast. This was even

after I had told her the night before that Linda and Patty assured me that they were going to prepare all kinds of food. However, you know how parents are, and my mum harped on me that I had to eat and that I needed the food, in order to stay warm, while out in the cold all day. I pulled on my hat, my work boots, and gloves, waved goodbye to everyone, and ran out the back door all the way to Harry's house.

I loved the cold weather; it did not bother me in the least, and this day was certain to test my mettle, as it was around ten or fifteen degrees. The sun promised some warmth, as it was just starting to peek over the horizon. I turned onto John Street and there it was, right in front of the Redmond's house, the big, giant truck from the shop.

It was an old, open rack body truck, and from what I could tell, it was once brown. It was an obvious veteran of many hauling jobs. Once, it was proud and straight, but it was now full of dents and dings and it was all rusty and worn. It had big, dual wide tires on the rear, and old, bent, metal stake racks lining an old wooden deck in the rear. It smelled like diesel fuel and I could see big ice chunks and snow stuck under the tire flaps. The truck had the name of the shop painted on the side of the truck in faded, old white letters. Through the accumulated snow and ice on the side you could read "Taylor Industries and Metal Fabrication."

Wow, I thought to myself, as I stared at the old truck, I hope this old bomb of a truck makes it all the way out to the country. I looked up and down John Street and all you could see were cars parked all over in every little available space, nook, or driveway.

The Redmonds never unplugged any of the Christmas lights or decorations; they just burned all the time. They left everything on twenty-four hours a day once the holiday season began. After Thanksgiving, that was it; they plugged all of it in and just let it go. I bounded up the front steps to go on the porch and set off the "HO, HO, HO" motion detector and rang the special musical doorbell.

"JUST COME ON IN!" someone shouted from inside and I opened the front door and stepped into a maze of people.

Harry and Jeff warmly greeted me and Ronnie immediately slapped me on the back. It seemed like everyone from the entire neighborhood was crowded into the Redmond's home. The crowds of people were all eating, drinking coffee and tea, laughing and talking. Some were in large groups, some gathered in smaller groups, but, as usual, everyone was having a great time. Linda and Patty had prepared a vast breakfast buffet spread out on a large folding table set up in the dining room. There were eggs, sausage, bacon, muffins, cornbread, juice, cups of hot chocolate, and anything else that you could ever want or imagine. People flocked around the table. Most of them were wearing winter vests and boots, and they were stuffing their faces and bellies full of food and drink. Christmas music blared in the background, kids were running around in every direction, and Cocoa and Marshmallow barked and begged for food handouts.

What a magical scene it was!

Everybody was excited and looking forward to a huge celebration. You could just feel the spirit in the air. Mr. Redmond called for quiet while he gathered everyone around in the living room. He was waving his hands over his head and motioning for the entire crowd to come in and hear what he had to say. A neighbor turned down the music, out of respect for the big man, who was running the show. Even the dogs and kiddies sat down to listen to him.

"Look gang, this is what we are going to do, so listen up, while I explain our plan." Mr. Redmond began his speech.

"After we finish breakfast, we are going to head out. Some of you have been many times before and know the way, but if you do not know how to go, here are some printed direction sheets for anyone who needs them."

He turned and handed the sheets to Jeff, Harry, and me to hand out to folks.

"The truck is a big one with sixteen gears and it is very hard to drive, slow, and ugly, but it will hold a lot of trees," he chuckled. "Ronnie, Bill Porter, and I will ride in the front of the truck, with the boys and Cocoa in the back, along with all the food, tables, ropes, tools, saws, and other supplies. The rest of youse guys can team up in your cars and follow us, or we will all meet at the base of Christmas Tree Mountain."

We started to hand out sheets to some people, and many people started to finish eating and get ready to pull out.

"It is going to be cold today, so make sure you bundle up. It is going to be a great day!" As Mr. Redmond ended his speech, everyone started to clap, cheer, yell, and holler. Christmas Tree Mountain was getting closer!

Even though this was my first experience with the annual trip to cut down trees, I could just feel the tradition as well as the excitement. For many of the neighbors, this was indeed the highlight of their holiday season.

"You boys are in charge of tying down the trees and keeping all the tools and supplies accounted for," Mr. Redmond instructed us. "We have saws, ratchet ties, ropes, and all kinds of supplies for the base camp, so we need your manpower."

The three of us nodded our heads in agreement; we were ready. I could now begin to realize what a major operation this was, and I wondered what the base camp consisted of. I did know that there was no one that could plan a party, event, or outing better than the Redmond family. Linda and Patty had a bunch of coolers and igloo containers. They were loading up food, hot chocolate, coffee, tea, and other supplies and they were working hard to clean up the breakfast buffet.

Jeff, Harry, and I helped them and we started lugging

out all the supplies, carrying them outside, and began loading up the back of the truck. Saws, tables, chairs, ropes, food, coolers, and all kinds of other gear all went on to the back of the truck.

Mr. Redmond was handing out work gloves to everyone who needed them and instructing them on the proper use of saws and chainsaws. "Please, we do not want anyone hurt!" He reported loudly for all to hear.

Linda brought out her portable cassette tape player, along with a large amount of Christmas tapes, and she asked me to put them inside the tool chest, on the side of the truck for safekeeping.

"We need Christmas music for the base camp," she explained as she handed me the equipment. We were loading up the truck when I noticed Ronnie come out of the front door of the house. Bundled up in a heavy coat, and with a Santa Claus hat on, Ronnie moved along slowly, carrying something under his arm, similar to how a running back would carry a football.

"PLEASE, DO NOT MOVE!" Ronzo yelled as he moved slowly and carefully down the front steps of the house. Everyone cleared the way, stopped in their tracks, and turned to watch Ronnie carefully navigate his way with his prized possession tucked safely in his arms. "Clear the way, stay away, stay away!" He was yelling out a warning.

The crowd moved away and a silent hush came over them all. Like the parting of the Red Sea, the crowd cleared a path to the truck for Ronnie.

I then realized that tucked carefully in his arms was his precious glass jar of Boryeungous!

Ronnie moved along with his jar, carefully watching his every move and step. Mr. Porter now joined in to help him, and he opened the door to the truck. No one moved as the tension filled the air. One wrong step, one little misstep, and all that incredible preparation and work would be lost.

It would ruin Christmas!

On the front seat of the truck was a specially fabricated foam container, custom made to fit the special glass jar, as well as a large, special leather harness that held it in place. Jeff, Harry, and I jumped down from the truck. We watched from a distance and held our breath, as Ronnie, and Mr. Porter carefully lifted the glass jar with the heavenly mixture into the container. The lid dropped down upon it and the jar strapped into place safely in the middle of the large front seat.

"Please stay away," Mr. Redmond yelled out to the anxious crowd. "We need to make sure the Boryeungous is in place, folks."

My goodness, how dramatic a scene it was!

Once it was set, Ronnie stepped back, exhaled a huge sigh of relief, and shook Mr. Porter's hand. The mixture was going to ride, front and center of the old truck, with the men guarding it with their lives. I looked at Linda, who was now shaking her head.

"Wow," I said to her, "that was a big deal."

"Oh, Paul, that is a year's worth of work . . . all for this day. That mixture has been fermenting for an entire year. When they bite into one of those raisins, then they will know how high a proof Ronnie has concocted this year, just by how the fruit tastes. It will set their mouths on fire, it could be a million proof for all we know, and it is a mixture that youse guys need to stay away from," Linda warned.

For all the men, it seemed to be a highlight of the season. It was obvious that this was some kind of traditional Christmas ritual, but for me, it seemed like an awful lot of fuss over nothing.

I was a long way from discovering the powerful effects of a bit of Christmas cheer.

We were all loaded up now, and a long caravan of cars began to line up on John Street. The sun was now up in a clear, blue sky, but it remained a very cold day. The snowplows removed most of the snow from John Street last night, but the blades had left a thin coating of polished snow upon the asphalt, and the coating had turned rock hard overnight. Everything now had frozen solidly and this snowy and icy world was daring the bright sunlight to try to melt it. Linda and Patty gave us some large, wool blankets to keep us covered and warm, and they provided us with a few old sleeping bags to sit on in the back of the truck. Harry whistled for Cocoa, and the faithful dog came running from the backyard. Cocoa, happily and energetically, jumped up next to us in the back of the truck. Cocoa, of course, brought his favorite squeaky toy, which was a large plastic pig whom we called Piggy. Piggy was the most annoying dog toy in the world, as it had the loudest squeaker that I had ever heard inside of it, but Cocoa would never dream of leaving home without it. It was now almost time to take off.

Mr. Redmond made the signal and waved to the caravan, and then Mr. Porter, Ronnie, and Mr. Redmond climbed up into the cab of the truck. Ronnie slid over to the driver's position and grabbed the wheel and gearshift. With a turn and twist of the key and a pump or two of the gas pedal, Ronnie started the big diesel engine.

BRRMMMM! BRMMMM! BRMMMMMM!

The big engine roared to life, with a big gargantuan bomb of dark, black smoke that spit out of the tailpipes. The blast and concussion of the engine turning over had set off the motion detectors on the front porch, tripped the music, and the Santa Claus voice. Ronnie put the big truck in gear and lifted the clutch and we pulled away to the sounds of, "HO, HO, HO" echoing from the speakers in front of the Redmond's home. Choking giant fumes blew out of the rear of the truck and encircled us like an atomic mushroom cloud. Ronnie was going through gears and shifting like a racecar driver and we had only gone about ten feet! The entire rest of the caravan fell into line behind us, and at least twenty-five cars began to follow the truck.

All of us went to Christmas Tree Mountain, making our way out of Haledon, New Jersey. Down John Street we went, turning out onto Belmont Avenue, then around to Burhans Avenue, and off to the main drag of Union Boulevard, we headed with the entire crew in tow.

It had been a cold night and the old truck was not very happy about having to roll in this cold. Slowly, we drove our way through the city of Paterson, making our way through the back roads of the city, crawling all the way to the interstate highway. I sat in the back with my buddies and Cocoa while we rolled off into the morning.

My first real adventure out on my own, and it was going to be a great day. I could feel the Christmas spirit in the air, off to some far-off distant mountain, to climb to the top and cut down real Christmas trees. I was building one of the first of a lifetime of memories of adventures with my buddy Harry and his family. Right now, I just did not realize how far I was going to travel with all of them on life's journey.

Chapter Four

Christmas Tree Mountain

Harry, Jeff, Cocoa, and I were huddled together in the back of the truck. All four of us were staying under the blanket that Linda had given to us. Our backs were all up tight along the rear wall of the front cab in a vain effort to stay warm. Cocoa kept his backside under the blanket and just stuck his head out from under the edge with Piggy stuck firmly in his mouth. Ronnie was driving with Mr. Porter, the precious jar, and Mr. Redmond in the front seat. We could hear all of them laughing and singing Christmas songs from the inside of the front cab of the truck. We turned and looked through the rear window and saw that all three of them were now wearing Santa Claus hats, and they were smoking big cigars.

The big, old bomb of a truck started to warm up more, and it was spitting out less black smoke from the tailpipe, but while the truck was getting warmed up, we sure were not! I loved the cold weather, but I had to admit that this was cold. The wind as we rolled along got underneath the blanket and worked into the layers of your clothes. We were used to playing hockey outside in the cold weather for hours on end, but at least then we were moving around. I knew that the three of us as well as Cocoa were tough and, to be honest, the excitement of the day was enough to keep us warm. Cocoa stayed as close as he could to us, as he was part husky, and he had a beautiful fur coat of light brown and tan colored fur, to keep us all warm. We sipped on hot chocolate and we were not doing too badly a job at preventing mass frostbite from settling in.

Ronnie turned the truck from Union Boulevard in Great Falls onto Route 46 northbound. He carefully steered the big truck onto the long entrance ramp, shifting gears wildly in an effort to gain some type of speed, without losing the four of us who were holding on in the back of the truck. The neighborhood caravan continued following behind us.

The car that was directly behind us was the Porter's 1969 Galaxy Super Glide 500 with Mrs. Porter at the wheel, along with Linda in the front seat and Patty, the Big Spike, and two neighbors riding in the rear. A few cars now broke out of the formation, passed the truck now that we were on the highway, and sped by us. These folks obviously knew the route to Christmas Tree Mountain and did not want the fumes of the truck to suffocate them any longer.

Now that the truck was attempting to hit highway speeds, there were big, black bombs of smoke puffing out the rear tailpipe every time Ronnie shifted.

Mr. Redmond stuck his head out the side window and yelled at us, "Are you boys doing all right back there?" I think he was concerned that we were all choking to death from the fumes. We answered that we were fine, and he went back to singing and laughing with Mr. Porter.

Cocoa thought for a brief moment that Mr. Redmond wanted to play a game of fetch the Piggy, so we had to tell him no and hustle him back in under the blanket.

Mrs. Porter gunned the big engine of the Galaxy and she moved alongside the truck to pass us up and head north. As the car raced by us, we all waved and yelled out to her, and she went to beep the horn and wave back.

Now, Mr. Porter was also quite the prankster, and unbeknownst to his wife, during the week he had installed an electronic device in place of the horn. When Mrs. Porter hit the horn, sure enough, out blasted a few loud and clear opening bars of "Rudolph the Red-Nosed Reindeer!"

Mrs. Porter shook her head and all of us howled in

laughter as we watched the Galaxy quickly out pace us.

Off Route 46 we went, over to Route 80, and across the wide-open interstate. The big truck rolled on, with some of the caravan still in tow. We went up and down hills and mountains, around twisty turns and curves carved out of stone hills, down long flat stretches of asphalt. We started to sing in the back of the truck, our own Christmas songs, and the men in the front continued crooning their own versions. Christmas was now in full swing!

The sun was now up high in the sky and it was beaming down in the early morning light through a crisp, clear blue sky. It was about a three-hour ride to Christmas Tree Mountain, and for an urbanized street kid like me, I might as well have been going to the moon. This was an adventure of a lifetime, rolling along the snow-covered terrain, taking in all of this fresh, clean air. We were used to the more polluted, heavy choking types of air that we had floating above us in our home city. This cold, clear variety of air sure was different. I hoped that my lungs knew what to do with it!

Gradually, the wide-open interstate gave way to a smaller, narrower road, and the terrain started to change to a rural setting with fewer and fewer cars and more open fields alongside the road.

Harry, who had made this annual excursion many times, chimed in and advised us, "We are getting closer guys. I recognize these roads and some scenery here. This is the last main road we are going to be on. We will now turn off by a big red barn, and drive up a little country road for a few miles. Christmas Tree Mountain is right at the end of that road."

Jeff and I felt the excitement building now. I started looking around to see if I could see the mountain off in the distance. The anticipation was increasing; even Cocoa was barking and moving around when he heard his master mention trees. After all, he was a male dog, and he would have an entire mountain of trees, all to himself.

Sure enough, just as Harry had predicted, Ronnie turned onto a frozen gravel, snowy country road. The big truck bounced as he made his way onto the frozen surface. Ronnie was expertly shifting gears and guiding the truck along the path, with a few of the cars behind us that were also feeling their way carefully along the icy road. I watched and noticed there was nothing alongside us on each side, nothing but open farm fields and hills covered in white, glistening, undisturbed, snow. We passed a few barns, and one of them had a small herd of cows hanging close to the barn doors, the steam rising from their mouths in the cold air. Until now, I had only ever seen cows on television, so this was a first for me. I strained my neck to catch a glimpse over the rack body of the truck at the cows.

I was now like a kid in a candy store as I looked over the undisturbed snow lying for miles and miles on the pastures. It was like a white heaven, framed by a wide forest of pine trees covered in clean snow, and crisscrossed with tiny frozen brooks and streams. The sheer beauty of the landscape was something that I can still remember, to this very day.

It was just like a scene from a Christmas postcard.

The road had now turned steeper, and slowly we crept our way up the road, with the truck tires clawing and grabbing at the surface to gain traction.

Harry jumped up from under the blanket and held onto the rail and pointed dead ahead as he shouted, "There it is, youse guys! Christmas Tree Mountain!"

Ronnie swung the truck into a hard-right turn, and we pulled into the base of the mountain, and parked on the side of a wide-open gravel driveway recently plowed of snow from edge to edge. Mrs. Porter had arrived earlier than we had, and she sounded the Christmas music horn loud and clear to greet us on our arrival. Some neighbors had also beaten us to the mountain, but slowly, the rest of the caravan that had followed along pulled behind us, and rode through the lot looking for a place to park.

We had finally arrived!

At the bottom of this large, snow-covered mountain was a red barn, and off to the side, there was a path leading up the side of the mountain. I looked up, and it seemed like the mountain towered to the sky. The landscape featured decorations here and there with clumps of trees scattered across the landscape, as if they were tiny points of bright green on a white backdrop. Next to the path was a small, brightly painted farmhouse, with a full farmer's porch wrapping around the entire exterior of the home. Everyone jumped out of his or her cars and trucks, and Ronnie cut off the big engine. The entire crowd was now laughing and greeting each other and discussing the long journey we had all made together to the site.

Mr. Redmond got out of the passenger seat of the truck, pulled his Santa Claus hat tightly down on top of his head, and made his way towards the farmhouse. Out the front door of the house came a long, lanky man, with a heavy wool coat on, and a knit hat on his head. He bounded out the front door and down his front steps, waving and shouting a greeting to us all.

"Good morning, good morning!" He shouted as he moved towards the large group now gathering in his driveway. It turned out that this man was Mr. Boatwright, the owner and proprietor of Christmas Tree Mountain. Mr. Redmond trotted towards Mr. Boatwright, and the two men embraced and exchanged greetings.

"How are you, Tim?" Mr. Redmond asked. "How has this past year treated you and your family?"

Mr. Boatwright answered, "I am doing just great, Harry. You are looking great. It is so good to see you!" It was quite a warm greeting between the two men.

In a loud booming voice, Mr. Boatwright continued, "Merry Christmas to you and yours, and welcome back for another year to the Boatwright's Christmas Tree Mountain."

Mr. Boatwright's entire family then appeared on the front porch and two dogs ran out of the barn to greet Cocoa. It seemed like one huge, happy reunion. This was a familiar scene to the participants, and it was clear to me, this same scene occurred repeatedly, many times before in past years. The Redmonds and their friends were celebrities who would come and visit once a year.

No matter where they went, it seemed as though people knew the Redmond family for their incredible charisma, charm, and fun-loving attitudes. They truly were infectious people, who you just enjoyed being around. Mr. Boatwright's son came out, and then Mrs. Boatwright, then a Boatwright daughter, then another, until the entire group was out in the driveway, meeting and greeting all the folks who had traveled so far to come and visit the mountain. They were not unlike the Redmonds, a huge, loud, happy bunch of people who seemed that they did not have a care in the world.

One of Mr. Boatwright's daughters was about our age, and the three of us noticed her right away, as she walked slowly towards the truck. She smiled at me, and Harry gave me a nudge in the side. She was dressed in a black overcoat, with a bright red hat and scarf, and the gal was very pretty, with a bright, but shy smile. We were just coming to the age where young women mattered and suddenly this little excursion had more pretty scenery than just the landscape!

Because Mr. Redmond was a longtime customer, it was obvious that he was going to receive special treatment. Mr. Boatwright called out to his son to run to the barn, and pull out the electrical power cord to plug in the diesel truck to keep it warm, so that it would start. The young gal looked back to me, waved, and then she followed her brother back to the barn to help him.

Ah yes, it was great to be a teenager.

It was bitterly cold here in the mountains and Mr. Boatwright was speaking to Mr. Redmond, Ronnie, and Mr. Porter next to the truck. "A lot of snow and cold on top of the mountain Harry, not like last year, when you could have come up here in shorts and tee shirts," Mr. Boatwright explained. "We really got hit hard this week with snow and by the end of the week; we had a good foot and a half here."

"Oh, not a problem, Tim," the never-daunted Mr. Redmond said. "I have all the boys here, Harry Jr. and his best buddies, Jeff and Paul. Look how big and strong they all are. They are ready to haul all the trees down from the top of the mountain and load them up on the truck for us."

Mr. Boatwright nodded his head. "I can see that, Harry. I will give them the wooden sleds to help haul the trees down the path. The path was groomed and plowed yesterday, but there could be a bit of ice on it, so your boys will need the sleds." Mr. Boatwright then turned to his son, who had just plugged in the electrical cord to the old truck's heater, and he instructed him to pull out the sleds and line them up at the base of the path. I thought to myself, this was like a Christmas wonderland. I never even heard of special sleds to haul trees down from mountaintops!

My goodness, this is all so amazing!

I thought about how much I was enjoying this while we all jumped down from the back of the truck. I was just thinking about wandering over to chat a bit with Mr. Boatwright's daughter, when Linda and Patty came over to the truck. Linda told us that it was now time to unload the truck and she then pointed to a clear spot right next to the bottom of the path and in front of the barn.

"Please set the base camp over there in that spot," Linda told us as she walked over to the clearing while still pointing in the direction that she had picked out. Patty saw me glance over to the young woman, and she came over to me, put her arm around me, and led me back to the truck.

"Work to do right now Paul, you can talk with the pretty gal later."

I smiled back at Patty, and I was impressed that she had read my mind.

"You caught her eye too, Paul," Patty said, while she pushed me jokingly in the back and led me over to the truck. "I can tell. All of us gals know these things. You will learn that. All that long blonde hair hanging out from under your hat, with that little beard starting to grow on your face, she thinks you are the bomb!"

Patty was awesome.

I smiled at her and she laughed at me, and she continued to push me towards the work. I jumped back onto the truck bed to help Harry and Jeff unload. Over by the barn, there were already tables and chairs set up by the Boatwright family. In typical Redmond family fashion, I then realized that the base camp was where the party headquarters was going to be. The Boatwright family, as well as the Redmonds, all seemed to be cut from the same mold. We started to unload the truck and the endless parade of coolers, containers, coffee, hot chocolate, and Jeff, Harry, and I handed down other assorted goodies to the ground team who set it all up on the tables.

Mrs. Boatwright had also prepared food and drink, and Mrs. Boatwright and her daughters carried various items out of their house and set it all up along with Linda and Patty. Some folks were getting cold, and they dove into the hot tea, coffee, and chocolate to get some warmth moving around within their bodies.

Mr. Boatwright had started a wood fire in a large steel drum set up over by the tables, and the enticing aroma quickly filled the cold air with a hearty wood smell. You could hear the snap and pop as the wood caught fire quickly in the cold morning.

It smelled like a little chunk of Heaven on Earth.

There is something about a wood fire on a cold day or evening, it just has an aroma that is like nothing else on earth. In the bitter cold, it was comical to watch as folks quickly gathered like moths to a summer flame, in order to warm up around the drum. After all the food and drink were set up, the music started playing. Soon the tape players were blaring out Christmas tunes, and all was well in the party world.

Ronnie suddenly stood there in front of the crowd, held up both of his arms over his head, and asked everyone to be quiet and listen up. Linda reached over and shut down the music for the moment so that we all could hear Ronnie.

Ronzo called out to the crowd, "It is now time to move the Boryeungous from the front seat of the truck! I have to ask you all to stand still, and move away from the main table, while we carefully transport it over to there."

Once more, it was a dramatic moment, and Ronnie played the crowd like a fine violin. A quiet hush came over the group, and everyone turned to the truck to watch. All the families, neighbors, and folks who had been milling around getting their saws, and work gloves, ready for the trip up the mountain, just stopped and froze in position exactly where they were. Even Cocoa and his dog pals knew that it was a moment to stop playing, and he and his friends immediately sat down next to Harry and watched. This was a serious moment.

I could once more feel the tension in the air as the decisive moment grew closer and closer. In my mind, I thought about how this was going to be a precarious journey from the truck to the table, and then across the snow and ice of the driveway. It was, as a diamond splitter must feel like before they strike the fatal blow.

Ronnie, Mr. Porter, and Mr. Redmond went to the cab of the truck and opened the side door. You could see Ronnie fiddling inside with the strap and special container. He undid the lid of the transport container. He stepped back, unzipped his jacket, pulled his pants up tight over his large belly, took his hat off, and then wiped his brow. Ronnie then took a deep breath and exhaled twice.

It was as if he was going into battle.

This was indeed some serious stuff! No one dared to move a muscle, cough, or twitch. Hold those sneezes! The tension was building as Ronzo reached into the cab of the truck.

All eyes in the entire country must certainly now be focused on this mission. The President of the United States himself was standing by in the White House Oval Office right next to the red telephone, awaiting news of the safe and careful delivery of the jar. I could imagine the news bulletins flashing across the television screens of the nation! I envisioned television audiences glued to newscasts and live coverage of the moving of the precious jar which interrupted regularly scheduled programming, in order to cover Ronnie moving his precious jar across the snow-encrusted terrain.

Ronnie lifted the precious jar up and out of the truck with his two escorts, watching his every move. Slowly, Ronnie moved and shuffled along the side of the truck, and then he carefully moved across the ice and snow to the front path, which led to the tables. Mr. Redmond, Mr. Porter, and now Mr. Boatwright helped Ronnie by holding his arms and back while walking along with him, as he slowly made his way to the table carrying the jar. One slip on this ice and snow and it could be a catastrophe!

Everyone just stood there holding their breath, some folks holding their gloves over their mouths and holding each other in fear of a little slip or nudge to Ronnie that could cause him to tumble. Ronnie made his way over to the special table that had been set up in the middle of the other tables. This table had a Christmas setting that the Boatwright family had prepared of a large holly ring in the middle, lined with red and white candles. This was obviously the place of honor for the glass jar to be set in.

As Ronzo was moving along, suddenly his foot hit a little patch of ice, and his right foot and leg slipped off to the side just a little!

"OH, NO!" In unison, the crowd gasped in horror. Ronnie, aided by his escorting support team, quickly regained his balance, and he was back on course.

"It is all right everyone, please remain calm. We have it under control," Mr. Porter bellowed out.

It was only fifteen feet or so from the truck to the table but it seemed like miles, and it was an eternity waiting for Ronnie to make it to the finish line. The tension was tremendous, and it was nerve rattling.

Ronnie finally reached the table, then he very carefully lifted the Boryeungous up and over the holly ring, and down into the final resting place. Bedlam erupted into the cold morning air as a wild celebration broke out. Everyone cheered and clapped for Ronnie, and the rest of the men started congratulating each other in celebration. Ronnie turned to the crowd, bowed at his waist, and he was beaming with a giant smile that covered his entire face. His mission was now complete, and he was a hero.

In the White House and across the nation, America returned to normal once more!

The music turned back on, dancing broke out, glasses held high in celebration, and all was well in the land. Cocoa and the other dogs started barking and running around, and Ronnie waved his clenched hands over his head in a continued celebration, as the precious mixture of heavenly Christmas cheer was now in place.

What a moment!

I didn't even notice that during the entire time while my eyes were fixated on the transporting of the Boryeungous that Mr. Boatwright's oldest daughter had been standing right next to me.

"Wow," she turned to me and said, while smiling, "was that nerve wracking or what?"

I smiled back and answered her, "It seems to be the center of attention that is for sure."

I was just going to ask her what her name was, when Mrs. Boatwright waved to her, and she said a quick, "I have to go," and she dashed off.

I thought to myself . . . how she wants to speak to me, but she remains elusive, but she surely was a cute young lady.

Oh well, timing is everything in life, I guess.

Chapter Five

Up the Mountain

Now that the precious and immortal mixture of Boryeungous was finally in place, it was time to head up the mountain and pick out the trees. I was now even more convinced that no one on the face of the entire earth could throw a party like the Redmond family. Here we are in the middle of nowhere, at the base of a frozen ice, snow-covered mountain, and the Redmonds have music, booze, food, and a party going on.

I was sure that history was wrong. In fact, dead wrong. The great mountain climbers and their guides, upon reaching the summit of Mount Everest, most likely found the Redmonds already up there, set up with a table and chairs, holding their glasses together, waiting for them to arrive in order to get the party started.

It had to be a coverup of the truth. It just had to be.

While I stood at the base of the path and looked up, the mountain looked as if it went on forever to me. We all gathered our tools, supplies, and Mr. Boatwright walked over to us.

"I understand that you boys are going to be the labor here. You will want to each take one of these wooden sleds that we have here, in order to move the trees around in the snow. The sleds will help you bring them down the path off of the mountain."

We all nodded our heads in agreement at his instructions.

"You also need to take these tags and this marker," Mr.

Boatwright continued with his instructions. He handed to me, a stack of long, blank paper tags with thin wires attached to the ends and a black marker. I stuck the supplies down inside one of my larger coat pockets while I listened carefully to Mr. Boatwright as he explained the proper procedure.

"Whenever, people select their trees, please write their name on the tag, and wrap it securely around a branch near the base of the tree with the wire wrap. That way, you will be able to tell which tree is which, when you load them all up and go to sort them out at home. Load the trees up on the sleds and bring them down the mountain. My son and I will help you wrap them, and load them on the back of the big truck."

It seemed as if the team had designated me as some type of logistical coordinator of this operation, even though I was actually a Christmas tree procurement rookie. I must have looked like I knew what I was doing, but nothing could actually be farther from the truth.

The instructions seemed clear enough to me, and we were all ready to go. About twenty-five people moved in line. The three of us, along with Patty, grabbed the ropes for the sled. Together, we started the long trek up, what I thought were thousands of feet into the air . . . up the side of Christmas Tree Mountain.

Ronnie waved over to Linda for her to come over by him. When Linda came close by, he said, "You know, honey?" Ronnie was stammering a little here. "All the men and I are going to stay down here at the base camp. You have the boys to help you this year, and they are all big and strong. Besides, honey, baby doll, you always pick out a nice tree. You do not need me for that." Ronnie was buttering up his wife for an obvious ulterior motive, and Linda was looking at her husband with a knowing and suspicious eye. "We are all going to stay here and uncork the Boryeungous."

Ah, ha! Now the picture was becoming clearer as to why we dopey teenagers were such an important cog in this celebration wheel. All over the base camp, husbands were having the same type of individual discussions with their wives and families, and laying their souls bare as to why they were going to stay at the base camp.

Linda folded her arms and asked Ronnie, "You are not even going to come up the mountain even one time?"

"Well, honey, you know I would love to, but I made this special mixture this year, and I really have to take the top off myself and take the first taste." Ronnie fudged his way precariously through the confrontation. He looked nervously at his wife as he studied her eyes for a reaction as to how this proposal was going to be accepted.

Linda was not buying what Ronnie was selling, but she waved her hand at him and answered, "Well, I know you worked hard on your concoction this year, so be careful and enjoy it."

Linda, Patty, Mrs. Porter, and the rest of the wives were none too happy, but they accepted the situation. They moved on with the rest of us as we headed up the path. Cocoa raced ahead of us with Piggy held tightly in his mouth and he ran up the path. All the while, he kept looking back, as if he was pleading for us to move faster.

We started walking up the snowy and ice-covered path, dragging our transport sleds behind as we began the long climb. Harry, Jeff, Patty, and I turned around when we were about thirty feet up the path and looked down at the base camp over to the tables.

"Look!" Harry reported. "Ronzo is going to open it!"

We stopped on the path and turned to watch as all the men had gathered around the table while Ronnie unscrewed the top. We clearly heard a loud "pop" in the air even this high and far away from the base camp. A few men jumped back from the jar in surprise. Then Ronnie moved his nose over the top of the jar. He proudly signaled, and then gave his famous two thumbs up salute. The rest of the men gathered around to stare down into the jar while they broke out into a large cheer and joyous celebration.

All the men grabbed shot glasses, gathered around the jar, while Ronnie took the cups and dipped them into the mixture to fill them. Once all the glasses were full, the group moved over to make a circle around the large steel drum with the roaring fire.

They all gave a loud, "Hip-hip-hooray" cheer and down their gullets, the special mixture of joy and warmth went. The entire group of men erupted into a loud hooting, hollering, cheering, and yelling ruckus as they jumped up and down and shook their heads, almost as if they were in pain.

It was a wild scene! Bunches of the men went over to Ronnie and they were slapping him on his back and were congratulating him. Some less fortified men of the group still just stood in their tracks shaking their heads back and forth and smiling.

Linda sighed and said to us, "Let them have their fun. Come on, boys . . . let's go get some Christmas trees."

Up the mountain we went, towing our sleds, and higher and higher, we climbed. The path was long and steep, but even though it was snow covered, we did gain enough traction to make our way up the side easily. We stayed on the main path and looking out to both sides of the main trail were open fields with rows and rows of Christmas trees, all neatly lined up like soldiers at attention as far as you could see. The rows of trees followed the curves and twists of the mountain, planted in the valleys, as well as flat spots of the sidewall of the mountain.

Mr. Boatwright had sent his young son as a guide to provide us with support and direction as to the particulars of the mountain. Mr. Boatwright had decided to stay back with the rest of the men to sample the Boryeungous.

I guess he had other things on his mind beyond selling some trees.

When we reached a spot on the path about three quarters of the way to the top, the young man pointed out which trees were which, according to the various types and sizes.

He stood in the path and pointed in various directions as he spoke out to the entire group, "Balsams, spruces, black pines, yellow pines, and Fraser Firs." You could see his excitement as he individually announced the order of the trees while pointing to the separate Christmas tree rows.

I surmised that someday, he would run the entire operation when his father decided to retire, because he already seemed as if he was a tree expert to me. He showed and pointed out to everyone, the sizes of the trees in each row and explained, "Here are the six footers, that row over there, are about five feet high, and as you walk up the path here, the trees become larger in sizes, all the way up to ten or fifteen feet high."

When Harry heard the ten or fifteen-foot-high mark announced, he turned and looked at his sister Patty. Patty gave her brother a hand and head bob signal and pointed up the path; clearly, she wanted to head in the direction of the larger trees.

Now, the teams had broken off into different directions, and they each wandered into the rows on their own, in an individual quest to pick out the trees that they wanted.

Jeff went off with his mother, and Harry, Cocoa, and I stuck with Patty and Linda. Patty was a great gal; she was full of fun and adventure. She was big, and she was tough, and she was very strong. I had seen Harry as big and tough as he was; back down from his sister a few times.

Mr. Redmond often instructed Patty, "To get her brother back into line" and Patty was very willing to comply and bring order to her wayward brother's life.

"I want a big tree this year," Patty proclaimed. "In fact,

let's find the biggest tree that we can find. The tree should reach all the way to the top of our cathedral ceiling in our living room. I want at least a ten-foot-high tree, and you two have to help me find the perfect tree." Patty was on a mission and her instructions were loud and clear!

We tied our sleds off on a tree trunk and we made our way into the rows of trees. Linda had her eye on a smaller tree while she and Patty ventured up into the higher rows right on the very top of the mountain. Slowly but surely, folks from our group picked out trees, and you could hear the sounds of a chainsaw starting in the air, or the sound of a hand saw rubbing back and forth against a trunk of a tree. I would see some trees carried out to the sled, and I jumped into action. Grabbing one of the tags, I wrote the name of the family on the tag and attached it to the tree trunk. One tree, then another, then another, and I suddenly became a busy guy.

In the meantime, Patty and Linda were still wandering around, searching for the perfect tree. Jeff came along with a nice sized tree that his mother had picked out, and we tagged it and hurled it up on one of the sleds. One-by-one, people picked out Christmas trees, cut them down, and gathered them on the path to be loaded on the sled. Linda grabbed a nice six-foot fir tree that we easily cut down, tagged, and packed away on a sled.

It seemed as if everyone had picked out a tree. Except for Patty.

Through row after row, we wandered.

"Too small, too tall, too skimpy in the middle! These are, too big at the top, too skimpy at the bottom," Patty pointed out the flaws in tree after tree, as we waded through deeper and deeper snow at the top of the mountain, while checking out tree after tree. Patty was a finicky Christmas tree picker outer!

Harry was becoming frustrated with his sister and complained, "Come on Patty, these are great trees, please just pick one."

"No, no, Harry. I am looking for a special tree this year," Patty answered as she was standing in knee high snow while surveying the situation. It was obvious that Patty had a special tree in mind for her special way of decorating a tree. She had a large living room, with a tall cathedral ceiling and she really did need a big tree. Patty, unlike the rest of the Redmonds, put her tree up earlier; she did not wait until Christmas Eve to put up the tree. Patty would put on many lights, and then intertwine them with her special, Dinky the Orange Teddy Bear decorative lights.

Dinky the Orange Teddy Bear was a popular cartoon at the time, which was, in my opinion, a stupid cartoon. Harry's little nieces watched it all the time, and it drove us crazy. The cartoon was about a teddy bear whose best friends consisted of a male dog named Sniffy, a female fish named Finny, and the most peculiar character of the bunch, a talking fire hydrant named Plugger.

The fire hydrant did not get along very well with Sniffy for some obvious reasons.

The Big Spike despised the lights, as well as the entire decorating process, and he made it very clear to Harry that he wanted nothing to do with it. Harry claimed in private to us guys, of an ulterior motivation for helping with the lights. He told us that George would slip him ten bucks, so that Harry would do all the work while he drank beer in the kitchen.

Harry stopped in his tracks, turned his nose up and complained to his sister, "No! C'mon, please don't tell me you are picking out a tree for those stupid Dinky the teddy bear lights!" Harry was now protesting the wonderful, ongoing tradition of the installation of the Dinky lights and all the merry joy they bring far and wide.

"Yes," Patty said. "I also bought about five more strings to add to my collection, so that is why I need a taller tree! You and the guys will need to come over and help us put them on." That is just the thing that Harry wanted his best buddies to hear, that his sister was counting on him coming over to decorate her Christmas tree once more, with Dinky the Orange Teddy Bear lights. Even to earn ten bucks, there is no way for a guy to live a thing like this down on the streets back home, no way for at least five or six years. In the quest for the perfect Patty tree, we had wandered off the beaten path and Mr. Boatwright's son came along to help guide us through some uncharted territory.

The view from the top of the mountain was spectacular. While Patty, Linda, Harry, and Mr. Boatwright's son debated over Dinky lights and trees, I walked along a little ridge and looked out at the scene. Miles and miles of crisp, untouched snow, and tree after tree, for as far as I could see. There was an old wire fence line about two hundred feet down from the edge where I was standing, and it was half buried in the snow drifts, with only the top of it poking out from underneath the snow. I can remember to this day, just standing there looking out over the hills, breathing in the fresh, cold mountain air.

I was thinking to myself, for a kid from the streets of Paterson, how this was absolute Christmas heaven. In retrospect, it was only a three-hour ride from where we lived, and it really showed how diverse the State of New Jersey was, going from a gritty, urban environment to the fantastic rural setting that we were all in now. Cocoa followed me to the spot where I was standing, leaping and jumping through the high snow, and he stood next to me, with his Piggy still entrenched in his mouth.

Even though he was a dog, he seemed to be also taking in the serene, quiet wonder of it all.

The wind was blowing fiercely along that ridge, and it shook you to your bones. But I loved it. I took my hat off and my long blonde hair blew out from under it. Like many young guys during this era, I wore my hair a little on the long side, after all this was 1973! It was just such a fantastic day that I was impervious to the bitterest wind or chill.

"It is pretty, isn't it?" A soft voice asked me from behind. I turned and looked, and there stood Mr. Boatwright's oldest daughter. Her presence had taken me by surprise, and I did not know what to say.

I searched for the right words, and simply responded with a low, almost inaudible, "Yes, it sure is. You sure are lucky to live here." I continued searching a bit for the right words. "Where I come from, it is a whole lot different."

"I have heard," the young woman answered. "Is that your dog?" she asked. "He is beautiful," she said as she reached down to pet Cocoa.

"I wish. He is actually Harry's dog, but he likes me, and follows me around all the time."

The young woman was now studying me carefully, and she smiled at me. Cocoa looked up at her and then back at me.

"He is a good judge of people," the young woman said, and she winked at me. She walked closer to me on the edge of the ridge. Her collar turned up on her coat in defense of the wind and her long, brown hair blew sideways under her hat from the gusts. I saw that she had large green eyes, and she squinted while trying to look at me in the bright sun.

"The cold does not bother you, you seem to not even notice the wind or chill," she said to me.

"No, I love it," I answered. "it seems, as if I have waited my entire life to this point, just to be able to stand on this spot and look out at this. It is the most beautiful sight that I have ever seen. I can see the hand of God in these hills and shimmering trees. It is really fantastic and you, well . . . I think you just add to how pretty it is."

There, I said it, and I meant it, as much as a young man of fifteen could have believed it. The young woman looked down, embarrassed, this brash kid from the city, standing on her family's mountain, flirting with her, oh my, what a time it was!

"Hey Paul, Cocoa, come over here," I heard Harry shout and the moment of peace was broken.

We all turned back to the tree stand, and I yelled back, "I am on the way! We better go."

"That is, it, Harry! Just look at how perfect that tree is," I heard Patty speaking as we walked closer. The three of us returned to the stands of trees, where Patty, Harry, and Mr. Boatwright's son were surveying a huge, giant Fraser Fir tree.

"Patty, it has to be ten feet tall," Harry complained.

"If it does not fit, we can limb the tree up from the bottom . . . yup, this is the tree. Harry, let's cut it down," was the definitive answer from Patty. She had finally made her final selection. What a tree it was! I was now wondering how we would bring it down the side of the snow and ice-covered mountain path.

We soon would find out.

Chapter Six

The Chase

Jeff and Mrs. Porter joined us now, as well as some more neighbors as they were all wondering what Patty was doing, with her considering cutting down this huge tree.

"Patty, that tree is huge. You will not have enough Dinky lights to fill that tree up," Mrs. Porter said.

"That will not be a problem. I can always pull out the extra Dinky character lights that I have in the attic if I need more lights." Patty reported in with a satisfied smile and her backup game plan.

Harry moaned and groaned about the Dinky character lights, having previously had to suffer through stringing endless; plastic molded and illuminated Plugger, Sniffy, Dinky, and Finny characters onto his sister's tree in past years.

We grabbed the handsaw and Mr. Boatwright's son walked over to Patty and told her what a great tree it was. He was a little sad to see it go, but he knew that if no one selected the tree soon, it would have grown too big, and no one would have ever enjoyed it. He was happy that it finally found a good home for Christmas. Harry, Jeff, and I worked the saw along the base of the tree and started to cut it down. We cut, cut, and worked at it, as it was a thick trunk. Patty jumped in, grabbed it, and pulled it over for the final cuts.

The tree gave way with a large snap, and it was down. We grabbed the tree and dragged it back to the path, with the entire group now waiting for us at the top of the mountain. This was a heavy tree, and it took most of our strength to drag it through the snow over to the waiting sleds. It was crowded now at the top of the path, as everyone was milling around and waiting for us to load up the sleds. Patty's tree was so big that we had to move all the trees around in order to put her tree on a sled by itself. It did not require a tag, as it was very easy to tell that huge, giant tree apart from all the others. All the trees were now tagged, loaded, and lashed to the sleds, and we were all now ready to head back down the path to the base camp.

This was going to be an adventure because we now had to navigate these sleds down this slippery slope. It was basically a point and hope type of operation, as you had to point the sleds in the right direction, and then hope that they made it down the slope. There really was no opportunity to steer them in any way.

Down the mountain we began. . ..

Since Harry was the biggest guy, he went ahead with the sled that was holding Patty's tree, and the rest of us lagged behind, working the sleds as best that we could. It was a slow descent, gradually with the loaded sled's weight pushing you along. Harry was a big, strong guy, but we could see he was struggling to make his way down the path, with that huge tree lashed to the sled.

The rest of the group, including friends, neighbors, dogs, and Mr. Boatwright's son and daughter, followed the group down the path, while staying in a group behind the sleds. Patty's tree looked like the annual Christmas tree that they put up every year, in downtown Paterson at Paterson Center, and we could hear Harry complaining and bantering with his sister over picking out such a large and cumbersome tree. Patty was ignoring him, or on occasion, she was answering Harry, with their usual sister and brother combative banter.

About halfway down the path, we could just now start to see the top of the barn and the base camp, when Harry stopped and turned to everyone and asked, "What is all that noise down there?" We pulled all the sleds to a halt, now stopped, and listened.

Coming up from below and resonating up the side of the mountain path from the base camp were many loud, male voices. They were all singing, laughing, hollering, and shouting at the top of their lungs. It sounded like a hundred men singing Christmas songs, or at least making some vain attempt at singing Christmas songs as loud as they possibly could.

Mrs. Porter had been leaning in, studying what the noise was all about, and she now spoke up, "It sounds like the men down at the base camp are singing. It sounds . . . well, it sounds like they are all half in the bag!"

Just as Mrs. Porter said that, Harry lost his grip on the sled with the giant tree!

Harry started running after the sled and tree, while Patty shouted out, "Harry, get it, get my tree!"

Harry was running as fast as he could behind the sled, when he realized that he was not gaining any ground on it and he made a last ditch, desperate dive for the back runner of the sled. Harry hit the snowy path with a thud, grabbed the runner, and held on . . . but only for a second. He lost his grip, and the sled broke away, bumped, and knocked into a snowbank on the way down the path. The sled gained speed and banged off one side of the snowy banks along the path, and then it glided across and hit the other side.

It was like a bobsled run in the Olympic Games.

Harry took off behind it, running hard in a vain attempt to catch up as it hurtled like a missile towards the base camp.

The big guy was now screaming and running the best he could down the snowy path. He was yelling the first thing, and the only thing that came into his mind.

"LOOK OUT, RUNAWAY CHRISTMAS TREE!" Harry

screamed at the top of his lungs.

The tree was careening down the side of the mountain like a rocket ship, with Harry in tow. Patty and Cocoa took off racing behind him in an unsuccessful attempt to warn the onlookers below. We all had our own sleds to handle, and we could not offer any assistance, so we just looked at each other in a hopeless manner.

"This is going to be a disaster," Jeff said.

There was a five thousand-pound-Christmas-tree-sled, loaded with a huge tree while flying down the path, banging off the sides of the snow banks and gaining speed, as it zeroed in on the unsuspecting, and what seemed to be, drunken, joy-filled, revelers gathered at the base of the path. Yes, Jeff was correct.

"Look out below!" Everyone, except for the group at the base camp, could hear Harry shouting. We all picked up the pace as best we could to make it around a bend in the path and see what was going to happen. We stood in horror at the scene evolving before our eyes. The entire group stood and watched while Harry, Cocoa, and Patty did their best to warn the men down at the base camp while the sled continued to fly down the path in front of them. They were screaming, Cocoa was barking, and Patty and Harry were waving their arms, trying to attract their attention away from the glory of the Boryeungous.

The group of intoxicated men really needed to look up, and see that. There was a sled with a huge tree attached to it approaching them at thousands of miles per hour. It was about to crash into them and pulverize them all to bits!

Suddenly, Ronnie looked up and heard the screams. Deep inside of his cloudy, booze-filled mind, he seemed to realize the danger they were all in, but rather than flee for protection, he realized that his precious mixture might actually be in danger. Ronzo ran across the bottom of the path, wrapped his arms around the jar, whisked it off the table, and carried it to the side.

All the men now gathered around Ronnie to protect him. It looked like a scrum in a rugby match, as the men were willing to risk life and limb to save the precious mixture. The sled reached the base of the path, zoomed by the group at supersonic speed, and crashed into the table holding the hot chocolate, coffee, tea, mulled cider, and donuts. Food and drink launched everywhere, and the resulting explosion of the table, urns, containers, and food all splattered over the base camp, as the men ducked for cover, still protecting the glass jar as items flew into the air like shrapnel. The sled and tree blew up the table, then impaled into a snowbank on the side of the base camp, and finally came to rest.

They saved the precious mixture!

The men were now laughing and rolling all over the snowy ground. They seemed to have already forgotten how close they all came to splattering all over the base of Christmas Tree Mountain. We all made it down to the base camp and parked our sleds when we realized the sight that was unfolding in front of us. The men were laughing and still singing, some were lying over in snow banks with their feet sticking up in the air, another group held onto each other with their arms wrapped around each other's shoulders and waists.

It was quite the scene.

Mr. Porter and Mr. Boatwright were singing a duet of some unrecognizable Christmas song, and then they collapsed together into a snowbank in front of the barn. Ronnie set down the glass jar. A few men came over with their little shot glasses, and Ronnie poured out the last precious drops of Boryeungous for them. I noticed that on one of the remaining tables, there was a plate full of fruit that the men were sticking forks into and eating the little bits that had soaked in the mixture. We all realized that all the men in the entire base camp were like drunken sailors hitting port; there was not a sober man amongst the bunch.

They could hardly even stand up!

Linda came down from the path and Patty ran over to the snowbank to check her tree. Harry, Jeff, and I helped her pull it out of the snowbank.

Linda and Patty walked over to where Mr. Redmond, the Big Spike, and Ronnie all were standing, or at least they were doing their best to stand.

"What on earth is going on down here?" Linda sternly asked, with her hands planted upon her hips. "What are you guys doing?"

Oh, oh, Linda was angry now! I was thinking that Ronzo was in some serious trouble now.

Ronnie could barely answer her and he slurred out with, "I am sorry honey, but I think the mixture was way too strong this year. I can hardly even talk or stand anymore."

Ronzo was gonzo.

Linda shook her head and said, "Ronnie, you are absolutely blitzed." Mr. Redmond was bombed, as well as Mr. Porter and Harold Clipclock, who were also three sheets to the wind.

The Big Spike turned to Patty, and he tried his best at speaking. After repeated starts and stops, he put his hand to his head and wiped his brow in an effort to inspire the words.

He finally managed to slur out of his mouth, "When I bit into one of the raisins it was . . . like a time bomb went off in my head!"

No sooner than he had finished the sentence, his knees and legs gave out, and the Big Spike crashed into a snowbank, gone and down for the count.

It turned out that it was a super-enhanced mixture this year and the fermentation process had turned it into a time bomb of alcohol. Let me tell you that the women in our group were quite angry over the outcome of the consumption of this year's holiday concoction. There were three or four of the neighbors that had simply passed out in the snow. They left them there, snoring their brains out, as everyone milled about, until a spouse or relative came by to wake them and claim them.

Ronnie and Mr. Redmond stumbled about doing their best to act sober and help. We unloaded the sleds and started to haul all the trees up onto the truck. It took all of our combined strength, in order to pick up Patty's tree and throw it up and into the bed of the rack truck, but slowly we were getting the job done. Back on the truck went the tables, the food, the music, and the containers. Up went the gloves, blankets, saws, ropes and other gear, and soon we were packed and ready to roll.

Mrs. Boatwright and her family jumped in place of her husband and she worked out the prices as everyone lined up to pay her for the trees. Mr. Boatwright was down and passed out in a snowbank. Therefore, he was no help at all. Mrs. Boatwright did not miss a stride in covering for her drunken spouse.

The base camp was broken down and Cocoa and his dog pals were in charge of eating all the food knocked over by the runaway sled and tree mishap. The Boryeungous had taken out the entire group of men. Most of them could not even stand at this point.

We were almost all loaded up and ready to go when Harry turned to Linda and asked, "Nothing for nothing, but who is going to drive the big, giant, truck back home? Dad is blitzed, Ronzo and Mr. Porter and the Big Spike are bombed too, as well as all the other men. What are we going to do?"

It seemed at this point to be a legitimate concern. It was a big, giant, diesel, stick-shift truck that seemed hard to drive even when you were sober.

'Here, we are,' I thought, 'stuck and trapped in the middle of nowhere. There are a bunch of drunk guys who sucked down all the Boryeungous, they are stumbling around too blasted to see or even speak. We have fifty or so, fresh-cut Christmas trees, one giant tree like the one in Paterson Center, all these supplies, all these people, and no one can drive the big truck to get us home!'

After a polling of the group and searching for one sober man who might be able to drive. It was looking mighty grim.

All of a sudden, Patty came over to the side of the truck. Confident, happy, Patty, fully equipped with her dream of her beloved Dinky the teddy bear lights, Christmas dreams, and her giant tree, all still fresh in her mind.

Undaunted, she walked up to the truck and proudly announced, "What are you guys worried about? I can drive this truck." Everyone looked at her and Patty said, "Sure, I have driven trucks for years. I have a commercial driver's license, stop all your worrying, and get on in. I can drive this truck blindfolded."

It was a done deal. Patty had come to the rescue! Now that Patty had solved the truck-driving dilemma, we turned our attention to the cars. We piled the men into the cars that we could, dividing the drunken men, and pairing them up with persons who could drive. We managed to get everyone into cars with safe drivers and still get everyone back home. Jeff, Harry, and I jumped up into the back of the truck, along with Cocoa and his Piggy.

The women exiled Ronnie, Mr. Porter, Mr. Redmond, and the Big Spike to the back of the truck with us, since they were still half in the bag, and hardly even knew where they were, anyway. Patty, Linda, and Mrs. Porter along with the now (thankfully) empty glass jar went up in the front cab of the truck. Another neighbor's wife took the Porter's car as it could fit a large quantity of drunk guys in the oversized back seat. Mrs. Porter warned the driver to be careful of the horn in her car, since it was a little tricky. The truck was unplugged from the cord and heater and it was ready to roll. It looked like we were finally packed up and all set to head home.

I was moving some things around to settle into the back of the truck when I noticed that Mr. Boatwright's daughter was standing next to the truck, looking up at me.

"Oh, hey," I said. "It was a great time, thanks for everything."

She looked up at me and said, "You're welcome, it sure was exciting this year!" I had to laugh at her correct assessment of the day.

"Well, one thing about the Redmonds is that it is never dull. Please, tell me your name." I leaned over close to the rails to speak with her.

"Debbie, I am Debbie," she said.

"Paul John Henson is my name. It was nice to meet you." I took my glove off and extended my hand through the steel rails. She did the same, and she handed me a piece of paper as we shook hands. I stood up and saw that it had her name, address, and telephone number written on it.

"Sorry, but we do not have a telephone at my house. We have to use my grandfather's phone next door," I confessed, "but I will try to call you sometime. For sure, I will send you a card from Paterson."

"That would be nice, and please come next year. Merry Christmas and goodbye," Debbie said. I nodded, carefully folded, and placed the paper in my coat pocket.

"Merry Christmas," I said just as Patty turned the key and the big engine came to life.

"Ah, just give her a big smooch, will you, Paul! She is a cutie," Ronnie blared out of his drunken stupor, while he sat next to me on a pile of trees. He was now wearing his Santa Claus hat and smoking a big cigar. "Forget all that goodbye stuff!"

Ronnie and Mr. Porter were starting to sing Christmas songs again. They now had put cigars in their mouths, and they were all wearing their Santa Claus hats again. The Big Spike and Mr. Redmond were leaning up on one another, sound asleep on a pile of trees. Patty slipped the big truck into gear as the giant truck coughed up the usual giant smoke bombs.

BRRRRRMMMMM! BRRRRRMMM!

Once more, the engine serenaded us with its loud roar.

Mrs. Boatwright came over to say goodbye, and she thanked us for coming and she added, "Maybe next year, Ronnie can tone down the old Boryeungous. This year's batch sure was potent."

I thought how that was an understatement! In reality, a time bomb hid in that cupboard.

Linda and Patty agreed, and with a last wave to everyone, the big truck started to move.

Chapter Seven

Upside Down trees and other Oddities

Patty spun the wheel, popped the clutch, and she shifted gears. We bucked and jumped a little and we banged our heads on the back of the cab, but Patty had the big truck rolling!

"Wooohhh!" Ronzo cried out as he teetered back and forth and held onto Jeff and me so he did not tumble over. "LADY DRIVER!" Ronnie bellowed out and Harry looked over to Jeff and me with a coy smile. Harry knew that if Patty had heard him, she would have parked the truck, gotten out of the cab and decked him with one punch.

Once Patty got the hang and feel of it, it was off to the races, down the snowy roads she steered the big rig, not really missing a beat. The men were still sloshed out of their minds, telling us what great kids we were, how God was great, and how wonderful the world was. All that the men did was to babble on and on with drunken gibberish layered in between verses of Christmas songs.

The afternoon was waning now, and it sure was cold. I could say that it was even colder in the back of the truck now than it was on the ride up to the mountain. Mr. Redmond and the Big Spike were still sleeping. Ronnie and Mr. Porter were just sitting there in a drunken haze with their hats on, with the cigars hanging out of their mouths, while they were singing intermittently. Many of the cars pulled away from us once we reached the interstate, because they now knew the way home. However, Patty just kept the big truck rolling steadily along. We noticed a large amount of big, giant fumes and clouds of smoke coming out of the tailpipe; we surmised that since the truck was still cold, it was smoking like a steam train.

"Wow," I said, "the old truck, sure is smoking."

"Yeah, yeah, yeah, that is because it is so cold out," Harry answered. "This old truck hates the cold weather."

We were riding along southbound on Interstate 80 heading for Paterson, with a huge cloud of smoke following us, when all of a sudden; we heard police sirens sounding as if they were getting closer. Even through the smoke bombs, it was easy to see the flashing lights of a New Jersey State Trooper's cruiser making its way down the highway behind us, and we all watched as the car worked from the hammer lanes, all the way over to the slow lane where we were traveling.

He rode right up behind the truck with his lights flashing and the sirens blasting when the trooper got on his P.A. system. "The big truck with all the Christmas trees, pull over there, pull over!" The speaker blared.

"Oh, no!" Jeff sounded off. "Patty is getting pulled over. What are we going to do? We have all these trees, and we have all these drunk guys in the back of the truck with us too!"

Harry leaned into us so the drunken men would not hear him. "Stay cool, stay cool." Harry warned. "I do not think there are any laws about hauling trees and having drunken relatives . . . even here in New Jersey." Suddenly, this was really turning into a nightmare of a Christmas adventure.

Patty pulled the big truck over on the side of the interstate. She stopped, and we waited. We could see the state trooper sitting in his car for a long time talking on his radio when he finally opened the door and slowly walked towards the truck. He put his big wide hat on and stopped at the rear of the truck while studying it for a long time. The trooper came up alongside the truck and looked at us.

The Big Spike was still soundly asleep on the trees. Mr. Redmond passed out and snored his brains out.

Ronnie looked at the trooper and slurred out in a long slow drunken drawl, "HELLOOOOO Mr. State Troopppppper!"

Mr. Porter then chimed in with a loud drunken, "Merrrry Christmassssss, Mr. State Trooper!"

The trooper just looked at them and then at us, and we simply said hello in unison.

"What the heck are you boys doing?" Mr. State Trooper asked us.

"Well, we cut these trees down for Christmas out in the country, and we are heading home to Paterson with them," Harry explained.

Cocoa then came over with Piggy, and he squeaked the toy into the rail in front of the trooper, hoping that he could entice the nice trooper into playing a game of "fetch the Piggy" with him. The trooper shook his head, adjusted his hat and gun belt, and walked up to the driver's door of the truck.

"Driver's license, registration, and insurance card, please . . . Miss," he boomed out to Patty.

Patty had the documents all ready at hand. She handed them to the trooper through the window, and looked the trooper in the eye and said, "That will be Mrs.! My name is Mrs. George Pinia."

The trooper frowned at Patty, and then he glanced down at the paperwork. "Oh, I am sorry, Mrs. Pinia," he answered while looking through the documents. "yes, I see that here, Pinia."

No one intimidated Patty, not even grouchy state troopers.

"Do you realize how much smoke is coming out of the back of this heap of junk, Mrs. Pinia?" The trooper asked.

"Well, I am sorry about that sir. You see, this is our work truck from the shop and we borrowed it. I am sorry. I am doing the best I can at driving this truck and it could be that I may be not shifting the gears quite correctly," Patty explained. "Do you see all the men in the back?"

The trooper cut Patty off and tilted the brim of his hat up higher on his head. "Oh . . . you mean all those drunken guys?"

Patty nodded her head, and she said, "Yes, those drunken bums back there are our husbands." Patty pointed to all three of the women in the front seat and then moved to Linda and herself while she continued.

"But the oldest one, who passed out and snored so loudly, he is our father."

The trooper shook his head a little, and he almost smiled, but instead he asked, "What on earth are youse people doing?"

All of a sudden, Mr. Porter broke into an intoxicated rendition of "Silver Bells" at the top of his lungs, and he was singing so loudly that he was drowning out the conversation between the officer and Patty. Jeff tried to get his father to stop singing, and Mrs. Porter was now angrily banging on the rear window, so we all joined in an effort to hush him up. We tried in vain to stop Mr. Porter from singing, as the trooper walked back to the side of the truck and looked at Mr. Porter with a suspicious eye.

Mr. Porter ignored us.

He was just happily singing "Silver Bells" along with his Santa Claus hat on, and a big cigar in his mouth.

The trooper walked back over to Patty and he said, "Look, you are going down the highway here. Where exactly are you going, Mrs. Pinia?"

"We are heading straight to our father's house to unload the trees. All the neighbors will be waiting for us," Patty explained.

"I realize that this is not your truck. Is this where you work?" The trooper was still digging for information.

Patty answered the trooper. "No, it is where my dad and

brother work. My brother works there part-time, he is one of the young men in the back, and he can tell you about the shop. Of course, my dad, he is asleep on the Christmas trees, and it would be hard to speak with him right now."

At that point, Patty also mentioned that the other drunken bum, snoring, drooling, and unconscious next to her father, is in fact her husband. The trooper tried hard to hold back a smile and remain his highly trained, stoic self, but he seemed like he had reached a point of too much information.

He answered Patty while moving closer to the window of the truck. "Please tell the owner of the shop to get this truck fixed because it is a hazard. It looks like a forest fire going down the interstate. I am going to let you go. Please just get these drunken men back to your home and get your trees unloaded."

He handed Patty the paperwork back, and Patty thanked the officer.

He turned and walked past us and we all yelled, "Thank you, sir!"

Mr. Porter stopped singing, "Silver Bells" long enough to yell out, "Merry Christmas!"

The trooper waved half-heartedly over his head. He walked back up the road towards his cruiser, while shaking his head back and forth, and went back into his cruiser. Patty put the truck into gear, pulled back out, and we were back out on the highway.

Slowly we made our way back. We could see the outline of the cities in the distance, and we were leaving the country behind. It was becoming later in the afternoon now, and the sky was getting that purple and red haze that it usually gets late in the day during the wintertime. The Christmas trees all piled in the back had a wonderful aroma that was quite enjoyable, while the heavenly scent drifted into the cold air.

Mr. Redmond started to stir, and Ronnie and Mr. Porter

were hugging each other, while sharing little bits of smuggled Boryeungous fruit and Dingleberry beer that they had stashed in their pockets. Ronnie and Mr. Porter were now both singing "Silver Bells" in a duet. Cocoa packed it in. I guess the drunken activity was too much, and he curled up and went to sleep, and the three of us huddled together, while we rolled along.

The Big Spike woke up, along with Mr. Redmond, and they sat next to the other men, had a few sections of the fruit, and joined in the melody. On occasion, the women in the front seat would pound on the window in an effort to try to get them to shut up, but they were oblivious to the whole situation.

Back we went, through the familiar streets of the City of Paterson, Patty working the gears, until we finally returned home and parked the truck in front of the house at good old 20 John Street.

All the neighbors were waiting as they wondered why it took us so long to return home. Patty apologized, and she explained the delay, due to an unexpected visit, with a representative from the State of New Jersey. First, we got the drunken guys out of the back of the truck, and then we unloaded the trees, handing them off to the correct people according to the names on the trunks. The truck was becoming lighter, and lighter, as we first unloaded all the trees and then the containers, the food, the coolers, supplies, tables, and tools. Everyone was tired now after such a long, long day and we unloaded in silence, being almost methodical in our work.

Remaining now, in the back of the truck, were very few trees, the Redmond's tree, the Porter's tree and Patty's giant tree were the only trees that still had to be unloaded. The unloading of the other trees and the supplies was now complete and neighbors waved goodbye, hugged each other, promised to be part of the trip next year, and thanked everyone for a great time. Jeff, Harry, and I unloaded the rest of the trees and tossed them on the ground.

The men had retreated to the backyard, while we were unloading the truck and there, they had started a big fire in a steel drum. They had quickly gathered around it, still laughing, singing, and having a great time as they slowly recovered from the impact of the mixture.

You see, I had come to realize that a Redmond family party never ends. The endless good times just never seem to expire. Just when you think they have sputtered out due to sheer exhaustion, they come back to life, and the party is back in full swing.

It was simply amazing!

Linda cautioned them to be careful to not burn the house down and Patty yelled almost nonstop at the Big Spike about various subjects, some of which dated back to the beginning of their relationship!

I think the women had their fill of the drunken revelry.

"One more thing to do, men, and we are done," Patty said as she met us back at the truck. I had never seen or heard of this one before and I have to admit that, in looking back, I have never seen or heard of it since then. It may have been a Paterson tradition, or it was a Redmond thing, but it sure was another interesting facet of Christmas with Harry and his family. Harry, who was a Christmas tree veteran, knew exactly what to do.

"Come on guys, grab these ropes, we have to drag the trees out to the backyard to the big oak tree, and get the trees upside down."

Now to me, the Christmas tree novice, I was confused as I could ever be, when I heard Harry mention upside down trees. I really had no idea what I was about to learn, but I knew that if it had something to do with the Redmonds . . . then it was going to be interesting. It took all of our combined strength to drag the giant tree to the backyard, and we set it down alongside the others, next to the large oak tree. The men were still around the fire, and they were all starting to come around and sober up.

"That's it, boys," Mr. Redmond piped up when he saw the ropes and us. "Get those trees up there in the oak tree and they will be nice and fresh for Christmas!"

Patty showed Jeff and me how to tie the ropes onto the trunk of the trees. Harry retrieved the ladder out of the garage and set it up on the trunk of the oak tree. He then scampered up the ladder and onto a large branch hanging out over the yard. We tied ropes on the Porter's tree, then the Redmond's tree and then Patty's tree. I then realized that the mission was to pull these trees up into the oak tree like giant icicles hanging from a roof edge!

Patty could see I was in awe, and I was dazed and confused, so she explained to me, "This is how you keep the tree fresh. You pull it up on the branch and let it hang there upside down until you are ready to set it up in the house. This way, all the sap runs back up into the tree, and it never dries up."

Well, pulling the first two trees up there was not too bad. Harry pulled and the three of us on the ground hoisted them up to him while we took the weight off the rope. However, pulling Patty's tree up that high into the oak tree was a major operation. Since the tree was so tall, Harry had to climb even higher into the tree to find a strategic branch. We lifted it, spun it, and swung it, then up the tree it went! Harry tied the ropes off and we were done.

What a Christmas card scene this was! It was not exactly a winter wonderland, a picture postcard scene made here in the Redmond's backyard. You had all these drunken men singing, "Silver Bells," smoking cigars, wearing Santa Claus hats around a big fire, framed by three Christmas trees hanging upside down from an oak tree, in the back of this house, in urban New Jersey. Not exactly what famous artists creating Christmas card scenes would have painted or imagined.

Of course, Linda had prepared food and coffee, and she was bringing out refreshments for the remaining group to enjoy around the fire. Ronzo and the entire group were coming back to reality now. The group had gathered around him, and Ronzo was receiving many congratulatory handshakes and slaps on his back from the men. They all agreed to what a wonderful job he had done this year in his preparation of the now historic Boryeungous.

Ronnie was now lamenting that it was all over, and the last fruit and drop of his grand creation was gone. He was already working and plotting on a mixture for next year.

Linda offered and suggested less potent solutions and recipes to her husband, but Ronzo shook his head.

"No, no, no, Linny," Ronzo denied the suggestions, "I may have made it a little too strong this year . . . but it really was not that bad after all."

If that was not too bad, I wondered what in the world he would classify as bad. I do not think the State of New Jersey could handle anything stronger; they may have to call in the New Jersey National Guard.

Ronzo looked at the three of us with a wry smile on his big round face, a sly twinkle in his eye, and he winked at the three of us. I knew that he was already formulating his recipe and concoction for next years' time bomb in the cupboard.

This long day, and all the magical adventures that had gone along with it, was finally ending. What a great day it had been, what a wonderful number of memories I had accumulated. Little did I know what other fantastic adventures awaited me. This was only the first big outing and escapade that I would share with my best buddy Harry and his quirky, but fun-filled family. I had hung with him and his family in their backyard, attended many backyard parties, and had some fun with him here and there, but this was the first of many out-of-town adventures we were to have together.

However, all those other adventures are a whole other story. In fact, to relate all of those stories would take up volumes of written words.

I tapped my coat pocket, opened it, and checked for the paper that Debbie Boatwright had given to me, and I smiled. I did write her a letter that next week, but that also is another story.

I rewound the day in my mind, while I stood and watched the flames flickering in the drum, and the occasional loud "pop" of some pinewood that threw some sparks up into the cold winter air. I stood next to the fire, listened to the conversation and exaggerations of the events that the men were now weaving into tall tales to last forever.

In my mind, I could still see the runaway tree careening down the side of the mountain. I could hear the singing of the men and the fresh smell of the cold, clear air. I sighed a little when I thought of that beautiful young woman and how bright and clear her green eyes were, as she looked at me, framed upon a backdrop of snow on top of the mountain. The look on that trooper's face when he spotted Mr. Porter and witnessed his individual Christmas celebration and rendition of "Silver Bells" was priceless!

Standing there, I could not help but think of how badly Mrs. Boatwright may have berated Mr. Boatwright for participating in the sampling of the mixture. There was no doubt that he was a big part of the now famous incident that lives in infamy to this day, on top of Christmas Tree Mountain.

Chapter Eight

Bang!

Right after New Year's Day of one year, I looked around on the internet for a recipe. Then I went to the hardware store where I found and then purchased a jar . . . the type of jar used for canning and preserving vegetables. It was one of those jars that you have a metal lid on to seal the contents and preserve it for a while. Following the instructions of the recipe, I threw some raisins in there, some dates, some apricots, and some figs. I mixed it around and then, according to the recipe, I added sugar, bourbon, and some rye whiskey, a touch of rum, and some molasses and honey. I stirred it all around again, carefully filled it right to the top of the glass, and heated it very gently over a low flame on the stove. While it was hot, I sealed the jar tightly, and placed it carefully in the top of a kitchen cupboard, way in the back, in a dark corner.

To be honest, I really forgot about it.

A couple of weeks before Christmas of that same year, I was sitting around the house with my wife in front of a nice, warm fire in our fireplace. We were listening to some Christmas music on a Saturday evening, just relaxing together in a quiet time. It had been a cold day; it was now a cold night, and it was very peaceful.

For no real reason, I thought to myself, wow, this was around the time we would make the annual excursion up to Christmas Tree Mountain, with all the Redmond family. I then suddenly remembered the mixture, the cupboard, and the glass jar.

I got up from my chair, and my wife was surprised that I had jumped up so quickly.

"Where are you going, Paul?" My wife asked.

"I need to check on something," I answered her.

I hustled into the kitchen, and opened the cupboard door, and sure enough, there it was hiding deep in the back of the cupboard.

Man, oh man, I thought this could be exciting!

This was only a small jar, not anything like the huge creation that Ronnie would have made. I took the jar down, placed it on the counter, and looked at it.

It looked good.

I could see the fruit moving around in there and the dark liquid sloshing about inside the jar. I did not know what was going on inside of there, but I thought—let me give it a shot. I unscrewed the metal lid very slowly, and then took a small opener and pried at the corner of the metal lid, with the rubber seal on the top of the glass edge.

"Whoosh!"

The lid popped off, and it surprised me. The air filled with a powerful aroma of whiskey and a fruity smell. I looked down in the jar because I was now very suspect as to the condition of the contents.

Taking a spoon, I stirred the mixture around, fished out one of the raisins, along with a little of the liquid, and put it on the end of the spoon.

"Well, here goes," I said aloud.

"Hip, hip hooray," I yelled out as I swallowed it down and took a bite of the raisin.

BANG!

It was as if a time bomb went off in my head!

I gave out a loud cry and shook my head back and forth.

My wife called me from the other room. "Are you all right in there?" She asked.

"Yes, I am fine. I am good, as a matter of fact, really good."

When I recovered, I took a little shot glass, now bravely poured some of the mixture into the glass, and took a few little sips of it. In a few minutes, there was a warm, warm, fuzzy feeling that started to come over me.

It is somewhat hard to explain.

I walked back into the living room; I sat down in my chair and broke out in a rendition of "Silver Bells."

I thought to myself, merry Christmas, Ronzo.

THE END

Harry's Resort

Chapter One

An Invitation Stirs Up a Memory or Two

I was walking out the door of my office late on a Friday when I heard the telephone on my desk start to ring. I did not know if I could make it in time, but I did, just before the person calling hung up. I greeted the caller and then heard the voice of an old friend on the other end.

"Hey, twenty-seven, it is Jim O'Malley here. I am glad I caught you. I was afraid that I might have missed you for the day." It was my old friend, O'Malley. Every once in a while, he calls me to chat a bit.

"Hello, Jim. It is nice to hear from you. How is everything?"

"Good, Paulie, really good. Hey, it is going to be a great day tomorrow, and I was hoping that you and Mrs. Henson could come over to a get-together at my house on Saturday afternoon. I know that a Sunday would be no good for both of us, but I was hoping that you could make it tomorrow. It has been a while since I have seen you. It will be nice to catch up. No hockey brawls, I promise. The wife and I are having a big summer barbecue cookout, some friends, beer, soda, some hot dogs and burgers. We would like to invite you and your wife over if you are not doing anything."

"Fantastic, Jim. I appreciate that," I answered. "I was just wondering what I was going to do this weekend. I know my wife will be disappointed. She is out of town this weekend, but you can count me in. Thank you and please thank your wife for the invitation. I will bring some Big Boulder beer and chips for us."

Jim laughed on the other end of the line. "Ha! You still drink that same brand of beer after all these years. That should be good, it should be a blast. I have some music out on the deck, and a big screen television now hooked up on the patio, so we can catch the baseball game. We are going to start around three in the afternoon, so most of the heat of the day will be gone. If you would like to go swimming, please make sure to bring your bathing suit. I just finished installing the new pool in the yard."

I laughed and told him, "Man, you have everything there, buddy, a pretty wife, a pool in the yard, a big television, cold beer, what a lucky guy you are!"

"See you on Saturday, Paulie!"

We exchanged goodbyes and hung up the line. I stood in my office and smiled. Jim is a nice guy; he sure has changed since the days when we played ice hockey together. In many ways, I owed Jim O'Malley an awful lot for what he taught me, but that is another story. I really enjoy his company to talk about the old days now and then. Wow, a big backyard cookout, with a new pool in the backyard, this sounds very familiar. While I gathered up my papers to finish for the day and get ready to leave, I found my mind taking me back to a very long time ago, when a simple backyard pool created a lifetime of memories for me.

I was heading back in time, in fact, all the way back to growing up and the important lessons that I learned from some very exceptional people.

Good old Paterson, New Jersey, one of the unique places on earth. It was where I was born and where I grew up. It is gritty, poor, determined, hard-core, rundown, dirty, and beautiful, all in one complex package. Paterson has everything that you could ever imagine, and want—from historic places, to mobsters, gangsters, and fantastic food like Taylor's Ham pork rolls and hot Texas weiners served, "all the way." It has a variety of "youse guys" and it even has mountains that tower over the city, poking strangely out of nowhere.

Folks who grow up there have the most interesting and different accents, like no place on earth. At first, non-northern New Jersey natives who are speaking to a true northern New Jersey speaker think they are from New York City, but listening closely it is much different. In fact, I know of no dialect like it. I speak it fluently, and even after living all over the country, it has never left me.

I hope that it never does.

When my sister and I were growing older, our parents wanted us to attend better public schools. The schools in north Paterson were getting a bit on the rough side, and our parents wanted to move us to a more comfortable educational environment.

When I was around ten years old, and my sister was a little older, we moved just over the border of the city to a borough called Haledon, which was really just an extension of the city. Haledon had a different school system as opposed to the city, and that was the primary reason for us making the move to the borough.

We had a house on a main drag street that went from the southern border of the city, all the way up into the northern reaches of this borough, and then south, directly to the center of downtown within the city. The main public service bus lines ran right out in front of our house, so transportation was very convenient. Our house was about fifty feet over the city line, and it was an interesting location. We were the farthest away from the public schools of any kids in the entire Haledon school system!

I remember my old man calling for some police intervention one time (which happened quite often) and the Paterson police officer who responded told my father, "Sorry, pal, you will have to call Haledon, this is out of my jurisdiction. It is five and one-half feet over the border."

Well, you had a better chance of seeing Santa Claus, the Easter Bunny, and a lucky leprechaun than you did of getting the Haledon police that far down into the gritty south end of the borough!

There were not too many kids our age in our neighborhood and the school really was far away. Therefore, it allowed us to voice the classic growing up complaint of kids all over, who when they grow up, they tell their children that old, tired, speech of, "In my day, we had to walk sixty-two miles through blizzards to get to school."

Our house sat directly in the middle of a city block on a very busy main street. Surrounding it was a tailor shop, a restaurant, a locksmith, a hair salon, and a gas station, all in a row right along both of the sides of our family home.

We had an apartment house next door above the lock shop, where one of our next-door neighbors was a middle-aged couple named Ada and Al. They were an unusual couple, but they were nice. They just had their own little world that they lived in. There was a large, walk up, six-story apartment right across the street from us. Many Italian families lived in the apartment house, and the families would hang out under a grape arbor, drink wine, and sing Italian songs when it was hot in the summer. The gas station on the corner was a very old station owned by a little Italian guy named Vince Baroni. Vince was a great guy. He was short, stocky, and close to the ground. He had a flat head with virtually no neck—it looked as if poor Vince had a heavy safe land on his head at one time, and it had pushed his entire neck and head down into his body. He was always nice to me and he would let me use his tools from the shop to fix my bike. Vince and his mechanics would even help me fix it occasionally when I did not know what I was doing.

Across from the gas station was a liquor store with a bar

in the back. I would slip in there with my shoeshine kit to shine shoes and make a dollar or two on a Saturday afternoon. Next to the bar and liquor store was a warehouse yard with Clipclock's Moving and Storage Company, which later on when I was old enough, I used to make a few dollars working with Harold Clipclock in the moving and storage business.

We had an old, wooden framed two-story house that used to be home to a family doctor, who had a small general practice. Years later, folks still would come to our front door asking if they could see the doctor. My dad would offer up some medical advice, and see if he could charge them for it, until my mother would intervene, and advise them that the doctor was long since gone.

We had a small backyard, which, after moving out of the city proper, we thought it was a miracle to be able to have some grass. My old man loved it, as he had a place to carve out a small vegetable and flower garden, and I turned it into an imaginary baseball stadium in the summer and a hockey rink in the wintertime.

In every old city in New Jersey, New York, and Connecticut, there is always without exception a doctor from some foreign country who moves into the neighborhood and establishes a family medical practice. They usually rent some old buildings and the doctor's office is generally on the second floor. It requires you to scale a long, dark, dimly lit, wooden staircase to the upper stratosphere and climb like a mountain climber to get to his office. I think they do this on purpose, so that you almost break your neck trying to see the doctor, and they can drum up more business.

Our neighborhood was no different. Soon, Dr. Salami moved into the old brick building right across the street from us. It had the obligatory second floor office and staircase, and the building smelled like mothballs.

One day he came door-to-door introducing himself,

asking folks to consider him for their family doctor. He was from the Middle East somewhere, was tall, round, and had a nice smile and dark mutton chop sideburns.

He was a nice guy and always stopped to say hello, shake your hand, and he would smile and say, "I am, Dr. Salami" in his charming accent.

He was quite the salesman.

My old man and mom signed up, and we went to him for years and years. The neighborhood sure was diverse, and it was home to us!

Interfacing into a new school when you are a kid is never easy, but my sister and I did it, and I soon became friends with Jeff Porter. Jeff lived all the way on the other side of town, on Oxford Street. I would pedal my bike to his house, and we would hang out together. My sister would do the same, as of course, all the new friends she made were also far away from our house.

In those days, you took the public service bus for a dime or you pedaled your bike. Mom and Dad did not run a taxi service for you.

About two city blocks away from my house, over on a street called John Street, lived a kid who was about my age named Harry Redmond. I did not know him other than to see him walking or riding his bike once in a while because he went to Catholic schools. There were many kids such as that whom you would only see in the summer because they went to the parochial or religious schools. Our area was very diverse, with Italian, Irish, Jewish, Polish, and some Spanish families, who all tended to send their children to the religious private schools.

I used to see Harry more in the summer, when school was out, but other than a nod of my head, I really did not know him. Lo-and-behold, one day, Jeff told me that his family was going to move, and that they had rented a house right over by me on John Street!

This was fantastic, as now my buddy was going to be

only two blocks away from me. Jeff and his family moved to 30 John Street, which was only a few numbers away from where Harry lived at 20 John Street. In fact, there was just an old lace factory that occupied the ten numbers between where Harry and Jeff lived.

Therefore, as things go, Jeff and I would be hanging out and we would run into this new kid, Harry. We would play stickball, pepper, kick the can, and street hockey in the streets out in front of Jeff's house, and Harry would come out and join in. We also would throw around the football and eventually, the three of us were hanging around together all the time.

Harry was big and strong and a happy, go lucky kid. He did have a wild side to him and occasionally, he would get himself into a little trouble here and there. Harry did not stir up any major trouble, just some ordinary kid-like mischief.

When we were twelve years old or thereabouts, Harry's mother became very ill, and sadly, she passed away. She had always been a very nice woman to me, and she always told me that I was a good friend to Harry, and that I kept him calm. She told me that Harry looked up to me for guidance and that he respected me. I missed her; she was a special person. Now, it was just Harry and his father in the house.

After a few years of just the two of them living in the house, and Mr. Redmond working hard at keeping Harry in line, and keeping the house up, as well as a job, Harry's dad decided to ask his oldest sister, Linda and her family to move in to help Harry's dad with running the household. Harry also told us that he no longer would attend the Catholic school system; his dad had decided that in September, he would begin attending the public schools.

Now, we would be able to all hang around together all the time, both in school and out of school, and that really kicked off our adventures together. Soon, the three of us became inseparable.

In the summer of 1973, Harry's sister Linda moved in with her family and that started one of the greatest summers of our young lives. I started to hang around more at his house and I soon came to realize that I had not only a good friend in Harry, but now, with a lot of other folks coming over and living at 20 John Street, it was as if I had joined up with an entire second family!

This was the house and neighborhood in which Linda had grown up in, and for her, it was just as if she was returning home. She brought her two young daughters, her husband Ronnie, and her love of life and fun personality. Linda was a large gal, and Ronnie was a large man; however, it was so much more than that! Not only were they physically large persons, but they were big in their hearts and souls, too. They loved to laugh, smile, and they were easygoing and friendly. That was the true measurement of how large they were!

Ronnie was a great guy and he fit right in with the rest of the neighborhood. He was a maintenance electrician, and he worked in downtown Paterson in a large department store doing all the electrical maintenance work. In our neighborhood, our fathers and neighbors were all tradesmen, laborers, truck drivers, and very hard workers of all types, shapes, and sizes.

We did not make a lot of money, but they sure all knew how to have fun! My old man was a machinist; Harry's old man was the supervisor of a metal fabrication shop and Mr. Porter drove a truck and worked in a seafood distribution establishment in the northward of Paterson.

The other neighbors included the Clipclock family who ran the moving business, Joe Hink (who we all called the hinky doos) whose dad ran an ice cream truck around town that sold more than just ice cream. My old man had warned me early on to avoid that truck. Unfortunately, little Joey Hink may have inherited some of his family's criminal tendencies. When he grew up, he developed a bad habit of stealing cars. Next door to Harry, on the other side of him, was the Healy family, who also were truckers. We did not have too much. In fact, the only kid we knew who had a nice house was this Italian kid named Rosilini. His dad was an engineer, and although we did not know what an engineer was, we knew it must have been important because he had a nice house, and they seemed to have new cars and a lot of money.

We thought we had it made; we did not really know any better. Growing up here amongst the old buildings, factories, mills, and gritty, worn-out streets may have made us a little street tougher and smarter, but for sure, we were all very happy!

Chapter Two

Fun and the World's Smartest Dog

I soon came to realize that the Redmond family was all about two things—work and fun! Mr. Redmond was the family patriarch. He was tall, round, and he had a full chock of thick white hair. He smiled all the time, and laughed, and he had a long face with full, puffy cheeks. His eyes were clear blue, and he observed everything and missed nothing. He ran a large metal fabrication shop where Harry, within a few years, would work as an apprentice. His company made stainless steel diners. These were the kind of diners that you would see on every street corner in New York, New Jersey, and Connecticut, and that were so popular during this day and age. He was very friendly to all of us neighborhood kids and you could tell he was very kind. Harry told us that his dad could speak fluent German. Mr. Redmond also told us how during his army days in World War Two, he was part of a group of American and British troops that liberated a German concentration camp, and saved many Jewish people's lives.

Harry's dad worked from dawn to dusk. He would leave for work very early, and you would not see him return until about seven or eight at night. Ronnie also was a hard worker, gone most of the time, earning a living and he quickly earned, for some unknown reason, the nickname Ronzo. Ronzo was a big, tall, strong man, who had a large, round face and thinning blonde hair that he combed over to the side. He was a good-looking guy, with a sly sense of humor and a hearty laugh. Harry warned us that he had recently returned from Vietnam, and he had a rough time over there, so we really should avoid ever asking him about it.

Linda was about fifteen years older than Harry was, and she was a big woman with a kind smile and a warm heart. She was very pretty with clear green eyes and a big, hearty laugh. I quickly learned that she could sing. She had a wonderful voice and could really belt out a tune!

One afternoon, Harry introduced us to his other sister Patty and his brother-in-law George. Patty was about ten years older than Harry was, so she was the middle child between Linda and Harry. She also was a big woman, with short brown hair and a quick, easy smile. She also was very pretty, she laughed and joked with us, and she was very easygoing. George was big and very tall. He was about six feet seven or so and he weighed about two hundred and fifty or so pounds. George was just a very large human being. Thank goodness, like many large people, he was a gentle giant. He was very soft-spoken and very easy to talk to and get to know.

Harry then told us some interesting facts about George. "He went to college, and he is an accountant. They have an apartment over in Buckley Park," Harry explained to us after Patty and George had left.

Jeff and I were in awe, as we had just met the first person that we ever knew, other than teachers in our school, who actually went to college.

"The Big Spike was a great volleyball player in college. He won all kinds of championships and awards, and that is why they call him, The Big Spike. George played rough and tough volleyball, not that winky dinky stuff that we play at school. Believe me, I have played with him, and when he spikes that ball over the net, it comes at you with some serious speed." Harry motioned with his hands and arms at how the Big Spike would bash the ball over the net at you.

Jeff and I just nodded and made a mental note to avoid a backyard volleyball game if George was going to be involved.

Harry looked like his father and his sisters did, and he was also strong and stocky, but he was not overweight at all. He was just big and strong, and as we soon came to find out from playing with him in sports. He was a solid guy.

The Redmond's house was a small Cape Cod style home set in a row of old houses, and for a house within an urban setting, it had a decent sized backyard. It backed up to an old storage building on one side, the old mill on the other, and one of the Clipclock's warehouses in the far rear corner of the property. The Redmond's house always had something going on, with little kids running around, music playing, two dogs running all over the place, and one thing that no one in our neighborhood had; a basketball goal on the garage. In fact, no one in the rest of the neighborhood even had a garage.

If Harry could convince Ronzo to move some old junk cars that he had lined up in the driveway in front of the hoop, Jeff, Harry, and I often would pass the time by shooting baskets in his backyard. Ronnie and Mr. Redmond had a collection of old, junky automobiles and extra parts for the broken-down cars lined up like old warhorses in the driveway.

There were older two door sports cars, four-door sedans, and even a convertible or two. Harry's old man was a big sedan type guy; he only ever drove the big, fancy, long cars. Ronzo had his prize 1967, rally sport Sonicmobile, with white racing stripes, the famous rally package wheels, and a crossed racing flag's logo on the front grille.

What a car!

The Redmonds also had an old rusty pool in their backyard, or what you might say was, at one time, a swimming pool. It was an old pool, and I had never seen it filled with any water inside of it for the few years I had been coming over to Harry's house.

Nonetheless, it was at one time a pool!

No one had a pool in his or her backyards in our neighborhood. I had actually never seen a pool in someone's backyard before. If you wanted to go swimming in our world, you would have to go to the city pool or the Police Athletic League pool, which was miles away and was a major trip even on our bicycles.

One day, I asked Harry about it, and he said it had not been filled with water the last few years since it had become so old and rusty, and the liner inside leaked a lot of water.

Harry went on explaining to me, "It was really cool to have when it was filled! I do not know what my old man is going to do with it, he keeps saying he may buy a new one, but that would be a major job to chuck out that one and put up a new pool."

Harry's backyard was amazing, not only with the basketball hoop, and with the fact that it once had a pool, but it had many other things that I had never seen before in a small city backyard.

On the other side, right next to the house, was a horseshoe pit. It had the sand pits around the pegs, it was long, and it extended from the front side of the house to the rear side of the house, in essence, the entire length of the home. Mr. Redmond and Ronzo would play horseshoes all the time, and on the weekends, the neighborhood men would come over. They would divide into teams, drink beer from a keg set up on the patio, and play round robin tournaments all weekend long. You could hear the laughter and the loud, "clang" of the metal shoes hitting the pegs all the way over to my house.

The front of the house had a big flagpole, which to us was special. Since they were Catholic, the Redmonds had a statue of the Virgin Mary out in front of the home, sitting next to the base of the flagpole. Now, Mr. Redmond, Mr. Porter, and Ronnie were all war veterans, and the flag would always fly on the pole in front of the house. My old man had also served in the military and he had a flag, but he could only stick it out the front door, next to the mailbox. The only place that I had seen an actual flagpole was at our schoolyard. I was a flag boy at school, and I knew my flagpoles, as well as all the rules and regulations for flying the flag. The stern, retired, Marine Corps Institute maintenance man Mr. Hutton, who drilled us dopey kids as though we had all enlisted, taught all the rules to me in school, while I was a member of a battalion of flag boys.

In the Redmond's backyard, there also was a concrete patio in the back of the house. It had a big barbecue grill and a covered roof over the patio. It even had speakers mounted under the canopy roof. They hooked up to a stereo and radio system, and Mr. Redmond would have music playing all the time.

For me, it was an amazing little chunk of the suburbs, tucked away in this nook, surrounded by what seemed like endless cement and asphalt.

It was late June now. We had just left out of school for the summer, and we all would be going off to high school in the fall. All three of us enrolled in a trade school in June, but going back to school right now was the last thing on our minds, as we had the whole summer to have some fun and adventure. The more I hung around the Redmond's house, the more I realized how much fun it was. During the week, they worked like dogs, working from sunup to sun down, but come the nighttime, they would sit on the patio, play music, play horseshoes, and have a few beers. They would laugh, dance on the patio, and sing songs all night, while they cooked food on the grille, sat around, told stories, and shared in each other's lives.

The weekends, well, they were a whole other story!

The entire neighborhood would gather at the

Redmond's house, starting late on Saturday afternoon. The horseshoe games would start, the grille fired up, a keg of Dingleberry beer, a keg of Big Boulder beer, and a half keg of Boylan's Birch Beer would be delivered from Trio Liquors. Before you knew it, a full-blown party was going on.

They were the most fun loving, happy bunch of people who I had ever seen or met! Hot dogs, burgers on the grill, soda, chips, and pretzels, they had it all going on there and the music would be blasting from under the canopy from the two loudspeakers hanging on the house. They would have steaming corn cobs cooking in a big barrel boiling over a fire pit. You could just reach down there and grab an ear of corn from the water.

Jeff's mom and dad would come over, Mr. Porter would bring some clams from his seafood shop, and they would make steamers. Mr. Porter, on occasion, would even cook an entire "catch of the day" over some hot coals. They would cook these fantastic, foot long hot dogs called Big Bob's Griddle Franks on the grill. The hot dogs had the most delicious flavor. They would snap when you bit them and they had spices that would stay with you for a while.

In fact, you could have a Big Bob's Griddle Frank and about five years later, have a little heartburn, and a little backfire, and you would taste them clear as could be in your mouth. "Oh yeah, that was that hot dog I had over at the Redmond's Memorial Day picnic in 1973," you would say to yourself.

They would play all kinds of music; rock, country, classical, folk, everything from one end of the music spectrum to the other. Mr. Redmond would bring out his big band records, play his records and dance with Mrs. Porter, and then take a turn or two with the neighbor's wives on the patio. Dogs and little kids would run around, all having a great time together. It was really the place to be in our neighborhood.

Harry had many pets, he had hamsters, gerbils, ferrets, a few parakeets in a cage, and even a rabbit that lived in a cage attached to the side of the Clipclock's warehouse in the rear part of the yard.

He also had two dogs, one was Cocoa, and the other dog was a very tiny, almost microscopic dog named Marshmallow. Now, the best way that I can describe Marshmallow, was that he looked like a softball with four little legs that stuck out of it. He would appear like magic out of nowhere and then disappear just as quickly.

People would be dancing and hollering on the patio, people would be standing around drinking beer and talking, the grille would be going, and all of a sudden, Linda would yell out, "Look out for Marshmallow! Be careful of him," she would warn. This little puffball of white would magically appear, with four little legs propelling him along through the crowd at a good clip. If you were not careful, you could easily step on poor Marshmallow. He was so small.

I would turn and ask Harry, "Where did he come from?"

Harry answered, "He is always around, but he is really, really old. He has been in our family for years and years."

He may have always been around somewhere, but he hid well. Marshmallow was a mystery as you very seldom saw him; I never, ever, saw him in the house and the dog only appeared on rare occasions, in the backyard. The Redmonds seemed to take it all in stride, but I found the little magical dog to be very unusual.

Harry's other dog was Cocoa, and he was a legitimate dog. He was our companion and friend as he followed us around constantly. He was only about three years old and he was a beautiful dog who was a half husky and half collie mix, with a wonderful, smooth, cocoa color coat of fur. Cocoa was always outside and the dog mostly stood guard out at the front of the house, standing watch inside the fence and gates that lined the front of the house along the street. They say that dogs mimic their masters and with Cocoa that was certainly true, as he was a happy and friendly dog who loved everyone. He did not have a mean bone in his body. He would run around, bark, and interact with all the partygoers, and he actually danced with anyone who was dancing to the music on the patio. He would run up whenever he saw people dancing on the patio and he would spin around, jump, hop, and chase his tail all in rhythm to the music! It was amazing.

Harry had taught us a few years ago that Cocoa was indeed, as the Redmonds would proudly tell everyone; the world's smartest dog!

Harry explained to us, "He is really, really smart, guys, so, please be careful what you say around him, because he can get his feelings hurt easily." Jeff and I really did not know what to make of that statement, but there was little doubt that Cocoa was smart.

We just did not realize how smart he really was.

Cocoa would hang out in front of the house watching cars, and it did not take us long to see that he knew and could identify different cars. Cocoa ignored strange cars, but he knew all the neighbors' cars by sight and sound, and he would bark and jump around when he would see one of them go by. Cocoa had piles of rubber toys; in fact, he had the largest collection of toys that I have ever seen. Some had squeakers in them and some did not. He had rubber steaks, pork chops, dogs, footballs, baseballs, cats, rubber hamburgers, hot dogs, Santa Claus, the Easter Bunny, and on and on. If they made a doggie toy, chances are that Cocoa had it. The Redmonds kept all of his toys in a large mound in the yard, at the top of the driveway. Everyone would just gather them up on occasion, and mound them all into one huge pile about five feet high. Of all the toys he had, the number one favorite toy was Piggy. Most of Cocoa's waking life was spent carrying Piggy around or having him somewhere nearby.

Piggy was a pink colored, rubber pig that stood upright as if he was human and he could stand on two feet. Piggy's other legs crossed in front of him as if he had human-like arms and he had this stupid, dumb smile on his face. Piggy had the world's loudest squeaker, and it was so loud that it would wake Ronnie up from a sound sleep while he was sleeping in the second-floor bedroom. You would want to have hearing protection on when Cocoa would squeak it.

One thing I learned right away that was the worst mistake you could ever make, was to engage in playing a game of "fetch the Piggy" with Cocoa.

A game of fetch the Piggy in theory, never ends, at least not without some pain and suffering. He would fetch Piggy for at least a week and a half straight. If you tried to quit, then Cocoa would haunt you. There truly was no escape, as he would be stalking your every move and continually squeak Piggy and bump him into your leg, until you conceded defeat and threw him just one more time.

You could climb to the top of Mount Everest in a vain and futile effort to escape, and Cocoa would be waiting at the top already with Piggy in his mouth. It was always interesting to watch, when a new person would come over to a Redmond's picnic or gathering, and Cocoa would immediately target him as unsuspecting fresh blood. All it would take was for Cocoa to approach some guy sitting at the picnic table with his beer and a hot dog, and the guy to see him with Piggy in his mouth.

Generally, the scenario went like this, "Oh, what a pretty dog, give me your toy." The poor sucker would throw it once, and that was it! Forever more until the end of time, he now had to play a game of "fetch the Piggy."

We all would watch and all you would hear were the low murmurs through the crowd, "Poor guy, oh no, wow," and on and on the sympathy would go from the more seasoned and experienced Cocoa Piggy players.

Fourteen hours later, the guy's wife has an ice pack on

his throwing shoulder and Cocoa is still going strong after fifty million throws and fetches.

Since Jeff had moved into the neighborhood, Cocoa's favorite person in the whole world became Mr. Porter. Now, Mr. Porter came from the same mold as the Redmonds. He was a happy, round, jolly man who was always laughing and telling jokes. He and his wife never were anything less than a big, happy barrel of fun, and I had known them now for a long time.

Mr. Porter always kept a long, brass bullet in his pocket that he had drilled a hole in, and he kept his keys on it.

When he would see us, he always pulled the bullet out, and he would show us and say, "Hey youse guys . . . stay cool, bite the bullet." It was always the same greeting for as long as I knew him. Cocoa knew what time Mr. Porter arrived home from work and he would position himself inside the fence within a few minutes of his arrival. Car after car would go by, and Cocoa would hold Piggy in his mouth, look at them and ignore them, knowing that a game of Piggy was unlikely from a stranger. Mr. Porter drove a 1969 Galaxy 500 Super Glide, and as soon as he hit the corner of John Street and Belmont Ave, Cocoa was barking, leaping, and jumping to see his buddy.

Mr. Porter would park in front of his house, jump out of the car, yell to his wife in a loud bellow that he was home, wave to all the neighbors, walk over to pet and say hello to Cocoa. He kept these little dog treats in his pocket, and he would flip two or three to his doggie pal, and be on his way back home.

Cocoa loved him.

Mr. Porter would occasionally play a quick game of Piggy. He was the only known human being that Cocoa would allow to quit a game after only a throw or two. I think it was out of his love and respect for Mr. Porter because all that Mr. Porter would need to say to Cocoa was, "No more Piggy," and the game would be over. Perhaps

Cocoa was afraid if he pushed too hard, Mr. Porter would shut him out of doggie treats.

One afternoon, while we were shooting baskets, Harry showed us what really made Cocoa the world's smartest dog. Cocoa was hanging out with us and watching the game, just sitting on the side of the driveway with Piggy.

We were talking about how smart he was when I said, "You told Jeff and me a long time ago to be careful of what we say around Cocoa, because he understands English."

"That's right, youse guys," Harry answered and put down the basketball. "if you do not believe me, then just watch this. Be warned after you see this, one of you will have to play Piggy with him for a while."

We nodded our heads in agreement. Suppertime was still four or five hours away, and to see this, it just might be worth playing a game of Piggy.

Harry was now yelling back at us as he was walking toward the mound of dog toys in the backyard.

"Watch this, youse guys." Harry picked up Piggy. First, he proclaimed a loud, "NO!" which signaled to Cocoa that there was no game on, and he gathered all the toys up and mixed Piggy into the bottom of the pile. Harry then looked at Cocoa and said to him, "Go get your pork chop!"

Bang! Off Cocoa raced to the pile of toys. The dog ran around it while loudly barking. He stopped, sniffed, scanned it, moved toys with his nose and paws, picked out the pork chop, brought it over to Harry, and dropped it at his feet.

"Good boy! Now, go get your football!" Harry instructed. Bang! Cocoa was off once more and the result was the same, with the football dropped at his feet. On and on it went, with Cocoa correctly identifying every single toy by name without a single error.

"Wow," Jeff said, "I can see that he really is smart, he knows the name of every toy." Harry downplayed it; I guess the Redmonds were all used to it by now.

"Yeah, he is a pretty smart dog," Harry acknowledged.

I would say so!

Then, in a final blow, Harry delivered the reward for a hard afternoon of work. "Get your Piggy and bring it to Paul. He will play with you until Mr. Porter comes home."

In four seconds, flat, Cocoa correctly identified and removed Piggy from the pile, and Cocoa was at my feet with Piggy in his mouth while he wagged his tail. I looked at my watch and sighed as it was still about three hours until I could count on that big automobile to come rolling up John Street to relieve me.

I would go home and tell my parents and my sister about how the Redmond household, with all the new additions of people living there and activities, had turned into the hot place to be in our little world. I told them how Linda, Ronzo, and all the others were the jolliest, most fun-loving bunch of folks that I had ever met.

"No kidding," my old man said one day while we were weeding the garden together. "I would hear all the laughing and carrying on while I am in the yard here, and I wondered where it was coming from." Our backyard actually lined up with the Redmond's yard even though it was a few city blocks away, and you could look right down from the side of the old lace mill and almost see Harry's yard.

The description of the activities clearly impressed the old man. He commented, "I can hear it really clear on a Sunday afternoon, when the traffic is not so busy in front of the house, now I know where it is coming from. I guess the horseshoe pit, explains the loud clunk you hear every few minutes."

I also told my family about Cocoa and the fact that he was the world's smartest dog. My sister and my mother were amazed, but my old man was a skeptic and a nonbeliever.

"He knows English and he can identify every toy by

name," I was telling him, while my old man was just shaking his head back and forth.

My dad went on to explain, "You see, dogs do not really understand words, they just understand common sounds and the inflections in your voice. They do not know actual words, but they have a sense of what you mean."

Well, I respected my father as being a pretty smart man, but I still felt in my heart that one day he needed to meet Cocoa and he would be a believer too.

Chapter Three

Mr. Redmond Makes an Announcement

If not, too much was going on over at the Redmond's house during the week. We would go fishing in Molly Ann's Brook, we played street hockey, some football, did general teenage activities, and tried to stay out of trouble. When the weekend came, the Redmonds cranked it all up. If the weather was looking good, by two or three in the afternoon on Saturday, the party would begin over at 20 John Street.

The most amazing part of this was that Mr. Redmond funded it all. He never asked anyone for a nickel for all the food, beer, wine, soda and other items that went into making these fantastic shindigs happen. He was happy just to have the company and be the center of all the fun and excitement. Folks would bring some beer once in a while and other contributions, and Mr. Porter would bring some fish or clams, but for the most part, Mr. Redmond was just happy for you to come over and share in his life. He was always inviting my parents to come on over, but my folks were always busy and my old man worked many long hours. In addition, my father worked some Saturdays doing part-time work.

It was a Saturday afternoon, just a few short weeks before the big Fourth of July holiday, and the party was just getting going for the weekend. The buzz was all about a picnic that the Redmonds were planning as part of a huge July Fourth celebration.

Jeff, Harry, and I were hanging out when I noticed my

old man come through the gate and wave to us. He was coming over to check out all the excitement and see what these parties were all about at 20 John Street.

My dad knew Mr. Porter for years from coaching little league baseball together. He and Mr. Porter went off together, so that he could introduce the old man to Mr. Redmond, Linda, Patty, the Big Spike, Ronzo, and the rest of the gang. The old man was talking, watching the teams play horseshoes, and drinking a beer, when Cocoa spotted him and began lurking around him.

Ah ha, fresh blood!

Sure enough, all three of us watched, as trotting along, now heading his way was Cocoa. The dog was scouting out the potential possibilities for a game of Piggy, with my skeptical old man.

We walked up, and I said to my dad as I pointed to Cocoa, "Hey dad, there is Cocoa."

"Oh yeah, yeah, yeah, that's the dog that you dopey kids say, can understand English," the old man answered as he reached down and petted him. "Here, let me prove this to you guys. Dogs just really do not understand English, they only know some basic sounds and the inflections in our voices."

The three of us, and Cocoa, just stood there looking at the old man until Harry piped in, "Please be careful, Mr. Henson. Cocoa is listening, and he can get his feelings hurt easily if he thinks you are saying he is dumb."

My old man stopped and looked somewhat strangely at Harry; he cleared his throat, put his beer down, and continued. There were a couple of other neighbors who were sitting on the patio and were now listening too. They were half in the bag, but they sipped on their beers, and decided to check out the old man's sermon about dogs.

"Here, let me show you. Just watch as I change my tone to him," the old man said as he leaned forward, put his hands on his knees, and spoke to Cocoa in a loud voice.

"COCOA, GO GET YOUR GIBBERTY GOO!" The old man shouted to Cocoa, who was now intently looking at the old man, sitting, and staring at him.

Now, Cocoa did not know my old man from any other person in the entire world. All Cocoa saw was a potential guy to play Piggy with, but he did not react at all to the nonsense that came out of the old man's mouth. Cocoa actually never looked upon anyone as a stranger; he only looked upon them as a human being that he would be able to lure into a game of Piggy. A criminal who broke into the Redmond's house would merely end up playing a game of Piggy until the police arrived.

The old man remained undaunted in his efforts, and he continued, "Oh well, let me try this one . . . Cocoa, go and get your bliberty blop."

This time the old man made his voice go up and down, from soft to loud, then back to soft, while he spoke the words.

Cocoa just sat there, staring at the old man with a smile on his face.

Harry shook his head and said, "You need to tell him in English, those mumbo jumbo words do not mean anything to him."

All of us, including the drunken neighbors, were now staring intently at the old man while we were watching the scene unfold. Cocoa was looking hard at my father and you could just tell he was thinking, "What is this guy saying?"

My dad refused to give up. He tried the same thing about ten times, each time changing the tone of his voice, pretending as if he was happy or sad, and all the time while he was speaking in some strange tongue with made-up words.

Cocoa just sat there patiently, looking up at the old man.

The old man was now sweating and becoming a little uncomfortable. He took a few chugs of his Big Boulder beer, wiped some beads of sweat off his brow, and he shook his head a little, not willing to concede defeat just yet, in his dog language theory.

Finally, maybe the beer had set in, or it just came out, but the old man slipped up and said, "Go get your Piggy!"

BOOM! Like an F-16 fighter jet, Cocoa was off and headed to the giant pile of toys. He circled the pile like a hawk, moved some toys around. He knocked a few things out of the way with his nose and paws, until there it was; Piggy! Within supersonic time, Cocoa returned to the feet of the old man, with Piggy firmly entrenched in his mouth, and his tail wagging like a windshield wiper in a thunderstorm.

A soft, low groan broke out amongst the crowd. All of us, including the drunken neighbors, shook our heads, and we walked away, as everyone knew the fate of the old man.

My father got a funny look on his face, looked around and picked up the Piggy and he threw it. He did not mention a word. In fact, he did not have to, but we all knew that he was now a believer too.

Mr. Redmond had Linda shut off the music, and he waved for all the partygoers to gather under the patio canopy. My old man was still on the sideline throwing Piggy, but everyone listened as Mr. Redmond spoke.

"Folks, I am going to need all of your help next weekend. We have two weeks, until we have the biggest party celebration ever held here at our place for the Fourth of July, and I made a big decision this week."

Mr. Redmond turned around and pointed at the old pool in the back of the yard, and he continued to speak.

"See that old junky pool back there, it is a mess. It is all leaky and rusty, and we have not been able to fill it for a few years now. Well, you see, I have decided to knock it down and replace it! I measured it all out. I went down to Sal Zucchini's pool center in Paterson, and I worked a deal with Sal. I am going to buy the biggest above ground pool that they make! I would love to have it all put up and ready to go for the big Fourth of July party, and that is where I need all of your help. This will be a major operation as this new pool is thirty-six feet around."

I heard a few whistles going around the crowd and I thought to myself, thirty-six feet around. That is huge; it will take up the entire yard!

"Ronnie, Harry and his buddies, and I, are going to work on taking down the old pool during the week and have it all ready to go for the new one by next Saturday."

Mr. Redmond was now getting excited, and you could hear his voice growing in intensity.

"Weather permitting, we can meet here around nine in the morning next Saturday. I am going to borrow the old truck from the shop to go down to Sal Zucchini's store as soon as he opens and pick up the new pool. My hope is to have the whole thing ready to go for the big holiday!"

The entire group of neighbors erupted into cheers, and everyone was walking up to Mr. Redmond, slapping him on the back, thanking him and telling him that they were in. "You can count on us," was the consensus, and it seemed as if Mr. Redmond had successfully organized a huge pool work party for next weekend.

Between throws of Piggy, I heard my dad yell over to Mr. Redmond that he had to work, and then exchange the head on the engine of our 1964 Putter Classic model 200, but he would be here to help as soon as he could finish up.

Most every weekend, my old man, if he was not working at his full-time or part-time job, had to perform some kind of repair on our family car, which was a 1964 Putter Classic model 200. This was still the day and age where you could repair your own vehicle without a PHD in computer sciences.

After his big announcement, Mr. Redmond had told us, "I will be counting on the three of you to help with this project. I know there will be a lot of beer, it will be hot, and I will lose many of the adults. You are all big and strong now, and I am going to need you boys when the rest of them give out, or they are too bombed to work anymore."

I could see that Mr. Redmond was a realistic guy.

We all assured him that we would help in any way that we could. This was a huge event and was simply unheard of in our neighborhood. The news was spreading like wildfire that the Redmonds were going to have this giant pool in their backyard.

No one had pools in their yards! It was something of a revelation for our neighborhood!

The rich people living in Wayne Township and North Haledon had pools in their backyards—not poor schleps such as we were. The entire rest of the day was just one big buzz as the discussion was all about the pool, and the fantastic party celebration planned for the Fourth of July.

I was so excited that I ran home to tell my mother and sister all about it, when my mom asked me if I had seen the old man. "I thought he was with you, over at the Redmonds?"

"Oh, he is playing Piggy with Cocoa. He should be home in a few hours," I told her as I went on and on about the new pool.

My mother had a funny look on her face, as I am not sure she entirely understood me, but about two hours later, I heard the back door open, and my father walked in.

"Don't ask," he told my mother. He reached in the refrigerator for a Big Boulder beer and the old man sat down exhausted at the kitchen table.

"Do we have any of that rubbing ointment? My shoulder is killing me."

Yes, my father was now a believer.

Chapter Four

The Project Begins!

I was a very annoying kid. Once I was interested in a subject, and I had the subject on my mind that was all that I would talk about for days on end. I would talk about it constantly and never shut up. The dinner table discussions all week after Mr. Redmond's announcement was a constant babble about swimming pools. I spoke endlessly about how great it was going to be, to be part of the team that will help install it.

On and on I would go, and my mother and sister would try their best to very politely change the subject and divert the conversation. It was hopeless, though, as I would pick right back up where I stopped, until my father would finally just cut to the chase and tell me to shut up about the pool. It was to everyone's benefit, as all the family had reached the point where they were holding their heads, plugging their ears and wringing their hands, at the very mention of the Redmonds and pools.

Jeff, Harry, and I met on Monday morning and planned our entire week's activities around the installation of the pool. We all decided to cancel all of our other activities, because we were all so excited about the new pool. The cancelled plans included our regularly scheduled summer activities, such as fishing, kick the can, stickball, and hanging out over at the Foodworld supermarket, hoping that some young gals would come along to whistle at when they walked by us.

On Monday after work, Mr. Redmond, Ronnie, Jeff,

Harry, and I bashed up the old pool and gathered all the junk up to bring out to the front curb for the garbage men to collect the sad remains. Mr. Redmond had brought home a large, metal-cutting saw from his shop, and after warning us kids to stay far away, and putting on a face shield, he made quick work of cutting the old pool up into little sections. The whole time, while we were working, Mr. Redmond was teaching us about working safely, how to use tools, saws, and many other important tips for three fourteen-year-old kids entering a trade school in the fall. After we removed the pool, Mr. Redmond carefully showed us how to rake out the sand that was underneath the old pool and pick out all the debris and rocks.

"Check it carefully, boys! All that it takes is a little stone to put a hole in the rubber pool liner," Mr. Redmond instructed us, "Tomorrow after work, we will have to cut the grass and remove it to fit the new pool. The old pool was a lot smaller than the new one was going to be. I am having a load of fine sand delivered here tomorrow, so you boys have to make sure the delivery guy puts it as close as he can to this spot."

Ronnie was now busy moving all the junk cars out of the driveway so the sand truck could drive up very close to the pool's location. We could see that Mr. Redmond knew what he was doing. I concluded that he was a very experienced pool installer.

The next day, we watched as a big truck dumped a load of sand right up in the yard next to the pool location. The driver asked us to sign a paper and told us that Harry's dad had already paid for the sand.

That night, when Ronnie and Mr. Redmond came home from work, we watched as Mr. Redmond drove a stake with a string wrapped around it, in the ground in the middle of the old outline for the pool. He then measured, stretched the string out, and made a new outline on the ground.

"Now, Harry, take that string, hold this knife on the end, hold it taunt and go around in a big circle, and make a mark on the ground," Mr. Redmond instructed his son. Mr. Redmond watched as Harry scored the outline of the dimension, and we all were in awe at the immense size of the new pool.

You could see the passion that Harry's father took in managing the swimming pool construction project, which seemed to be on the surface—a mission to provide joy and happiness to our neighborhood, as well as add another element of backyard fun to the already legendary Redmond gatherings.

However, could it also have been that he had planned a twofold mission?

As we eagerly assisted in the work, Mr. Redmond was also teaching three young men teamwork, project organization, proper usage of tools, and trade skills and planning. Looking back, it was an education that I am sure at the time we did not even realize that we were receiving.

Ronnie stood back and observed the outline and after seeing how large it was, he walked over to the tool shed and returned with a pickaxe and shovel. Taking a long sip of Dingleberry beer, Ronnie then spit into his hands, rubbed them together, and grabbed the handle of the pickaxe.

"Now for the hard part, boys," Ronzo said as he raised the axe up over his head. "I trenched enough perimeters over in Vietnam, so I am really good at this part," he said, as the axe hit the ground directly on the mark that Harry had made.

Ronnie was like a human bulldozer as he had that big body steaming along as he went around, picking out the grass and debris for the new perimeter of the pool. We all followed behind with shovels and wheelbarrows, and soon enough, Ronzo had the new pool outline cut clean in the backyard turf.

Mr. Redmond was pleased. It was now getting dark, and it was time to quit. "Tomorrow, it will be your job to use the wheel barrels and spread the sand out inside the new pool perimeter," he told the three of us. "Right now, it is time to quit!" He shook all our hands and thanked us for a nice job, and then he turned to Ronnie and said, "C'mon Ronzo, I will buy you a Dingleberry beer . . . but you know that I will have a Big Boulder. Those Dingleberries are way too sweet for me!"

The next day we spread the sand out, and Mr. Redmond told us to report in front of the house on Saturday, at seven in the morning sharp. We were working as hard as we had ever worked in our entire lives, but we were enjoying every minute of it.

Saturday came and the excitement of the adventure was overwhelming. It was a clear, bright sunny day, but you could tell that by the afternoon it was going to be hot, sticky, and humid. All during the week, we had worked with Ronzo and Mr. Redmond preparing the pool location, and now the big day to pick up the pool and build it was finally here. I ate a quick breakfast, dashed out the back door, and headed for 20 John Street. My father was already out working on the Putter and he promised he would join in later once he had the car running.

He had his Super Whiz-Bang tool set from Substantial Industries spread out across the driveway. The old man only ever bought tools and other items from Substantial Industries and the company made everything from tools to cars and trucks. The company slogan on all their television commercials was, "When the wimpy stuff just will not do the job, then go Substantial!"

His dream was someday; to dump the old 1964 Putter Classic model 200, and buy their famous Substantial Industries Rhino 400 automobile, which in the television commercial advertisement collides violently with a tank. The tank falls apart, the gun turret falls off, the tracks pop off, and smoke comes out of the tank, as the Rhino car continues untouched as it travels down the roadway.

The old man loved it, and he would leap out of his chair when the commercial came on the television.

"Someday," he would say, "I will drive one of those puppies and all those cars on Route 23, better look out when I come down the road in my Rhino 400. Yup, someday."

Until then, I could see he was strapping on the six guns to once more battle the old car, and persuade it to roll a few thousand more miles.

The old man asked me, "How is Mr. Redmond going to get that big pool up from riverside, Paterson?"

"Oh, he is bringing home the big delivery truck from his shop," I answered. My old man nodded in approval when he heard the word "shop" and he went back to his tools.

You see, all of our fathers always went to the shop. It was what they all normally did. We knew that the shop was like the workshops that we all had in our basements, but only bigger, and in a roundabout way that was where the money all came from. Everything happened, "Out by the shop." My old man would get a haircut out at the barber by the shop. He would pick up a hot dog and a beer out by the shop on the way home from work. He picked up a part for the car, at a store next to the shop, and so on and so on.

It was the center of our father's universe. The shop was an unknown, mysterious, lofty place that our fathers would mention all the time. We all knew someday that our fate was that we would report to our own shops and they would become part of our lives, too.

When I turned onto the street and reached Harry's house, I saw that parked in front was a giant, old, rusty rack body truck that said, "Taylor Industries and Metal Fabrication" on the side door. This was the truck from the shop. I knew that we were going to use the old truck to carry the new pool back from the store. It was old, and very large, and it looked like a veteran of many types of jobs and assignments that it had to haul over many, many years. A thick, distinct odor of diesel fuel and oil hung in the air.

"How do you like the truck from the shop?" I heard Harry's voice from behind me as I was checking out the old relic. "It is not pretty but, it sure is strong!" He laughed and patted me on the back. Soon Jeff, Ronzo, Mr. Porter, and Mr. Redmond joined us as we all gathered around the truck to hear what the game plan was.

"Ronnie, you can drive," Mr. Redmond yelled as he tossed the truck keys to Ronzo, who climbed into the driver's seat.

Mr. Porter opened the side door to climb in with Mr. Redmond who told us, "You guys climb up and get in the back, we are going to need a lot of help to load this pool onto the truck, so get in there and hold on tight. We have to go down Tilted Hill you know."

We all jumped right in and we sat in the back of the cab. Jeff moved some ropes and straps that Mr. Redmond had put in the bed of the truck to help tie down the pool and the parts that would go along with it. We sat, three in a row on the bed, while tucking our backs tightly against the front cab.

Nowadays, you would probably get five years in the federal prison for allowing kids to ride in the back of an old truck like this, but back in the early 1970s, it was just what you did.

Ronzo started the big truck, and it roared to life. It spit out a few giant black clouds of smoke that floated out and into all the open windows along John Street. Neighbors coughed, choked, and stuck their heads out of the windows to see what had happened. Once they saw that the source of the noise and smoke was the Redmonds heading out to purchase the swimming pool, everyone began yelling encouragement and waving goodbye to us! Off we went, with Ronzo dragging the big truck through the gears, and slowly we crept along John Street, and headed for Tilted Hill.

Now, the world famous, Tilted Hill, was a street that led from the border of the borough, right down to the Paterson River, just before downtown Paterson. The hill was unique, because the city had a few hilly areas, but this stretch was by far the highest. It led from the northern outskirts, all the way down to sea level at the river. One side of Tilted Hill brought you to the riverside section of the city, and the other side had a large development of apartments known as the Christopher Columbus projects.

The unique thing about Tilted Hill was that it was not really a hill; it was more like a mountain inside a city. It was very long and steep, and it had three levels of flats that you would reach as you made your way along the road. Going down, you had to make sure you had good brakes, or you ended up in the river. Attempting to go back up the hill was another story.

My old man in the Putter Classic model 200 would have to get a head start down near city hall in downtown Paterson. He would then pray that he would not hit a red light, build up enough speed to climb the hill, and even then, half the time he would have to veer off, and go around the top of the hill to make it back to our neighborhood, as the powerless Putter would fade right at the last stretch.

Forget about it in the ice and snow. It was like a bobsled run. The people who lived on the hill itself would sit on their porches in chairs and they would be continually entertained at the various stranded and stuck junk cars, attempting various methods to make their way up and down the incredibly steep slope. One day, the old man and I even spotted some guy going backwards up the hill in some old wreck of a car! I guess he figured out that his heap of junk car could pull much stronger than it was able to push!

We turned from Burhans Avenue onto the top of Tilted Hill and down the hill, faster and faster, we went. Ronzo firmly hit the now smoking brakes as the old truck picked up more and more speed. Mr. Redmond tapped on the glass of the cab to get our attention and warn us to hang on. The front of the truck seemed like it was ten feet lower than the rear as we navigated the slope.

Booooom!

We hit the level part. The old truck hit a little air, and then slammed back down to the roadway and all the ropes, tie downs, and toolboxes, shook and jumped.

Boooom!

Up and down, we went, until we hit the final level and we were finally down.

What a ride, we loved it!

Mr. Redmond turned and counted the kid's heads to make sure we had not lost anyone on the ride down.

Ronnie turned onto River Street, and off we were shifting gears, spewing smoke, and making our way to Sal Zucchini's pool center.

A large Italian population heavily dominated the riverside section of Paterson. It was full of Italian restaurants, Catholic churches, Italian delicatessens and food markets, and was the closest thing that Paterson had, which you could say was a "Little Italy" type setting.

Everyone in our neighborhood went to Sal Zucchini's store, not for pool shopping, which was for the folks from the richer and more affluent localities farther away from our neighborhood, but we would come down for tools. This store was very hard to describe to people nowadays, who may not understand the northern New Jersey setting or culture, and still manage to stay within politically correct and safe guidelines. Suffice it to say that this was northern New Jersey, this was a heavy Italian area, you had this large store that used to be a supermarket, and now was a tool and pool center run by an Italian guy named Sal Zucchini.

That being the case, it is very hard to say what the exact nature of the business conducted within this establishment really and actually was.

It was a very strange store, as the tools would be pushed aside every year around April, and the inside of the entire store was set up with above ground swimming pools, all filled with water inside this huge, old building. It had pool accessories, pools, filters, parts, chlorine and everything you would need for a pool in your backyard all stuck in this strange store, located right in the center of this urban neighborhood along the river.

You see, this all was a sideline, for whatever the real business was that went on behind the scenes of retailing tools and pools!

In trying to tell anyone who was not from this area about a place like Sal Zucchinis, I always left it up to folks to make up their own minds as to what kind of operation it actually was. We learned a long time ago in our lives growing up here, that there were certain things you did not poke around and try to understand more than you should.

I learned my first lessons about all of these types of sideline businesses when I was about seven years old. I went home and told my father that the little candy store down the street that I bought baseball cards from, also sold these little cards filled with numbers on them that all of these men would circle numbers on, and then pay the store owner, money for.

"What were those cards, Dad?" I would ask.

"Stay out of that joint kid, it is a front for a bookie joint," was my father's answer. I still did not understand it all until I got a little older, and understood that these stores sold a lot more than just some candy, baseball cards, and ice cream.

Ronnie pulled into the parking lot and stopped the truck

and engine. We all jumped down from the back of the truck and joined the men as we all made our way across the lot towards the front door. The first thing that we realized was that there were about four or five thousand Italian guys standing outside the building. They were all dressed in fancy suits, with dark sunglasses on, wearing dark hats on their heads, and they were all watching us very carefully.

Now, if you were serious about buying a pool, you would not have driven up in an old wreck of a truck, like we just did and you would not have looked like we did either. Actual pool purchasers did not come from our neighborhood, and they would have driven up in a fancy car, been dressed better than we were, and would have come down to the riverside from one of the fancy suburb towns.

As we walked slowly to the front door, we realized that we were fish out of water. The forward watch of Sal Zucchini's operation was watching with great intent and suspicion to determine the actual purpose of our visit. Mr. Redmond led the way, followed by Ronzo and then Mr. Porter. The three of us lagged a little behind as we opened the front door and all walked inside the store.

Once inside the store, an intense smell of chlorine floated in the air, and it immediately hit you in the sinuses and overpowered your senses. The entire store was a large open floor layout, with some steel posts here and there to hold up the roof. It was as if it were an open floor supermarket without any shelves. Some dimly lit strings of light bulbs and old fluorescent strips of lights lighted the sales floor. The store workers pushed all the tools over to one side of the sales floor and the rest of the sales floor now had all kinds of shapes and sizes of pools on display. All different types of pools were there, child-sized pools, large and small oval pools, round pools, square pools. You name it, and they were there—all filled with water, while the quiet hum of pool filters circulating water around the inside of the pools filled the air. Many of the pools had beach balls and other toys floating around in them. It was very surreal to see all of this inside some old building!

A large Italian guy with jet-black hair, dressed in a dark, perfectly fitted black suit, who was wearing dark sunglasses even though he was inside, met us directly inside the front door.

We stopped dead in our tracks.

We were just some dopey teenagers, but we all knew the deal here. We were on the riverside section of Paterson. There was this very large Italian man staring at us, and we knew that we were going to follow his directions very carefully.

"Cannnahi helpah you?" The man asked with a thick accent.

Mr. Redmond cleared his throat and answered, "Good morning, I am Redmond, and I am here to see Sal Zucchini." All of us just stood back and held our breath a little while the large man sized up Mr. Redmond, and then he looked at the rest of our group. His eyes were going up and down, all of us very carefully.

All of a sudden, he lost his accent and spoke like any other regular Paterson guy. "Yeah, yeah, yeah, Redmond, Sal told me, youse guys were coming. You are going to buy a pool?"

"Not just a pool, but the largest pool that you have!" Mr. Redmond answered proudly.

"Oh yeah, I heard that. Do you have a truck? How are you going to haul this big pool, Redmond?" The front guy was now starting to walk towards a long, wooden front counter.

"I have the truck from the shop. Look at it out there," Mr. Redmond stopped, and he pointed out the front windows at the old truck parked in the front lot. The Italian guy stared out the window, but still refused to remove his dark sunglasses.

He nodded and said, "Yeah, yeah, yeah, a big truck, Redmond. We all wondered who was pulling up there. Come on over here and let's see if we can get this deal done."

We followed the man over to the front counter. He turned around and asked us to wait right here. We all stopped in our tracks, and we actually all bumped into one another when all of us stopped abruptly when the large man signaled us to stop.

The large man went over to the counter where an older woman was sitting on a chair. He leaned over and spoke to her very quietly. He then looked back at us and pointed. The woman nodded, and she looked through some papers on the counter in front of her. She then got up from the chair and disappeared behind a wall behind the counter.

The large man came back over to us and spoke, "You are all set, Redmond. You must have worked the deal a few days ago since your papers were all there. Go ahead on up there and they will take care of you. Oh, and ya better have the dough. This here pool—ain't cheap."

Mr. Redmond stuck out his hand and said, "Thanks a lot." The man shook Mr. Redmond's hand, pointed to the counter, and he walked away.

We walked up to the counter when the woman returned from behind the wall, followed by a tall, lanky, older gentleman with a bald head, beady, black eyes and a long, pointed nose. He was wearing a pair of black, thick-rimmed glasses. This older man sat at a stool at the end of the counter, folded his arms across his chest, and just intently stared at us. The woman handed Mr. Redmond some papers.

We all realized that the older guy just sitting there staring at us must be Sal Zucchini himself!

Harry leaned over to Jeff and me, elbowed us both, and pointed towards Sal Zucchini.

"That must be, Sal," he whispered to us as we all

nodded in agreement.

Sal was sitting there staring at Mr. Redmond, Mr. Porter, and Ronnie and then back at us kids with those dark, black, beady eyes. He was emotionless, and only his eyes moved as he sat there.

Mr. Redmond was studying the papers that the woman handed him. He looked up and caught Sal Zucchini's stare, and he nodded towards Sal with a slight nod of the head.

Sal nodded his head back.

He then asked, "You're Redmond?"

"Yes, I am Redmond," was the answer.

"You must be, Sal."

"Yeah, yeah, yeah, I am Sal. Sal Zucchini." Now, Sal was looking at him with a suspicious eye, as it was obvious that Mr. Redmond was studying the invoice and the price of this pool must have been a very large amount of money. Sal was looking carefully at the situation because it appeared as if Mr. Redmond was hesitating to pay for the pool.

We all feared the severe consequences of wasting a man like Sal Zucchini's time!

Eyes were going back and forth, back and forth. . ..

After what seemed like a lifetime, Mr. Redmond reached down into his pocket, and pulled out a giant, rolled wad of money about the size of a softball, held together by two large rubber bands. It was the largest amount of actual money I had ever seen in my whole life. Mr. Redmond pulled the bands off with a loud snap, turned, and smiled at Sal.

Sal nodded his head and smiled back.

I think for a brief moment, Sal suspected that we were all bums and Mr. Redmond did not have the dough, but now, all was well as they were speaking the universal language. He plunked down the giant load of money on the counter in front of the older woman, and she picked it up and thumbed through it.

She turned and nodded to Sal, who smiled, nodded his head twice, and waved back at her.

It was now a done deal!

The two men shook hands and Sal started to speak. "Now Redmond, you and your boys listen to me carefully, you see." Sal got up from his stool and put his glasses on top of his head. When a guy like Sal Zucchini explains something, you tend to follow the directions carefully; he is not the kind of guy you want to double cross. In these types of operations, the legit types of merchandise that guys such as Sal are marketing, is generally not at the actual store, it is always at some other remote location. The actual business conducted here at this location was not something that we were interested in knowing too much about. . ..

"Now Redmond, you and your boys, you see, take the truck from the shop and go out here, make a left, then two city blocks down make a right, and stop in front of the old warehouse, in the middle of the block. An old warehouse with the number one on it. It will have a big sign in front that says, Hank's Pickles on it. My boys will come out with your pool, and the rest of the stuff and they will load youse guys up."

"Thanks a lot, Sal," Mr. Redmond said as he shook Sal's hand, as did Ronzo and Mr. Porter. Sal nodded at the three of us and he play punched Harry in the arm as he walked by.

"Youse guys are all big, strong guys. Come on back in a few years if you are looking for a job. Be cool kids," Sal said to us as we passed.

We all got back in the truck, followed Sal's directions through the city, and stopped in front of the warehouse where there was a large group of warehouse guys waiting for us with all kinds of boxes. We pulled up and jumped out when the lead man told us to pull the racks off the side of the truck body. He and his crew then took a fork truck, and they started loading all the boxes onto the back of the truck. There were small boxes, big boxes, in between size boxes, and two very large, heavy boxes. We helped tie and strap them all in the back of the truck.

The lead warehouse man lit up a cigar while the rest of the boxes went on the truck and he said to Mr. Redmond, "Hey pal, how are you going to get this all off your truck? You will not have a fork truck to pull these off and some of these boxes weigh a lot."

"That's not a problem. I have half the neighborhood coming over to help us put this pool up," Mr. Redmond answered as he took out some more money and handed it to the lead man. "Here, you and your boys, go have a few beers on me."

"Thanks a lot pal. Hey good luck with your pool," the lead man said, as he and the rest of the crew waved and went back to the "pickle" warehouse. We all climbed back into the truck and we were off. There was hardly any room for us to sit back there now amongst all the parts and pieces of the pool, but we made room and sat down as Ronzo wove his way back towards Tilted Hill.

Well, the old truck was about to be put to the test, as Tilted Hill loomed in front of us, and the truck was loaded with thousands of pounds of metal, rubber, kids, men, prayers, and pool parts. Folks came out onto their porches along Tilted Hill, when they heard the roar of the big engine, smelled the smoke spewing out the back, and heard Ronzo shifting gears. The spectators lined up in lawn chairs in front of houses up and down Tilted Hill, to watch the anticipated failure of the truck from the shop.

Up the hill, it went and during the entire time, Harry was very confident.

"This old truck will make it," he predicted.

Sure enough, it crept along, shifting, smoking, coughing and sputtering, but it made it. The old truck from the shop was not pretty, but it was a beast! Soon enough, we had reached the top and were pulling back onto John Street. When we pulled onto John Street, I will never forget the wild scene.

The entire neighborhood was out in front of Harry's house waiting for us, cheering and yelling.

"Here they come! They got the pool! They got the pool, everyone! Look, here it comes!"

It was like a hero's welcome home parade and Mr. Redmond was leaning out the window of the truck, fist pumping in the air and hollering back, "We got the pool, we got the pool!"

The neighbors were all waiting, shouting, and smiling. They held rakes, shovels, socket sets, and other tools with them, as they appeared all ready to go to work. They were all dressed in their work clothes, and it was obvious that they all were very eager to get the pool assembled and ready to go.

Chapter Five

The Pool is Built

After the fanfare of our arrival died down and the congratulations and backslapping were over, it was time to go to work. There had to be thirty to forty people all there wanting to help. It seemed like everyone was there, the Healys, Joe Hinky doo and his dad, the Mangers family, the Lens, it went on and on, as everyone had heard about the event, and the big pool party planned for the Fourth of July. The Big Spike and Patty had arrived, and Patty and Linda were already organizing the food and drink. Mr. Redmond had a little engineer in him, as he gathered everyone around and organized the work parties into teams.

"Now Ronnie, you are in charge of unloading the truck and organizing the parts and materials of the pool into a supply line, as we need it at the site. Now Harold, you, Bill Porter, Jimmy, the Big Spike, and your teams will be assemblers. I will direct you myself according to the instruction booklets. Billy and his crew will haul the supplies from the street into the backyard. Harry and the boys will be my personal assistants, and they will help me with anything that comes up, just stick right next to me, boys."

Wow, we are going to be working side-by-side with Mr. Redmond, right in the heat of the battle! It was amazing, but within minutes, Mr. Redmond had organized the entire pool installation crew into teams and cohesive units.

Under the patio canopy, the women had already set up

the Dingleberry beer keg, along with a keg of Big Boulder beer and a half-keg of Boylan's Birch Beer. The grille was heating up, and the music had started to play. Cocoa was running around excited at all the new activity and he was seeing where he could contribute. Cocoa knew this was not the time for a game of Piggy. We all had jobs to do! Somewhere, in a dark obscure corner, within a hidden crevice, Marshmallow was waiting for the right moment to make his usual cameo appearance or two.

We had started with the bottom steel sections, and Ronnie and his team had given us the parts to begin. We had begun assembly of this steel track that now had completed a large circle outlining the pool perimeter. You could now really see how huge this pool was, since it covered the ground from the far corner near the rabbit cage, almost over to the garage.

It was now around ten in the morning, and you could feel that it was getting hotter and a little stickier with humidity. The work just flowed and flowed in the direction of Harry's dad.

My old man showed up with fresh grease on his arms and face, carrying his trusty Substantial Industries Whiz-Bang tool set. It seemed as though he had just completed a successful battle with the 1964 Putter Classic model 200. Due to his superior tool handling skills, the old man's assignment was with the assembly crew.

We laid the steel track down, then we leveled the sand inside, then we snapped these plastic protectors on the track and on and on it went. Mr. Redmond called my old man over, and they were discussing a plan and pointing at the pool sand. Mr. Redmond had a stick with a long string tied to it that he put in the center of the pool circle. My dad then took another stick, cut exactly to the height of the pool wall, and he placed it on the steel track along the edge. The two men then explained how they were determining the slope of the sand to get the proper depth. As they held the two sticks up and stretched the string out between them, Mr. Redmond instructed Harry to take a tape measure and measure the distances from the string to the sand from the edge to the center of the pool. This was very scientific, and we had learned another trick of how to calculate measurements with basic tools and some strings.

Harry proudly reported as he scooted along the string measuring the dimensions, "Four feet, four and one-half, five feet, five and a half . . . right here in the middle."

Five and a half feet deep! That was like the pool out at Palisades Amusement Park!

Mr. Redmond got a big smile on his face as he dropped the string. He was satisfied as he told us, "Let's go pick up those rakes, and then smooth out our footprints in the sand there, boys. We are ready for the wall of the pool."

It was nearly noon when Ronzo came in and explained that it was now time to get the steel wall box off the back of the truck, and there was a bit of a problem. This was the actual wall of the pool, and the steel pool wall was contained inside a huge box that the warehouse men had used a fork truck to place on the back of the truck.

"Don't get the parts mixed up now, folks!" Mr. Redmond warned everyone, when someone tried to step out of the plan and risked becoming a bit disorganized. "Stick to the game plan!" Mr. Redmond walked out to the street to assess the size of the box and he whistled a little when he saw how large it really was.

"It is big time heavy, Pop," Ronzo explained. "I put all of my weight on it and went and got the Big Spike, and we could not even move it one inch together. The box with the rubber liner is heavy too, not as heavy as this one is . . . but it is heavy."

We all watched as Mr. Redmond studied the situation. "Let's break for lunch now, while I come up with a plan to unload these."

Mr. Redmond walked back to the yard and announced,

"Hey gang, let's take an hour to eat and relax. We will meet back here at one o'clock. Linda, Patty, and Betty Porter have made all kinds of food, Big Bob's Griddle Franks, Taylor's Ham, burgers, soda, chips, and we just tapped the birch and the beer kegs, so go ahead, relax, and enjoy the food and drinks."

Mr. Porter, the Big Spike, Ronzo, the three of us, Cocoa holding his Piggy, and my old man, all stayed next to Mr. Redmond. We walked back to the truck in front of the house while the rest of the crew headed to lunch.

"What's the plan, Harry?" My dad asked, as it was obvious that Mr. Redmond had come up on a bit of an unexpected obstacle.

"I have an idea, Paul. I just do not know right now if we can make it work," he answered. Mr. Redmond then turned to Harry, Jeff, and me and clapped his hands loudly and briskly. "Harry, head to the garage and bring to me those big giant ropes and chains that I bought from Substantial Industries." He waved his hands toward the garage, "You know, the ones we used to put the Christmas trees upside down in the oak tree. Paul and Jeff, youse two guys, jump up in the truck, study those boxes, and see if they have any weights stamped on the side of the cartons. Hurry men, it is really getting hot and the crew will fade now that they are eating food and drinking beer!"

Off like a flash, we were on our missions, and Jeff and I read off the numbers on the two boxes in question.

"One thousand and fifty pounds . . . please use a fork truck and caution when moving," I read off the pool wall carton.

"Six hundred pounds, at least this one is a little less," Jeff yelled back to Mr. Redmond, trying to put an optimistic spin on the situation. Harry arrived with big, huge chains, and thick, heavy ropes, and he dropped them all next to the truck. Mr. Redmond was looking up and was studying a large tree right in front of the house. We all wondered what he was thinking of doing, but not one person said a word.

He then smiled, and turned to Mr. Porter and said, "Bill, please, go and get your Galaxy 500 and pull it around in the back of the truck under this big, maple tree branch."

"Will do, come on, Cocoa," Mr. Porter said as Cocoa sprung to life, grabbed Piggy, and followed Mr. Porter over to his car. He was more than eager to be involved in this part of the mission, especially if it meant working alongside his best buddy in the whole world.

Mr. Redmond was still studying the situation. He then pointed at the back of the truck. "Everyone else, jump up in the truck and let's strap up those cartons with this chain and rope. Ronnie, you jump in the truck and start it up, listen carefully to me, and I will tell you what to do."

We all jumped up, and we helped and watched as the men wrapped the cartons and tied special knots with these huge ropes and steel chains.

"Tie those cartons good, men. They need to hold a lot of weight. Now, throw the rope ends over that big tree branch as Ronnie backs the truck up close."

Ronzo kicked off the huge engine, and he slowly backed the truck close enough for all of us to get the rope over the branch.

The Big Spike took the ends of the ropes and he said, "I got this job guys." With one big vertical leap from the bed of the truck, George launched like a rocket ship up in the air, and tossed the ropes up and over the branch, while the other ends tumbled to the ground.

"That is why he is the Big Spike," Harry explained.

"I've got it, Harry! I see now, what you are going to do," my dad yelled, as the plan had now unfolded in my father's eye, and the two of them were on the same page. Mr. Redmond smiled back, and nodded his head, while we watched the big Galaxy 500 arrive on the scene.

Mr. Redmond guided Mr. Porter with Cocoa sitting in

the passenger seat up behind the truck, right under the branch, holding the ropes.

"Now, tie both of those rope ends on the big steel bumper of that giant Galaxy." Mr. Redmond instructed everyone.

My dad tied the ropes on the steel bumper and gave Mr. Redmond the thumbs up signal.

"All right, everyone off of the truck, and stand far away from the whole thing!" Mr. Redmond warned us.

Now a crowd had gathered to watch this major operation as many folks heard the truck start up and lunch was now winding down. Their curiosity had now captured them and low murmurs filtered throughout the crowd of, "What is he doing? What is going on?"

So, there it was in front of us, a marvel of street smart, "hood engineering" ingenuity. The cartons were on the back of the truck with ropes and chains tied around them. The other ends of the ropes were over the huge tree branch and tied to the bumper of the big giant Galaxy 500.

What a scene!

"Ronnie, inch the truck forward, and Bill, you hold your foot on the brake of your car."

The big truck crept forward as Ronzo let out the clutch, and the cartons started to move and wiggle a little.

"Ronzo, inch it forward, slow, slow, forward, forward," Mr. Redmond yelled as he watched the bed of the truck intently.

Everyone stood holding their breath while watching, and a loud cry went out when the cartons suddenly pulled off the truck bed and swung in the air! The ropes and chains pulled up tightly, the ropes and chains creaked and snapped, and we all watched to make sure the Galaxy 500 did not come ripping apart.

Cocoa had his paws up on the dashboard, while loudly barking, and Mr. Porter was sweating bullets, as he had both hands clenched on the steering wheel as if his life depended upon it.

"Good thing those ropes and chains are from Substantial Industries," the old man yelled out.

"Bill, pull the car forward, slow!" Mr. Redmond yelled as the big Galaxy 500 creaked and strained and Mr. Porter inched the car closer to the tree. As the car crept closer, the boxes that were hanging in midair slowly lowered to the ground. Lower, lower, and lower. The boxes went, until a group of men rushed in, grabbed them and guided them to the ground for the last few feet.

"Bannngggggg!"

The boxes hit the ground, and the crowd erupted into cheers! Who needs fork trucks when you have big trees, Substantial Industries ropes, chains, and a giant old 1969 Galaxy 500 automobile? Mr. Porter started to beep the horn on the Galaxy in celebration and you could hear him yelling, Cocoa barking, and we saw him hugging Cocoa in the front seat.

"Simple principle of chains, weights, ropes, and leverage, boys," Mr. Redmond said as he smiled and put his arms around us.

My dad came over, shook his hand, and simply said, "Amazing plan, Harry. Simply amazing."

"Let's get something to eat," was all the humble man said.

It was now really hot and humid, and the air was growing hazy and thick. Lunch was over and the work crew, as Mr. Redmond had correctly predicted, was moving slower and slower. The beer was flowing freely now, and you could tell some men were getting tired, tipsy, and a little lazier as they were drinking and sitting around a little more than they previously were.

We placed the big boxes upon large, industrial hand trucks that Mr. Redmond had borrowed from the shop, and a team of ten men each trucked and wheeled the boxes into the backyard next to the pool. Ronzo tore open the cartons and inside sat the huge steel wall and the precious rubber liner.

"This is the hardest part, gang, here take these work gloves, as that steel wall can be sharp," Mr. Redmond said as he handed out work gloves to everyone. "We will place the rubber liner inside on the sand and unfold it as much as we can without disturbing the sand base. We will then have to work the steel wall into the bottom track and latch it on the sides. It will take all of our people to hold this up because this pool is so huge."

The steel wall installation now began with all the available workers, Patty, Linda, and all the other ladies included, as we rolled out the steel wall, and made our way around the pool snapping, the wall inside of the track. Luckily, it was a dead, calm day as the slightest breeze made the steel wall shake and rattle. Another team then dropped the rubber liner in place inside as the wall slowly closed around it.

What a major, major operation it was!

Once the wall was all in place, Jeff, Harry, and I went around snapping in sidewall supports and some top sections to give it all stability. All the while, Mr. Redmond was directing the entire scene. Occasionally, my dad and Harry's dad would study the instructions to make sure it was all working out according to the book.

Mr. Redmond then picked up a long section of stainless-steel metal that had holes drilled in both sides of it and handed it to Ronnie.

"This is very important. Ronnie, this splice piece joins the two wall sections together. You need to tap it down and then install these nuts and bolts in the holes to hold it all tight. This is all that holds the walls together, so we cannot make a mistake here. It will be under extreme pressure, so make sure you tighten it all down good and secure. I have to go inside to make a phone call, and go to the restroom, but you can take care of this for me. Make sure that you duct tape the inside edge of the splicer so the nuts and bolts do not cut into the rubber liner."

Ronzo looked like he was becoming a little pie-eyed, but he reported that he could handle it, and off he went to install the splice piece.

It was now becoming later in the afternoon and many folks were leaving, as they had some things to do. Now, it was really hot and humid out and the heat and humidity took a toll on the workers. The larger and most difficult parts of the pool construction were now completed, and my dad gathered up his tools, spoke with Mr. Redmond for a while and he took off and headed for home too. The crowd was now dropping like flies. It was really thinning out and as people left, Mr. Redmond was thanking them for helping, while also reminding them of their invitations to the big Fourth of July party. The remaining workers were really getting tired, some were half in the bag, and many people were only standing around talking. We were all hot, sweaty, and tired, but Mr. Redmond knew he could count on us young teenagers once the rest of the crew was drunk or too tired.

"Grab the two step ladders and jump over the side, boys. Most of the crew is bombed or gone now, but all we have left to do, is to pick up the liner, snap it in under the top rail, and then smooth it all out."

Up the ladders we went and over the side. We did exactly as Mr. Redmond instructed us and worked our way around the entire pool until the liner was in place. It was really looking like a pool now, and it looked like it was close to completion.

The sun was now fading; this long, hot day had waned. The summer breeze had picked up slightly, and the heat of the day had started to fade just a bit.

Ronzo was gone, but we found him out like a light, snoring under the beer keg. The Big Spike and Mr. Porter were pretty well blitzed by now. And most of the other people had left.

Mr. Redmond stood on the side, folded his arms, and smiled. "Get the hose. Harry, throw it in there, and let's start to fill it!"

Finally, the project was finished!

It was the moment that we had been waiting for!

What a project and we were a big part of it! Harry carried along a tiny garden hose, and he tossed it into the pool and turned the water on. Of course, most of the city water pipes were very old; the city had installed them in the ground about ten minutes after Paul Revere told everyone that the British were coming, so the water pressure was not too swift. A little, tiny trickle of water came out of the end of the hose, and chased around the inside of the pool liner.

Mr. Redmond continued to direct us. "Take off your work shoes and your socks too. Roll up those pants and jump on in there, boys. Smooth out the wrinkles in the liner, now that the water is there to hold it down."

Looking at the feeble trickle of water peeing out of the hose, he then pointed out the obvious, "It will take a little while to fill the pool up."

The three of us followed the careful instructions of Mr. Redmond and jumped into the inside of the pool. Let me tell you after a long hot day—the cold water sure felt nice on our legs! Once there was enough water in the bottom, we smoothed the rubber liner out, and Mr. Redmond told us to come on out and dry off. It was dark now, and the mosquitoes were eating us alive.

"You boys did very well today." Mr. Redmond was very proud of us. He slapped us all on the back and shook our hands one by one. "You all worked very hard. Now go ahead and get those last hot dogs, and have a soda and relax. It is all finished," he told us.

As we sat and ate, I watched Mr. Redmond standing with his hands on his hips, scanning over the masterpiece he had created.

"Ronnie and I are going to set up the filter. He is going to help me build this fancy wooden deck around the pool and put up some lights above the deck during the week," Mr. Redmond told us. He then added, "I might even take a vacation day or two to get it all done in time for the big party."

A vacation day!

Guys like my old man and Mr. Redmond never took a vacation day; this must be really serious!

Looking back, this was the first real work project in which I was ever involved in constructing. I went on to work for a period, in a career where I built many things, fixed, and maintained them, but this was really where it all started for me.

We all owed that man a lot, as we did not realize it at the time, but he had taught us all an entire textbook of knowledge on one hot and humid summer day.

Chapter Six

The Fourth Arrives and Disaster is Not Far Behind

Due to all the time, I had spent working on the pool over the last week; I was way behind my time with my household chores, as my mom and the old man had painfully reminded me. I spent most of the next week leading up to the Fourth of July, working around the house and catching up. I saw Harry and Jeff here and there, but I had not yet had a chance to go over to the Redmond's house to see the pool all filled up and completed.

I knew the holiday was coming up in a few days and that the big celebration would start at around noon on the Fourth of July. Of course, I planned to attend the big party, but I did not have too much time to become overly excited, since I was so busy around the house. The days crept up on me until it was the day before the fantastic holiday celebration.

Around the dinner table, I reminded my parents, and they both told me they would stop by and visit during the day. I sure was excited now, and I did not sleep much that night dreaming about the pool and the big day ahead of us. The Fourth of July came, and it was a bright, clear, glorious day, not really too hot and humid considering that it was Independence Day.

Around noontime, I ran over to John Street. When I rounded the corner from Belmont Avenue onto John Street, the number of cars that I saw that were parked and lined up from one end of the street to the other astounded me. Both sides of the street had many parked cars and the parking for the visitors even overflowed over onto nearby Geyer Street. I opened the front gate and I could hear the music blasting from the loudspeakers on the patio as I walked up the driveway. Cocoa met me about halfway with Piggy in his mouth and I reached down, petted him, and said hello. I turned into the yard and stood there, amazed at the scene.

It was all there in front of me. The pool, the deck around the pool with fancy palm tree lights hanging down around it, the grille was smoking, people were dancing to the music on the patio, the little kids were playing on a spinning merry-go-round set up in the yard, the horseshoes were clanging, and on and on it went.

From one end of the backyard to the other, it was nothing but endless fun and games. The food lined up on three long tables, and they even had watermelons cut open and filled with crushed ice and sangria wine, fruits, and punch, three kegs of beer and a half keg of Boylan's Birch Beer, steamers in a big kettle cooking over fire pits, along with another barrel filled with corn on the cob.

It was Harry's Resort, and all the other resorts in the entire world had nothing on us!

The place was jammed with wall-to-wall people everywhere that you could see. It was hard to find Harry and Jeff, but we finally met up. Harry introduced me to relatives of his that came in from Danbury, Connecticut and Delaware to attend the big picnic and party. My goodness, people who had come all the way from Connecticut and Delaware arrived at Harry's house! Even Father Mark was there from Harry's church. He was the head priest at the church that the Redmonds attended, and he was best friends with Mr. Redmond. I had met him before, from time-to-time on some of these special occasions, and I liked him . . . he and I got along very well together.

I walked over to the pool and there it was in front of me,

the centerpiece of the entire celebration. It looked like a lake; the water was crystal clear, and it was beautiful. In the center of the pool was the crown jewel of it all, as the Redmonds had built a volleyball net that spanned the entire pool. In the pool, right in the center, was the legendary Big Spike himself. He was playing a game with a group of unsuspecting victims, whom he had lured into participating in what they thought was a little fun game of pool volleyball.

I heard Patty calling out warnings from behind me, "Now George, please take it easy with the volleyball game. These people just want to play a nice game now."

In the meantime, the Big Spike was sizing the opponents up to pummel a spiked ball off their noses, faces, shoulders, and other various body parts. Some victims of a happy little game of pool volleyball already had suffered some black eyes, bloody noses, and other injuries at the hand of George.

"Play nice, George!" Patty called out to her husband.

The rest of the pool, well, it was filled with kids, people floating on tire tubes, rafts and mats, and other folks, just hanging out talking and swimming, while keeping a close eye out for a rocketing volleyball being spiked in their direction. Small replica, life preservers with beer cans tucked inside of them, floated liquid pleasure around the pool here and there. It was a fantastic, unbelievable scene, this resort haven tucked inside of urban America in some old, gritty, hardened city. All of our hard work and sweat had been worth it.

Mr. Redmond stood on the sideline, eating food, drinking beer, and smiling like a Halloween pumpkin at the incredible creation that he had built and funded. He would mingle and move among the crowd, laugh, and talk and dance once in a while to some big band music; he was eating it all up. Ronzo and Mr. Porter were working the grille, wearing big Uncle Sam hats on their heads. The griddle franks and burgers were cooking up all over the place. The partygoers would gobble them up as soon as they came off the grille. Linda and Patty kept a constant supply of food, drink, and supplies flowing out of the kitchen and out to the patio, and they worked hard to keep up with it all. My parents stopped by, as did most everyone in the neighborhood did, at one time or another during the day. Even the police officer on beat patrol stopped by and had a burger with us!

The three of us went in the pool and we had a blast, but we were sure only to go in when the Big Spike had taken a break to drink some beer and eat a burger. There were American flags flying from on top of the garage, the pool deck, the flagpole, and on top of the house.

If ever a bunch of folks appreciated and exemplified what America was all about, then it had to be the Redmonds and the group gathered at 20 John Street.

When dusk came, Ronzo and Mr. Porter shot off all kinds of fireworks and firecrackers and put on quite a show. The party went on and on, well into the early morning hours, until it finally ended when the partygoers were either too exhausted or too half-in-the-bag to continue.

What a glorious day it had been!

July came and went, and every weekend that the weather would permit was about the same, with huge parties, cookouts and fun over at 20 John Street. The summer was slowly waning, and the dog days of August had arrived. Sometimes, when things sail along so happily, the last thing you could ever imagine was that disaster or some kind of adversity could ever enter the picture. The Redmonds were such positive people; I never even gave it a second thought that something terrible could happen to them.

Eventually, disaster always raises its ugly head.

August had brought those creepy, sticky, hot, humid

days where you felt all of your energy sucked out of your body, and you did not really want to do anything at all. I despised the heat and humidity, and all I wanted to do was lie around like a slug, and not do a thing at all on these types of days.

I remember this particular day as if it was yesterday. It was a Sunday, and it was hot and very humid. I had helped the old man put a water pump in the Putter earlier in the morning, before it had gotten too hot. Since working on the pool, I had gained quite a bit more confidence with tools and wanted to get involved with repairs and projects. After that, we had eaten an early dinner, then the old man and I had watched the New York Bugs baseball game together on television. It was around four or five in the afternoon now, and it was still just as hot as it was earlier in the day.

"Aren't you going over to Harry's house and going into the pool?" The old man asked after the game as we walked out to the backyard. He headed for the garden with his garden hoe to weed out the vegetables.

"Yeah, yeah, yeah, it is just so hot and I wanted to help you, but I guess that I will head over there now." I half-heartedly answered him, while following him over to the garden. We could hear the music playing over at Harry's Resort, the occasional clang of the horseshoes hitting the pegs, the water splashing, and people laughing, as well as other party related noises drifting over to our yard. I stood there watching the old man working the tool in and around his tomatoes and pepper plants . . . when it happened.

All of a sudden, while I was watching the old man work, a gigantic, loud, unbelievable, earthshaking noise occurred. It shook the very ground, and resonated as if a bomb had hit, or some type of other incredible explosion had gone off. I could feel the very earth of our neighborhood roll, rattle, and shake under my black canvas sneakers.

"KAAAABOOOOOOOOOM!"

The windows of the houses, stores, apartment buildings,

and every other building around shook and rattled. I have never heard anything like it both then and now, and my first thought was that a steam boiler in one of the old lace mills or dye factories had blown up. The old man ducked, as I did too, and he dropped his hoe in surprise.

"WHAT THE HELL WAS THAT?" The old man asked as he climbed out of the garden.

"I don't know, Dad!" I was looking around, working hard on getting my bearings.

My mother stuck her head out the window and she asked, "What was that?"

Ada and Al stuck their heads out of their apartment window and yelled over to us, "What the hell was that?"

"We don't know! It was so loud. It was unbelievable! It shook the ground!" The old man explained. Ada yelled out the window that the noise seemed to come from over by John Street over in the direction of the Redmond's house.

Harry's house!

As we stood there puzzled, we noticed that people were looking out their windows throughout the whole neighborhood and they all were trying to figure out what had happened. We all then became strangely aware of people screaming, yelling, and hollering from over in the direction of Harry's house. We also noticed that all the usual normal noises of the pool, horseshoes, music, and other party related noises . . . had ceased.

The old man looked at me and he yelled, "Let's go, something must have happened over there!"

Off like a rocket, the old man took off with me in tow. My father was in good shape and he could always run like a deer. Off we went, through the apartment house yards, down the stairs for the parking area, across Vince's gas station, and down Belmont Avenue, we ran.

The old man was flying, and I was right behind him as we turned onto Cook Street. Past Trio liquors, past Clipclock's warehouse, past the locksmith shop, we continued, when the old man yelled back to me, "I think it is Harry's house!"

As we turned onto John Street, I noticed that the street gutters at the corner of Belmont Avenue and John Street had water running down them, in and amongst the tires of the parked cars. It had not rained in a long, long time, so I was a bit confused as to where the water could have come from. I could see people running out of the front of Harry's front gate, holding their hands above their heads and screaming.

"Run! Run!" We could hear people yelling as they ran from his house, hollering and yelling.

We reached the front of Harry's house and ran into a rush of water, flowing out of the backyard like the Colorado River.

People were still running in all directions and wading through the water. We went through the gates and made it towards the backyard, where the water was up over our waists in some spots. There was water everywhere we looked! There was water flowing out the basement windows of the house, as all the glass had been broken out of the windows and water was pouring out of them.

There were hot dog buns, plastic wrappers, Big Bob's Griddle Franks, hamburgers, dog toys, beer cans, soda cans, hats, kid's toys, corn cobs, volleyballs, beach balls, mustard jars, beer kegs, birch beer kegs, lawn chairs, and anything else that you could ever imagine, floating in the backyard within this giant flood of water.

I saw Harry standing in the middle of the water up to his waist and I yelled, "Harry, what happened?"

Harry saw me, turned around with a dazed look on his face, put his hands over his head, and yelled, "I do not know, but I think the pool blew up! Do you see, Cocoa?"

"THE POOL BLEW UP!" my old man yelled back.

"Yeah, the pool is gone, we just don't know, but the pool is gone. It blew up. Look!" Harry pointed in the direction of where the pool was at the back of the yard.

Just then, I spotted Cocoa swimming across the yard and I pointed him out to Harry. "There he is. There is, Cocoa!"

My father saw Mr. Redmond wading through the water, calling for help, and my dad worked his way over to him. The grille was floating upside down in the water, along with grass, mud, and overturned tables and chairs. The water level was now starting to go down, and I could see people lying on the ground in the mud and dirt, still in their bathing suits. They had rolled and tumbled along the ground and they were floundering along the ground, stunned and confused. There was Ronzo, Mr. Porter, Patty, Billy Healy, and other neighbors. We reached them and helped pick them up.

I turned and looked at the top of the driveway, to see the rabbit that lived in the cage next to the pool, still inside his cage, as his cage floated on top of the rapids as if he was going for a ride out to sea. He rode in his cage, and the cage steered safely along the torrents, down the driveway, and finally came to rest out at the street in the gutter! A neighbor ran out to the street to recover the poor rabbit.

"Where is, Marshmallow?" I heard Linda call out.

A voice answered from an upstairs window inside the house where a neighbor had fled. "I have him up here, he is in the house!" The person must have been watching the scene from up high within the house. They had rescued the poor old dog from his hidden crevice before he had floated away.

It was like a scene from some strange and weird 1950s B level science fiction movie.

The water was finally leaving and going down now. We turned to look at the pool, and sure enough, the entire side of the pool was gone! The deck was overturned, the ladder and filter were gone, and the pipes for the filter were now sticking straight up in the air. The force of the water knocked down the fancy palm tree lights, and some of them wrapped around the top of the garage next to where the deck had once been.

It was an unbelievable disaster of an incomprehensible magnitude.

My old man, Harry, Mr. Redmond, and I reached the side of the pool, and we looked into what was left of the pool where the whole side of it had blown out.

There inside the bottom of the waterless pool, in a maze of debris, sand, mud, grass, and tangled in the volleyball net, sitting on a tire tube, was the Big Spike! He was stunned, dazed, and still sitting on the tube in the bottom of the pool, with the netting wrapped around him. The pool was now gone and was just an empty torn shell with remnants of a rubber liner remaining. The Big Spike then fell over, and he was lying on the remains of the rubber pool liner, floundering like a fish out of water as he was trying to free himself from the volleyball netting.

We all climbed in, helped the giant Big Spike to his feet, pulled him out of the netting, and got him out of the pool shell and into the backyard.

"Wwwwwhat happened? Wwwwwhat happened?" The poor confused volleyball champion kept saying repeatedly. We helped him over to the patio. I picked up one of the chairs, and turned it right side up for him to sit down in. Slowly, folks started to recover. Jeff and Mrs. Porter, who were at their house, rushed over too when they heard the explosion and they now assisted my old man and me in checking for anyone who might have been injured in the pool explosion.

"Is everyone all right, is anyone hurt?" Mr. Redmond was calling out. Everyone was speechless but they nodded their heads to acknowledge that they were all safe; most of them were wet, muddy and very dirty. Remarkably, no one seemed hurt; everyone was just dazed and confused as to what had transpired.

Along came the police and the fire department, and they

all rushed into the yard and started to check everyone out. My old man showed the police that it appeared that the side of the pool had blown out, and in a rush and explosion of water, swept away the people who were inside the pool at the time, as well as all the folks in the backyard attending the picnic.

"The police hotline was flooded with calls. People two miles away heard the explosion!" The police officer told Mr. Redmond and my father. "We thought we were under attack and war had broken out!"

Thankfully, everyone was unscathed. Some folks had some minor cuts and scrapes from tumbling in the dirt and mud, but other than that, it was a miracle that no one was hurt badly. The fire department set up big giant pumps, and started to pump the water out of the Redmond's basement, since the water was up to the first floor inside the home! Harry's backyard looked like the surface of the moon, with craters, debris, mud, and junk strewn all over the entire yard and driveway. In reality, the word disaster did not seem broad enough to describe what had happened.

In studying what had happened to cause the pool explosion, Ronzo, the old man, and Mr. Redmond determined that the source of trouble was along the pool wall. In fact, the trouble spot turned out to be that famous splice plate that Mr. Redmond had told Ronnie to make sure that he tightened all the nuts and bolts on. It seemed like Ronzo may have had too many beers at that point and not tightened a few of them down quite tightly enough. Then folks remembered that the Big Spike, in celebration of another volleyball victory, had climbed up on the deck, and jumped down onto the tire tube into the water. The force of the giant Big Spike landing and hitting the water was a little too much for the splice plate, and the explosion occurred!

My old man went over to Mr. Redmond, who was

standing watching the water pumping out of his basement windows with his head in his hands. He put his arm around Mr. Redmond and told him that he would help him clean up and it would be all right. Cocoa was standing next to them both as if to tell them he would help, too.

The disaster had far-reaching implications for poor Cocoa too, as Piggy seemed to be lost, and it appeared that he was a victim of the floodwaters. Piggy was gone . . . carried off in the raging currents to some unknown land. Cocoa was a wreck, and we all searched and searched, but it was to no avail, as Piggy seemed to be gone forever.

Before long, a remarkable thing happened.

The entire neighborhood, folks young and old, little kids, old men, old ladies, teenagers, the homeless guy who lived in a box on Geyer Street, policemen, firemen, ambulance drivers, the manager of the Foodworld market on the corner and his butcher, Vince from the gas station and all of his mechanics, my mom, my grandfather, my sister and her friends, the man who ran the Italian sausage factory on the corner, literally everyone, who lived or worked within a two or three-block radius, descended upon the Redmond's yard.

They all began to work as a team in the yard, picking up junk, debris, raking the grass, sand, and mud out, hauling furniture and boxes out of the flooded basement to dry, sweeping the patio, and picking up the furniture, helping Cocoa collect his toys back into a pile, picking up the grille, nailing the rabbit cage back along the side of the warehouse.

They boarded up the basement windows that had been blown out, and fixed the broken palm tree lights, and Mike the plumber from around the corner, fixed the broken filter pipes. Workers in every size, shape, and form came from what seemed like miles around.

They came, and they all worked, without anyone asking them to help, because they wanted to help the man who had been so generous, who gave us so much, and cared only about providing a good time to everyone.

It was getting darker now, and we all were working hard to clean up the mess. Mr. Redmond was sitting in a chair on his patio watching us; he was still stunned and shook up over what had happened. I noticed that he had tears rolling down his cheeks; it was apparent that he was humbled at the show of love and support that had occurred, and how many of the neighborhood people had come to help in the face of this disaster.

Suddenly, we noticed a big, black, luxury Galaxy 4000 car with blacked-out windows, pull up in front of the house. The car stopped right in the front of the Redmond's driveway. We all turned and stopped working . . . this was not the kind of car that visits our neighborhood very often.

The driver stepped out of the car and Jeff said to me, "That is the big guy who stands in front of Sal Zucchini's store!"

Sure enough, it was the big guy! He stood there, dressed in his dark suit with his dark sunglasses on. He looked around, walked over to the rear passengers' door, and put his hand on the door. Another big, black Galaxy 4000 with blacked-out windows pulled up and three more Italian guys jumped out, walked, and stood next to the first car. Then a big truck came roaring up John Street with "Hank's Pickles" emblazoned on the side and it stopped behind the other cars. The lead warehouse man who smoked cigars, who had helped us load the pool, and about five of his warehouse workers got out!

We were all standing there astonished, when Mr. Redmond got up from his chair and walked slowly out to the front of the house to see what was going on.

"What is the matter now?" He asked as he walked slowly to the front of the house.

The big Italian guy looked around a few more times, tapped his suit jacket pocket as if he was feeling for something, and he opened the car door.

Stepping out of the car was . . . Sal Zucchini!

He was wearing a dark suit and a necktie and he got out, straightened his tie and jacket, and walked up the driveway, followed by his men and the warehouse workers. The big man nodded to us. We just stood there with our mouths open, and we did not say a word.

"Sal?" Mr. Redmond said as he met Sal Zucchini in the driveway. "What are you doing here?"

"Hey, Redmond," Sal began. "I heard about the trouble you had with your pool and looking around here it sure is a damn mess."

"You did?" Mr. Redmond stood there shocked while looking at Sal . . . surrounded by his henchmen. His men were all around Sal and they were constantly scanning, with their eyes, the area all around us.

"Ah, yeah, yeah, yeah . . . you see, ah, due to the nature of some of my business, I tend to keep an ear out on the police radio, and one of my boys heard the call come in about the explosion, and the fact that your pool blew up. I want to tell you that I am here to take care of everything. Sal Zucchini stands behind whatever he sells and does."

Mr. Redmond shifted his feet uneasily and since he was a wonderful, and honest man, he said, "Well, Sal, that is really nice of you, but the trouble was that my son-in-law did not really tighten the bolts on the splice plate enough. You see, Ronnie was a little bombed, and not on top of his game and my other son-in-law who is really big, jumped on a tire tube, and blew it out. It really was not your fault, and it was not a defective pool." Sal was waving his hands at Mr. Redmond as an indication that he already knew what Mr. Redmond was saying to him.

"Yeah, yeah, yeah, I know about the Big Spike, Ronzo being pie-eyed and the splice plate, but that does not matter. I had my boys bring you out a brand-new pool. You see, they have it loaded up on the back of the truck right now. Get your boys over there, Redmond. Help my boys unload it off, and they will put it right in your yard. We brought a fork truck to unload it. I also heard about the tree, rope, and car thingy."

Mr. Redmond was dumbfounded, and he turned to Ronzo, Mr. Porter, the Big Spike, my old man, and the three of us, and waved his arms for us to go out to help Sal's boys unload the replacement pool.

"Sal, I do not know what to say . . . I can't thank you enough." Mr. Redmond stammered as the two men shook hands.

Sal nodded. He turned around and walked towards the car and his men followed behind him. He then suddenly stopped and turned around and faced Mr. Redmond.

"Redmond!" Sal shouted back.

Mr. Redmond had begun to walk back to the yard, and he turned around and said, "Yes, Sal."

"This time, you should stay and supervise that splice plate installation yourself and not go to the restroom."

"I will, Sal. I will."

Sal smiled and waved and said, "You're a good man, Redmond, a really, really, good man. You bring a lot of joy and happiness to people's lives, who otherwise, would have very little, and that is very important."

Sal then turned and headed for his car. When out of nowhere, Cocoa showed up with his pork chop toy! He had decided that Sal Zucchini was a new man in our neighborhood and he thought he might engage him in a game of fetch! Oh no, we all thought, as he squeaked the toy into the leg of Sal's fancy suit. We all hoped and prayed that Sal would not throw the pork chop. The big Italian man circled around and protected Sal when he saw Cocoa come over, but Sal motioned for him to back off.

"Nice, doggie too." He said, "I heard you lost your favorite toy in the flood. I tell you what there, nice doggie. Sal will send you a new Piggy and some treats. Stay cool, doggie." Cocoa dropped his pork chop, barked three times and wagged his tail twice at Sal who smiled, petted Cocoa's head, waved, got in his car and he was gone.

We had the new pool and all the parts off the truck, in no time flat and the fork truck made quick work of putting all the boxes, parts, and pieces in the backyard.

It sure went a lot quicker than it did the first time!

Mr. Redmond walked out to the truck, found the lead man of the crew, and thanked him. He reached down in his pocket, pulled out a bunch of wet money, and went to hand it to the lead man. The lead man put the money back into Mr. Redmond's hand and closed his fingers back over it.

He looked up and said, "No . . . Mr. Redmond, as Sal said, you are a really, really, good man."

Then all the warehouse men climbed back in the big pickle truck and they were gone, too.

John Street was quiet once more.

The next day, the delivery driver delivered a package to 20 John Street, and he left it on the front step. Harry picked it up and read that the label address was to, "Cocoa Redmond." He opened it up . . . inside was a brand new, identical replacement Piggy, and a box of dog treats.

Everything was well in the world once more.

Sure enough, the next weekend, it was all the same.

The work crews, the beer, the soda, the cookout, the hot dogs and hamburgers, the laughter, the fun, and the hard work.

The replacement pool went up.

This time, Mr. Redmond himself installed the splice plate. He and the old man tightened the bolts and nuts, and then triple checked them all.

Once the pool was all filled, and it was completed, Mr. Redmond pulled the Big Spike aside, and explained that he was banned forever more from any tire tube celebrations.

When the replacement pool was all set to go, the next

weekend was Labor Day and the end of the summer. The Redmonds threw a Labor Day party to remember. They drank Dingleberry and Big Boulder beer, Boylan's Birch Beer, they ate all kinds of amazing food, cooked out, played volleyball, laughed, and danced like there was no tomorrow.

I remember Mr. Redmond came up to us and thanked us for all that we had done that summer. He explained that we now had learned a lot about tools and projects. He felt that we were all prepared to take on vocational school next week and do well in our studies. In celebration, he told us that we should put on some modern rock-and-roll music that we enjoy and he wanted us all to dance on the patio together.

"Okay Dad," Harry told his father. He then went inside and selected a popular song at the time, "Spin Around and About" by the rock group, "No Way."

It blasted away on the patio and all of us, Ronzo, Patty, the Big Spike, the Porters, Linda, and my old man, all danced and danced.

Mr. Redmond joined the rest of us and he wiggled around as if he was having the time of his life, while Cocoa barked and danced next to us all.

There is a lyric in that song that seems very appropriate as it says something about wonderful, true summers, laughing, and always being there together and forever.

And that to me, just about sums it all up.

Chapter Seven

Memories

Memories, parties, shindigs, cookouts, pools, and fun. These were simple times, and in retrospect, we did very simple things, but they were, in fact, really very special. People cared about one another and shared in each other's good times and bad times. We did not know it at the time, but we really had it all growing up in our little spot in the world. People who had more would come into our neighborhood, and look around at our little piece of America and think, wow, my goodness, these poor folks do not have anything.

Little did they know about how rich we actually all were.

These were all special, hard-working people who played as hard as they worked.

Mr. Redmond was a unique man, as there is no way to measure what he gave us that summer. He taught us about tools, teamwork, the trades, skills, and about being kind, generous, ingenious, and smart. Later on, in our lives, we would realize, even more, what special things that Mr. Redmond had taught us.

Sure, he spent a lot of money. What he gave us all; you could not really put a price tag on.

He gave us memories.

They are mostly all gone now, all passed away.

Mr. Redmond, Ronnie, Cocoa, Mr. Porter, Mrs. Porter, a lot of them, but they will live in our minds forever.

When you think about it, time is the only enemy we all

really have. We only have so much time given to us to love, to learn, to think, to teach, to work, to play, to help others, and to grow together, before time in its wondrous power catches up with us all.

People such as Mr. Redmond, Ronzo, Mr. Porter, and all the others knew that. They fit all the joy and happiness of life that they could into their own lives as well as other people's lives as quickly as they could. They made the most out of every precious second. Time, in all of its power, can only make our memories fade and dim a little as the years pass. If we take some control and do not allow it, even time cannot erase memories completely from our minds.

In our minds, we can always remember the people we loved, their faces, their voices, their smiles, the words; it is something that even time cannot diminish.

Oftentimes, when it is hot and sticky, and the summer heat is bearing down, I lift a window, turn my ear a little toward the west, and listen very closely. I close my eyes, and no matter where I am on this good old Earth, if the wind is blowing a certain direction, I can hear it. The clang of the horseshoes, the splash of the pool, the laughter, the music; it is all still there.

If I ran into the magic genie in the proverbial bottle, and the genie gave me those three wishes we have all heard about, one of them would be to take me back to 20 John Street on a summer weekend in 1973. I would love to be taken right back there, and I would hug them all, shake their hands, pat them on the back, and thank them for what they gave us, because it was more than special; it was real, very real.

I went to the party at Jim O'Malley's house that weekend and I had a great time. I missed my wife when she was away, so this was a nice escape for me. I knew she would have enjoyed the picnic, too.

Jim had a nice pool, cold beer, good food, a big, fancy deck with a new sound system, and a brand new, big screen television that we sat in front of and watched the ball game.

It was a great time, but something was missing.

I noticed a little dog walking around, eventually; I was able to make friends with him, and the dog would come over by me.

I learned that the dog's name was Slinky.

When no one was looking, I got the dog's attention. I stood up and put my hands on my knees, leaned close in over the dog and said, "SLINKY, GO GET YOUR GIBBERTY GOO."

The dog just looked at me and wagged his tail. I then sat down, conceded defeat, and just for the whim of it, I said, "Slinky, go get your Piggy."

To my surprise, the dog ran off. About ten minutes later, he came back with a stick in his mouth.

I laughed and sighed, and thought, no something was really missing.

THE END

The Eye of the Tiger

Chapter One

A Warm Cup of Joe

I woke up early on this particular Saturday and I felt a little down. For no real reason, it was just one of those days that we all have from time-to-time. My wife was sleeping late, and I had some time to kill. After a shower, I came downstairs, and did not really know how to start the day.

Hmmm . . . music, I thought.

I decided to flip through old CDs in my collection, thinking that perhaps music would improve my spirits. After going around and around for a while through different selections, for some reason, I picked an old CD from a Canadian folk singer from the mid-1970s. I put the CD in my player in the living room and then wandered into the kitchen for a nice, hot cup of good ole Joe.

As I sat down to drink my morning coffee, I listened to the words of the song as the singer who, by coincidence, was singing about drinking his own cup of coffee. He also was telling the sad story of a long-lost gal that the songwriter loved, but somehow allowed to get away for one reason or another. The singer and songwriter nailed it on this song, I thought, as I nursed a cup of coffee.

I stared out the window, and thought how true it was that facing a day early in the morning, sometimes, could be so daunting. The coffee had not improved my frame of mind, and to be honest, neither did the music.

Oftentimes, music is the thread that binds our memories, the melodies can invoke past times, both good and bad, and the lyrics can parallel times in our own lives.

My mind suddenly became an old-fashioned movie house newsreel, flipping through many past times in short, fleeting moments. I stood up from the table and went to the sink to rinse out my cup. I stopped walking about halfway to the sink when I heard a car in the neighborhood driving down the street in front of my home. I knew that sound very well as of late, as I had heard it quite often. It was a car driven and owned by a young teenager from around the corner in our little development. It was a hot rod car that he had just finished modifying, and he would frequently test drive the car in and around our streets. The car shook the windows of our house and the entire neighborhood, with a loud reverberation from the exhaust system, as he went through the gears. He rode around a lot, showing it off and having a good time with it.

I smiled and remembered a time when I was young and being in a hopped-up car was so important to us all. It was a status symbol of youth, and as we called it in our day, a chick magnet.

It may have been the combination of the song, my melancholy mood, and then the car, but for some reason, my mind flashed back to a time long ago when my best buddy, Harry M. Redmond Jr. allowed a gal to get away, and how that event turned a summer weekend into one of our most memorable adventures.

Some adventures that Harry M. Redmond Jr. and I experienced together were unbelievable, and some were, of course, commonplace. In fact, some more unbelievable ones would be hard for even me to believe, except for the fact that I went through them myself. A single event triggered this wild adventure and the trigger, of course, involved a young lady.

We grew up together; Harry, Jeff Porter, and I, all in a little two or three city block area in a gritty, old, tough, northern New Jersey city.

We all hung together and faced whatever came our way. Looking back, I would not trade growing up there, in that old neighborhood for anything or any other location in the world, because it made you who you were. It was worth ten college degrees, because the education that you received free of charge from the streets was worth a million dollars.

Harry was a great guy; he just was a little different. He quickly became obsessive in his pursuit of certain things. You see, when Harry reached about sixteen or seventeen years of age, he thought about three things, hockey, cars, and women! He continually pursued women, almost as if it was a pastime or hobby.

Harry was a good-looking guy, tall, strong with a big beer barrel chest, and strong, powerful legs and arms. We played a lot of ice hockey together during this time in our lives.

It was our sport.

We started playing on the street, and then progressed to the ice, when we made a little money to be able to afford the ice time. Harry was a rough, tough guy on the hockey rink, where he played defense and he was quite a good player. He had longish blonde hair, and he grew a mustache that he sometimes let grow longer along the edges and side. As much as he tried with the young ladies, he always had this incredibly bad luck when it came to women. It seemed like every relationship was destined to be mired in some crazy twist of events, or was destined to end in a smoldering heap of tears and unfulfilled dreams.

To be honest though, Harry sometimes caused his own female troubles.

He, in fact, was a terrible womanizer.

In our lives, it was sports, primarily ice hockey, and since we now were in a trade school and we had full-time jobs through our apprenticeships, it was about cars and trucks.

I was a truck guy, and Harry was into cars. Once we both obtained our driver's licenses, our entire world changed. We mostly had wrecks for vehicles, or as we called them, "beaters." We would fix them up as best we could with the money we had, then ride them until the wheels rolled off, the floorboards rusted out, or they cost us too much jingle to repair. Then we would junk them or sell them off for some other pile of junk.

Harry had a good job for his trade training. He worked as a welder in the metal fabrication shop where his old man was a general foreman. I was working as an apprentice electronics and electrical technician and was just getting by. While the rest of us schleps were making around two to three dollars an hour in our trades, Harry was making about nine dollars per hour as a junior welder. This was unheard of . . . this was very good money for a teenager in 1975.

Harry's father had fixed him up in a great program. By the time he was seventeen, he was a certified welder, and he was able to earn wages that were only a few notches below the shop's full-time, experienced men. He welded stainless-steel countertops and equipment for the stainless-steel diners that you would see in every town in New York, New Jersey, and Connecticut, so his shop was always very busy. Because of his good fortune and skills, Harry always had a good amount of dough in his wallet, when the rest of us were mostly broke and we got by day-to-day and paycheck-to-paycheck.

In our day, there were only a few things that you had in your arsenal that you could do in an attempt to lure the young women into being interested in you. You could have fancy hairdos as we all had in the 1970s; you could wear fancy clothes like bell-bottom pants or leisure suits with wide neckties, metal chains around your neck and fancy boots. You could be an expert in music and have memorized, and be able to sing along on a fancy eight track tape deck, to all the words of the entire eighteen minute and forty-two-second-long, song, "Close to the Crevice" by the progressive rock group, No Way. There also was always the slam-dunk lure for a young woman, if you were the star player on a sports team. Since we played hockey, we quickly found out that it was a sport that really did not have the appeal with the young gals like the more glamorous sports of football and baseball did. After all, it was hard for the young gals to consider you a good-looking guy, when you had stitches all over your face, had a black eye, a bent nose, or were missing your teeth from the impact of the latest game. I was a goaltender, and Harry and Jeff played defense in front of me, so most of the time, we had some type of injury or other physical malfunction during the hockey season.

We came to realize our fate, as there really are not many odds in your favor when you come from the gritty, poor, urban streets of Paterson, New Jersey to win the heart of a young teenage gal. That did not stop us as we sure tried all the angles!

The one sure fire ace in the deck, however, was the chick magnet set of wheels, or in no uncertain terms, a nice car. Now, the car needed to look good, have a loud exhaust system, fancy chrome wheels, and be equipped with a very loud music system, which in our day was an eight-track tape deck, amplifier, and the preferred speakers were the famous three-way Tri-axils. You blasted music as loud as you could, while cruising around, and tried to get the attention of the young women by making yourself half-deaf in a vain effort for recognition as being cool or hip.

The key was to play current cool music and since we were not the disco types, we leaned towards other types of music, but our favorite was loud, progressive rock-and-roll.

We played music from progressive rock bands like our favorite, which was a band called No Way. We also listened to folk, pure rock-and-roll, along with a little country and some rhythm and blues. Disco music did not make the cut with us though; it was just not our bag. Music was in the heyday and we blasted it loud and often.

This was a great time to be a teenager, and music was a big part of our scene, and a tool in our often fruitless, female attraction attempts. The wrong music could doom you to a life of listening to big band era music, sitting in your living room with your parents, with no girlfriends in sight!

My wreck of a truck was a 1968 service van, which I bought from an auction of old New Jersey telephone service trucks. I fixed it up as best I could, and it did not look too bad, considering how little money that I had to invest in it, but it was not going to win me any points for being the coolest truck in the neighborhood that was for sure. Harry, on the other hand, since he was now earning and had more money than the rest of us, always had nicer vehicles, or at least, a step up from our previous heaps.

It was in the summer of 1976, and we were ready to enter, in the fall of the year, our last year of the trade school. It was during this summer that Harry pulled the ultimate magic car out of his magic magician's hat. I remember the day when I first saw it as if it was yesterday.

Harry surprised me and called me up on the telephone after work one day and he told me to come over to his house as quickly as I could. I finished supper, jumped in my van, and tooled on over to John Street, which was only two blocks away from my house.

When I arrived at the front of Harry's house, I saw it right there . . . parked right in front of his home. It was a 1975 Sonicmobile, with a four-speed stick shift transmission, custom hood scoop, bucket seats, and a special X4-2Z high output engine. It had the fancy crossed racing flags, chrome logo on the hood, as well as all the other bells and whistles.

The car was the most unusual color of white that I have

ever seen. Still to this day, I cannot say exactly what color it was, as I never saw another automobile that had that same color. The best way I could describe it was that it was a creamy, off-white color that had just a touch of grey metal flake chips in it. It had fancy chrome trim and that long Sonicmobile hood, with the distinctive, super deluxe, racing wheel covers. The car had a sandal light brown colored interior with dark brown highlights on the bucket seats.

The car was just so fantastic and perfect that it astounded you.

Harry saw it one day on his way home from work, on Union Boulevard over in the town of Great Falls, on the auto lot of Johnnie's Auto Mart and he knew that he just had to buy it. The car was one-year-old, but in nearly mint condition, and he plunked down, with help of a loan through his company, the unheard-of amount of three thousand, five hundred dollars to purchase it! I could not believe it, as Harry told me the story, and I just stood there in awe of it. Harry just spent over three thousand dollars to purchase his own sports car!

"What do you think, Paul?" Harry asked me as he sat on the trunk, beaming from ear-to-ear.

"Wow," was about all I could manage to say as I leaned in the window and checked it out.

Harry then opened the door and said, "Check this music system out." He turned on the ignition key and slid an eight-track tape into the deck. Out blasted, pure heavenly music as I saw that mounted in the rear decks were the coveted three-way Tri-axial speakers.

"Hop in," Harry said. We sped off into the cool evening air, the music blasting, and both of us feeling like we were big deals.

It was magnificent!

Still, to this day, it was one of the most fantastic and beautiful automobiles that I have ever seen.

Looking back on our lives, things have a strange way of getting better, while time goes on.

It is the same as many of the old TV shows that I thought were so corny or annoying when I was growing up. I remember how I could not stand some of those old cornball shows when I was a kid, and they would be on the television.

Nowadays, when I see them come on as reruns, I sit down and say, "Oh, I loved this show when I was a kid, these are so good." Time has a funny way of changing things for us.

Looking back at the Sonicmobile, I can honestly say that I know this car in my heart, really was as perfect as I remember it, in my mind's eye.

Chapter Two

Harry Gets Caught!

Since Harry had the fancy set of wheels and most people (including Harry) considered my old van to be lacking in the cool factor, it was just not a cool enough vehicle; to attract any young females. Therefore, the logical thing to do was to take the Sonicmobile whenever we set out on our adventures. I would throw in a few bucks for gas to go cruising for girls with. Our other buddy Jeff would go with us once in a while, but he had a steady girlfriend in our last years of high school, and he spent a lot of his free time with her.

Most of the time now, it was just Harry and me, going through life, and hanging out together. Friday nights were not the big activity nights for us, since very often both Harry and I worked at our jobs on Saturdays. We went to school one-half of the school day and then worked in our trades the other half. I worked every Saturday, but Harry worked every other Saturday.

Since there were laws regulating how many hours we could work while we were still in a trade school, we could only work until 2 P.M. on Saturdays. That left Saturday night as being ours, and Saturday became the big night for us! In the winter, we had hockey games on Saturday night or early Sunday morning during the season, but this was the summer and the off-season for us, so we were free.

Harry always had two or three young women that he was dating or pursuing all at the same time. He was amazing. He had to have at least one active, steady relationship with a girl or he was depressed and dejected, it was just his personality. I was different, and while I would have a date now and then, I did not have any steady girlfriends. Things were a little different back then, as many girls and guys would all go out together as a large group, and while some of them might be actually dating, most of us just all hung out together, and had a good time.

We would hang around the hockey rink and go to the open skating sessions at the Ice Land Arena, in Great Falls, New Jersey, where we would play hockey, and in the off-season, we would skate in general sessions to keep our skating skills sharp.

After skating, we usually hung out at a restaurant that we called the Greek joint. It was a pizza place owned by a bunch of Greek brothers who were nice guys and prepared fantastic Italian food and pizza pie. They had Italian flags, maps of Italy on the wall; they played soft Italian music in the background, and had all other types of memorabilia and items on the wall to give it the ambiance of an authentic Italian restaurant, even though they were all from Greece. We hung out there all the time because it was close to the ice rink and they made great pizza pie!

Harry was going through many particularly tumultuous relationships during the summer that he got his Sonicmobile. While I tried hard to keep up with the drama, it was difficult, as he often changed girlfriends on a week-to-week basis, so you felt as though you needed a scorecard to keep track of them all.

"How are things going with Karen?" I asked Harry on a summer night in late June.

"Karen, no, I dumped her, two weeks ago, Paul. I am with Joyce. Do you remember, Joyce?" Harry answered.

"Oh yes . . . Joyce." I faked my way through it.

Joyce was a nice girl who worked in a bakery in Clifton, New Jersey. I thought she was about the nicest of the girls that I had met that Harry had dated. She was tall, pretty, and she had a very nice personality, but you never knew when the moment would come, when Harry would seek out a new love. He had met Joyce at the bakery when the owner of the establishment had hired Harry and me to do some repair work at his bakery. Harry worked on the metal display cases and I reworked his electrical systems. The owner must have been really looking for a deal to let two young apprentices work on his bakery, but if I remember correctly, we actually did a good job, and we did not wreck the joint or burn it down.

Joyce had then turned into a steady relationship with Harry, but of course, it was up and down. All it took was one night when Joyce had to work and Harry would go cruising in the Sonicmobile. Chicks would spot him in the Sonicmobile; he would meet them and be off on another adventure with some new love. I would start out sitting in the front seat, and when Harry would pick up some new gal, he would exile me into the back seat. I sat there like a dope as the oddball man out, while Harry showed the young woman the whiz-bang, super deluxe, tape deck or some other fancy feature of the Sonicmobile.

It would make for a long night for me, that was for sure.

Keeping up with Harry's playboy lifestyle was like a soap opera that never ended. I secretly hoped and wished that Joyce would finally end all the revolving doors of women in Harry's life. She seemed in my opinion to be the one for him, that was for sure. Joyce would pop up at hockey games and she would skate and hang with us all the time. It really seemed at times that it was a long-term, serious relationship starting up.

Little did I know that Harry would whip up an intricate scheme to derail the relationship with Joyce.

In July 1976, we decided to change up our hockey-training regimen, and we traded our ice-skating routine, for a stint or two, at the nearby roller-skating rink. Generally, if you can ice skate well, then it is an easy transition over to roller-skating. We did not use the in-line skates that they use now, we used the old-fashioned, four-wheel rollers, and the rink we skated on had the traditional hardwood floors.

As a change of pace, we often would go to an open skating session at the roller-skating rink on a Saturday night. In the spring of this same year, the rink was brand new; it had just finished construction, and had been open only a few months, so it was quickly turning into a teenage hot spot. This was the place to be on a Saturday night for guys, as well as the gals, with big crowds, a disc jockey playing music during the skating, and it was a huge hangout for teenagers.

Guys would park their cars in the lot outside the rink and all the nice cars would line up and park in one spot and open the hoods, play some music and try hard to act cool. Guys would be swapping car parts and checking out each other's cars, working deals for music, or just staring over at the girls.

Harry would cruise on in with the Sonicmobile, and of course, attract a lot of attention with his vehicle. Once inside the rink, we could really get it done. Being hockey players and good ice skaters, we could both roller skate well.

Harry would ham it up big time, dancing to the music, weaving in and out of the traffic, flipping around backwards, doing tricks on skates, skate on one skate, and really put on a show.

I behaved a little more conservatively and while I could skate really well; my personality was generally to hide in and amongst the crowd and try not to attract too much attention.

Harry had everything going for him, his looks, extra money, a fancy car, steady and not so steady girls, but one thing he was not really too good at was keeping it all organized.

The next Saturday was the Fourth of July weekend, and Harry thought we should go over to the roller rink and meet up. He was picking up a new gal, and he said he would meet me for a general skating session.

"What about, Joyce?" I asked.

"She is busy for the holiday and is going away with her family," Harry told me.

Based on that plan, I met Harry and his latest gal at the roller rink. The new woman seemed nice enough. She was pretty, talkative, outgoing and friendly, but I still felt that Joyce was the one woman for Harry.

Harry was skating with her and I was going around by myself when I suddenly felt a tap on the shoulder from behind.

I turned around and there was Joyce skating right behind me!

"Hi there, Paul. What is Harry doing skating around with that girl?" Joyce asked me with a very unhappy and stern look on her face. "He told me that you two had a job to do this weekend and we could not all go out!"

Oh, no! Joyce had caught Harry and his luck had run out. Now I am stuck . . . between those horrible rocks and hard places!

You see, I think Joyce is really the nicest gal I have ever seen Harry with, but Harry is my best buddy. We are like brothers, and I have to do something to protect him.

For a fleeting moment, while I stood there like a dope, not knowing what to say, my mind threw around all these fantastic lies and stories.

Ah, huh, let's see, it . . . is . . . his long-lost cousin. No, no, correction. It is the next-door neighbor's daughter, who could never get a date, and her dad asked Harry to take her out as a favor, before she entered training to become a nun. On the other hand, it is really his half-sister that he did not know about . . . until last week, and other wild fantasies to protect my best friend all whirled around in my mind. It was obvious that Harry had gotten his signals crossed. He had woven a tall tale to tell Joyce about us working, and he was in big time, hot water.

I felt bad for her and in the end as I stood there mumbling and fumbling; I folded like a cheap camera.

"Joyce, I do not know what to say. You had better ask, Harry," I said. I had chosen to take the safe way out and just punt.

"I will!" She answered angrily and skated off in his direction.

Oh boy, being Harry's best buddy was sometimes a hazard, and it sure had some awkward moments that came along with being his friend. To be honest, Harry really was not treating the young women very respectfully, and he was self-centered as far as his love interests were.

Sometimes, in life, you get what you deserve.

I skated and then came to rest on the sidewall of the rink, content to watch from a safe distance as the scene was about to unfold. Joyce also waited and when Harry came around the turn, you could see the look of horror on his face when he spotted Joyce. He had some major explaining to do to Joyce, as well as to the new gal that he was courting this particular evening.

Well, as you can imagine, it was an ugly little display right there on the rink. Jilted love is never pleasant, nor is it easy when you are seventeen years old, in fact at any age. Suffice it to say after a big, loud discussion; Harry lost Joyce as his number one steady girlfriend, as well as the new gal that he had brought to the rink for this date. Both of the young women skated off angrily . . . leaving two-timing Harry alone in the rubble of discontent.

These things happen in the world of Harry, and he brushed it all off, but we left the roller rink shortly thereafter the confrontation. Harry and I rode home together; and it was a quiet ride back home. He tried to make out all rough and tumble that it did not bother him at all, but I knew him well enough to know that it was not true, and he was suffering big time at the loss of Joyce.

Chapter Three

A Plan Evolves

A day or two later, Harry and I kept up our usual pace and frequented our usual haunts. We cruised in the Sonicmobile, played music, shot some pool games here and there, and hung out at Pete's pinball parlor, playing some machines. The usual high spirits of Harry just were not there though; he was down in the dumps most of the time. He had a date or two with some girls that he had met here and there, and while he never mentioned it, I knew he still was missing Joyce and hurting from the big blow up at the roller rink.

I stayed away from the subject, but one night at the Greek joint over some sodas and pizza pie, I asked him if he had heard from Joyce at all.

"No, no, no, I haven't and I really don't care," Harry answered me, shaking his head. He knew that I was not convinced, and he became a little quiet and sad and put his head down. I did not say anything, but Harry then offered, "I called her house a few days ago, and her mother said she did not want to talk to me anymore, and that I should not call her."

I did not know what to say other than a low quiet, "I'm sorry, Harry, I know you really liked her."

It was a tough spot to be in, as I knew my best buddy was hurting, but I thought it best not to say too much. He really did bring this on himself, by being a Casanova and jumping from girl-to-girl, while giving Joyce the impression that she was his steady gal. I wondered if he had learned his lesson. After eating, we rode over to the ice rink for a quick skate in the Saturday night general session. And who shows up, but Joyce and a bunch of her girlfriends! They were all skating together, laughing, and looking like they were having a great time. Poor Harry spiraled downhill quickly, in a forlorn and sad reaction (all of his own doing—I might add) as he was upset at Joyce's reactions or lack thereof.

"Just go on over there and talk to her and see if you can patch it up," I told Harry.

Harry screwed his mouth up like a corkscrew. Big, rough, tough, Harry was being a pansy-la-la.

"I don't know, Paul. It just does not seem right. She does not seem like she is even missing me." Harry stood there in the corner of the rink and lamented. At one point, as he stared in her direction, he lifted his hand in a feeble attempt at a wave in her direction while she skated around the corner of the rink, right past us. Joyce never even acknowledged him or looked his way at all.

I had to admit that it looked bad.

Harry sighed, stood there a little defeated, and shook his head. He whipped up a quick excuse, "Hey, I have a bad edge on my right skate here. I am going to see if the skate shop will grind it for me, I will be right back." Harry then skated off the ice and out of the rink. I thought that he just needed some time alone, so I picked it up and just skated slowly around the edges of the boards by myself.

I was going around slowly when I heard a soft voice behind me call out my name. I turned around to see Joyce waving and skating to catch up to me. She was a good ice skater, but I turned in and allowed her to catch up.

"Hey Paul, how is it going?" Joyce asked.

"It is going good, Joyce. How is it going with you?"

Joyce never replied to my question, but she quickly asked, "How is, Harry?"

I stopped skating and glided to the sideboards, and

Joyce followed me. Leaning on the boards, I fudged it as best I could, but I would never make it in a poker game or as a spy.

"Oh, he is doing all right, I guess, not too bad." I was not convincing at all.

"Well," Joyce said, "I really do not want to talk to him, but would you be kind enough to tell him something for me?

"Sure, sure, Joyce, what's up?" I answered, hoping that she was going to ask me to relay some love note, or a sappy poem of some sort, to end all of this madness.

Joyce then went on to tell me how she is raising money for a charity, one of those major, mainstream, fund-raising charities that everyone knows about, and is constantly pitching for donations on television across America.

On and on, she went, telling me about what a wonderful mission it is. She told me how she was involved in the fundraising, and all kinds of other fantastic promotional information and mumbo jumbo that, quite honestly, took me by surprise. All of this charity information was really the last thing that I had expected to hear. I really had no idea of what she was talking about, but she was making my ears bleed.

Yet, I did not want to be rude at all to her, so I just stood there on my skates, nodding my head, smiling and being very polite as I listened, desperately hoping that Harry would return from the skate shop to rescue me, and meet up with her to patch things all up.

Joyce then went on some more to tell me, "I am going to be participating in the summer fund-raising event in two weekends to raise money for the charity. It is a marathon skate-a-thon at the new roller rink and you can sponsor me for a pledge. It is going to be the highlight of the summer, Paul. Everyone is going to be there. I will be there skating and even though I will not speak to Harry, you can let him know that he can support the charity and pledge some money. That is, of course, if he is not too busy chasing women around all of northern New Jersey."

Joyce then handed me a pledge card that she conveniently had in her back pocket, and she explained that I could pledge a dollar figure for each hour that she skates to raise money for the charity. Oh boy, I thought. Joyce is ensnaring me into a pledge for a charity while Harry was off getting his skates sharpened.

While she babbled on and on, all I could think about was how I was a little short all the time in the old cash department and that Joyce could probably skate for a while. I could be out a little more dough than I wanted to be!

"Well, it sounds like a really good charity, Joyce." I managed to squeak back as I took the pledge card from her as if it was a glass of poison. Then it hit me! Joyce knew that I was not exactly a descendant of some wealthy and affluent family, and she had only a slight chance at working me over for fifty to seventy-five cents at the most. It did not take me too long to figure out that her sales pitch was actually a covert effort to let Harry know she will be at the rink for this big event.

It was a glimmer of hope, on an otherwise very bleak love horizon! Joyce successfully roped me into this pledge thing, and I agreed to the terms and conditions, for the sake of giving my best buddy a shot of restoring his relationship with this charity-infatuated gal.

I motioned to Joyce to skate off the rink, over to where the grandstands were.

"If you have a pen or pencil, we can go over here and I can fill out the pledge card. Otherwise, we can fill it out some other time," I said while stepping off the ice. Of course, since this was a setup, Joyce promptly produced a writing instrument and handed it to me with a big, wide smile. Oh geez, she really was into raising dough for this event, I thought as I searched the card for the lowest possible dollar figure that I could find and circled it. I put my name on the card and faked a big, wide smile.

Ah, the traps that the young women set as they capture and lure us dopey male teenagers. Joyce had not only corralled me into pledging some few measly little coins that I would take home from my paycheck, but she also dropped a huge hint to Harry, for a possible opening back up of the romance door.

Much to my frustration, I was learning that no young women could ever come out and communicate directly to the male species their feelings. It is all secret code words and behind the scenes, secret agent, type subterfuge.

I gave the card back to Joyce, and she tore off one piece for me to keep for my records. She thanked me, excused herself to go join her friends back out on the ice, and off she went.

I sighed, and thought, well now, that was a whole load of fun. Mission accomplished for her. And now, I was a few bucks in the hole. I jumped over the boards off the rink by the player's benches and skated back out on the ice, sadly crying the blues to myself over my poor financial situation.

Just when I was thinking in my mind of finding a part-time job, or joining up with some monks, or coming up with some other radical fund-raising plan, I heard Harry cutting the ice hard behind me to catch up. He motioned for me to skate over to the boards towards the player's bench and I met him there. We both turned our backs to the ice and hung over the wall to talk.

"I saw you talking with her," Harry almost shouted at me. "Give me the inside scoop," Harry demanded. "What did she say?"

He was so anxious he was not even letting me answer. His eyes were darting back and forth, as he tried to pry the answer from me, as well as keep an eye out for where Joyce may be on the ice. He was head over heels in love with this gal, but he was way too stubborn to admit it.

I thought how Harry must have been watching from the sideline and he had seen everything, but he was lying in the weeds, playing chicken and letting his best buddy Paul fend for himself. It was obvious that by wanting to chat like this, Harry was playing it cool, not wanting Joyce to perceive him to be overly anxious to hear what had transpired in the discussion between Joyce and me. Oh boy, more silly drama, and way too much subterfuge!

"Well, it is not really that good right now. I think you hurt her really badly. She doesn't even want to speak to you," I finally said, when I had the chance to get a word in edge wise.

Harry put his eyes down, as if he was a little ashamed and hurt, and then he looked back up and answered, "Yeah, yeah, yeah, what else?"

He overcame the feeling ashamed part rather quickly.

I then continued with my update. "I can tell that she misses you though. I can also tell you what is going on in about two weeks from now. See, I have this pledge card, Harry," I said while pulling out the receipt that Joyce had given me.

"What's that? What pledge card?" Harry asked as he ripped the paper from my hand and started to study it.

"Yeah, yeah, yeah, you see, Joyce is going to be raising dough for this charity. She is going to be participating in this big skating marathon up at the roller rink to raise jingle for the organization. You see, you pledge so much money per hour that the person you are sponsoring is able to skate." As I explained the situation to Harry, I too suddenly felt myself feeling the excitement of the event planned at the roller rink.

Harry was studying the paper, and he was reading it intently, when he then looked at me and said, "Wow, Joyce is going to be there?" He chuckled as he added, "She even got you to pledge a few bucks," as Harry knew well, my financial situation.

"Yeah, yeah, yeah," I answered. "I did it for you!"

Harry stood there on his skates and now turned back to face the ice. He had a huge smile on his face. He folded his arms across his chest and puffed it out a little; his confidence was returning. I knew that face, as it usually meant that his devious mind was working on some far-fetched, hair-brained idea that usually had me playing some kind of a support role in his latest scheme.

"I've got to do it too!" Harry shouted at me as his eyes grew wide with enthusiasm. I was not exactly following him; he had confused me when he proclaimed that he had to participate in the skate too.

"You have to do what? Pledge some dough, yeah, but you will need to find another person to sponsor, Joyce will not speak to you."

Harry cut me off, impatient that I had not read his mind. He waved his arms and hands at me in the air to signify that I was not following him.

"No, no, no, not just a pledge, but I have to skate too, so that I will run into Joyce on the rink and she will see how much I care about the charity as well. She will see what a nice, caring, person that I am, and want to get back with me!"

No wonder I was not following him, as I always was thinking more about the logical or realistic truth. Harry caring about charities did not quite rise to the top of my list. I grew skeptical; this seemed like a dumb idea.

"I don't know about that, Harry. Look at this card, this is a big deal, it starts Friday night at eight o'clock and does not finish until that Sunday at noontime. This looks like a major commitment to make, Harry."

I was always thinking about the details while Harry dove right in, not really thinking out all the facts and potential repercussions. Harry, on the other hand, had a strategy and his plan was to win back Joyce by hook or by crook.

"Oh, I do not care about all that stuff." Harry waved his hand at me, revealing the truth. "I will get a few pledges from my old man, my sisters, and your mom, and go around a few times, get close to Joyce and it will all be over. It will be a done deal, you see, she will love the fact that I cared too."

Oh boy, I thought. This seems as if it is already a horrible plan. I rolled my eyes a little and shifted uneasily on my skates. Harry was scheming to his maximum mode, in an effort to impress Joyce and win back her heart.

"Well, Harry, I don't know. It sounds kind of far-fetched to me, plus, I don't even know where you would even sign up for this thing."

Harry pulled the paper out of my hand and he studied it some more.

"Look, let's blow this joint, jump in the Sonicmobile, and head up to the roller rink. I bet one of the managers there can tell us what we need to do to sign up."

Harry was back to his old conniving self. He was excited now, and he had a plan. At this point, I knew that there really was no chance of changing his mind. When Harry had a scheme or a plan, I knew that it was generally not going to be fun, easy, or normal.

We skated off the ice, went back to the locker room, changed into our street shoes, and drove off to the roller rink. Deep down inside, I had a funny feeling about the event. On the surface, it seemed innocent enough, but I knew Harry really well, and I felt like this little pledge card was only the tip of the iceberg of what my best buddy was thinking about getting involved in.

I could not help but wonder where I could find some monks on top of a mountain somewhere that I could go hang around with, copy manuscripts, and chant together, until this was all over.

Chapter Four

Pledges, Pledges, Pledges, and More Pledges

We cruised up the highway to the roller rink and sure enough, a manager on duty there knew about the big event. In fact, there were even posters on the walls of the rink advertising about the fund-raiser. The manager was a young man in his mid-twenties with a heavy New Jersey accent. Based upon the information he was providing; it did indeed look like it was going to be the hot event of the entire summer.

"Oh, yes." The manager explained, while handing us a paper flyer, "This is going to be a big event for the charity and the roller rink. Youse guys need to sign up and commit to raising a lot of money for a really good mission to support." On and on he went until Harry grew impatient and interrupted him.

"Yeah, yeah, yeah, that's all good to raise money, but where do we get the sign-up sheet?"

The manager smiled, and we knew he was cool. "Oh, I see, you want to meet chicks, huh?"

Harry apparently did not want the manager to think he was an uncaring, women chaser, and Harry realized that he needed from here on in, to convince people that he sincerely cared about the charity, so he shifted gears and decided to practice on the manager.

"Nah, nah, nah, well, yeah, girls are always fun to hang with, but this charity thing seems like it is a really good cause." The manager was still smiling, and I doubted that he was buying too much of what Harry was selling.

"Well, this will be the place to be two weeks from now that is for sure." He said while handing us both these large packets of papers, forms, and stacks of pledge cards. Harry and I thanked the manager, and we took the packets and sat down in the refreshment lounge to study them.

"Are you going to do it too, Paul?" Harry asked.

"I do not think that I can. I have to work on Saturday until two in the afternoon, and my old man wanted me to do a bunch of stuff that weekend. I cannot skate in this event, but I will help you out. I promised a few bucks for Joyce, but if you want me to give you a little dough for this thing, then just let me know." Harry was only half listening to me as he was reading the paperwork.

"Nah, nah, nah, Paul, if you can help me out, that will be good. I might need you to drive me back and forth and bring me food or some kind of supplies. This event looks like I will really need you. If you can be free to go out and buy a hamburger if I get hungry, or maybe you have to drive me around, then that will work out well. You can be my support team, you know . . . like a bench coach," Harry said as he looked up at me and smiled.

He was obviously sympathetic to my poor monetary situation and felt that he just may need me for advice. Harry leaned on me for female relationship guidance that he generally listened to, and then completely ignored, but he did also acknowledge my reputation as a problem solver. I think he felt he needed me there for many reasons, as well as some logistical support. He may have also felt a pang or two of guilt because he also knew that I was privy to the real reason that he wanted to participate in the skate-a-thon.

Harry signed up with the manager, gave him all the information, and he was set to go. The manager explained how the pledge cards worked and Harry was on his way. Early that week, back in our old neighborhood, Harry was soon peddling the pledge cards door-to-door. He hit up his old man, his sisters, and his brother-in-law. Then he hit up the next-door neighbors, like the Porters, the Hinks, the Nit Nat kid's mom and dad, Harold Clipclock and all the others for pledges. Soon, he showed up on my doorstep selling his newfound love for this charity to my mom.

Harry came to the right place. My mother was always sympathetic to all kinds of charities. She always wanted to give money to save lost penguins in Antarctica, build Eskimo people new igloos, raise money to save habitats for the Long Eared, Speckled Wing, Zippy bird and all kinds of other causes. My old man, however, was the guardian for any kind of smooth talking, flim-flam artist, who came sniffing around for some of his hard-earned dough.

As Harry stood there in our kitchen explaining his new charitable interest, and how my parents could sponsor him for each hour that he skated, my old man cast a suspicious eye towards Harry. After all, he knew him since he was a little boy.

"Since when do you care about charities and long, lost causes there, Harry?" My dad asked. "What do you want me to do, sponsor you for jingle while you skate around the rink for hours, chasing the girls around looking at their backsides in tight pants?"

My old man always cut to the chase and was not one to mince words.

My mother hushed my dad up and told Harry how proud she was of him for wanting to help, while she was filling out the card. Mum was buying it all completely. I rolled my eyes and my old man waved his hand and went back to watching the New York Bugs baseball game on television.

Harry signed up my family, as well as many of the other unsuspecting neighborhood folks to sponsor him on his covert mission. He used his gift of gab and silken tongue to convince some of us that he was now a caring, helpful, young man, whose primary mission in life was supporting these charitable communities and worthwhile causes.

Harry was doing well, and he played the entire neighborhood like a fine violin. Harry arm-twisted my sister for a pledge, ambushing her at a soft moment on a Sunday morning, before she went off to church. My sister was three years older than I was, and she already had a full-time job at this point, so Harry signed her up rather easily by appealing to her income status. He also manipulated my grandfather, who Harry caught when Gramps was buying a six-pack of Big Boulder beer at the corner liquor store. He worked through the rest of the neighborhood like a buzz saw, obtaining pledges from Vince, who owned the corner gas station, Big Frankie, who owned Trio's Liquor Store, and Ozzie, who was the owner of the local transmission repair shop. He even hit up old Pete, at Pete's corner candy store, which was really a front for a mob bookie joint that ran a local number's racket.

Harry was unstoppable in his quest for pledges and no one was safe from his selling! Harry was able to tap into a huge amount of people that he knew through his work because most kids our age did not work at an important job such as Harry did. He was working at a large shop and he was able to obtain pledges from most of the guys that he worked with.

"Why are you getting so many pledges, Harry? I thought you did not really care about raising money for the charity," I asked Harry one day after work as he sorted through the cards at his kitchen table. There were huge stacks of them that he was organizing into piles.

"You just do not get it, Paul. That is why I have all the gals and you scramble for one date," Harry lectured me. "All this charity stuff is all well and good, but the more pledges I get, the more Joyce will see how wonderful and caring I am, and she will be back with me in a second. I am going to show up with all these pledges and Joyce will be amazed at how much I care."

I hate to say that my best buddy was pushing the envelope of flim-flam, and I am sure he did care a little about the charity, but for the most part, it was all part of his grand plan. One day he was down in the dumps at his huge mistake of double-timing Joyce. The next day, he was on top of the world with his mission to win her back.

Harry was amazing; he never stopped with his conniving and scheming, and remained all fired up about the skate-a-thon. Day after day, for a week and a half, all Harry did was to whip out and sell his pledge cards. He became a wild selling machine, continually spouting attributes of the charity from one corner of the neighborhood to the other. He studied every aspect of the charity and its operations. Harry even could name the officers of the charitable corporation, and their wives, children, and pet's names too!

"Ya have to know your product to sell it," Harry told me!

I must admit he was very innovative in his marketing plan.

Harry could sell ice to an Eskimo.

He set a trap outside the bingo hall one night and hit up the old folks coming out of the weekly bingo games at Saint Peter's church. He had some of the old folks sobbing their eyes out as he explained about the poor, downtrodden charity, down to their last nickel. The old folks were clamoring over one another to sign up. He must have signed up half the congregation in one shot. Even the head priest, Father Mark, signed up for a pledge. He went back to the roller rink to replenish his card supply three times during the week because he kept running out of supplies!

Harry now had stacks and stacks of pledge cards. I cannot even tell you how many he had, but it was turning into a major operation to keep track of all of them.

"Help me organize these, Paul. I need some kind of system now, to track them all."

Harry spread the pledge cards on his kitchen table and piled them up on the surface of the table in Harry's house. I suggested we organize them by the location of the persons who pledged them, such as the neighborhood, school, church, and his workplace and so on, until we actually had a good system. Each card also had a number, and we copied the numbers and each name onto an individual list in a logbook, so it would be easier to track for payment. I really was being useful, and this was turning into quite the operation.

"Wow, Harry, this is an amazing number of pledges! How on earth would you collect all this dough if you go around the rink for any significant amount of time?" I offered up the question now that I had a chance to see the scope of the pledges that Harry had collected.

"You worry too much. Stop being such an old lady." Harry said while shaking his head, "I am just going to go around a few times, and hook back up with Joyce. She will see what a great guy that I am and it will all be finished. Joyce will give up quickly once she sees my undying commitment to the charity and then how boring this event is going to be. She does not like to skate for a long time, you will see. We will end up over at the Greek joint for pizza on Saturday, since this thing will be such a bomb," Harry predicted.

"Harry, I don't know. That manager guy, told us this was going to be some kind of big shindig."

Harry laughed and said, "You think he is going to tell us what a big stinker it will be? Come on Paul, what do you expect him to say? Please—think about it—geez man! A skate-a-thon! We can handle this skate with our eyes closed, we are professional skaters." Harry was quite adamant now as he gave me a little punch in the arm. "What is there to worry about? You goaltenders always think way too much."

Harry was primed and ready, and he really thought he

had a foolproof plan to win Joyce back and not exert too much of an effort in the big skate-a-thon.

If you would like to, then call me a Doubting Thomas, but I was not so sure about this plan.

You should never underestimate the competitive nature of the young male teenage species. Your hormones are bouncing; you have fancy cars, fancy clothes, and all kinds of music and all these other things going on. We also in our minds, all thought that we were big hot shots. Of course, we really were not very hot, but old Harry sure was driven. We were both hockey players, in good shape, pretty confident and tough, so Harry's testimony that he knew this plan was going to work had his mind convinced.

I remained a little skeptical.

The big day finally came and the Friday night kickoff for the skate-a-thon was here. The skating began at eight o'clock sharp. This really was a marathon because the schedule plan was for the event to continue all the way until noontime on Sunday. I thought in my mind that I cannot imagine anyone ever really skating that long. Perhaps the rest of the time was for entertainment and fund raising for the charity. Harry was right; I was way over thinking this whole thing. The instructions were quite specific, and they told all skaters to be there about one hour and a half before the kickoff to receive instructions and other directions from the organizers.

Harry and I met after dinner and work at his house. We jumped in the Sonicmobile, and we were off. I held the box containing the pledges and my paperwork in my lap in the passenger seat and I was reading and checking the instruction sheet given to Harry for skaters.

Tonight, it was a super-charged and fired up version of Harry! Dressed in a fancy shirt and pants . . . he looked all snappy, with a fresh haircut and trim. I was not dressed very nicely at all; I did not think I had to. I wore an old, No Way tee shirt proclaiming my love for my favorite musical group, and an old pair of black canvas sneakers. I wore my hair long at the time, down past my shoulders, and I would tie it all up behind my head when I played hockey or was at work. I was not that concerned with my appearance. I guess I missed the memo on dressing up for the event, but then again, I was not out this evening to win my steady gal back.

Harry was in great spirits. He was blasting and rocking out on the latest, No Way recording all the way to the rink, and he kept encouraging me that this was going to be a great night. It was a perfect, early August night in northern New Jersey, one of those special, rare summer nights. When the air is clear, the nighttime sky is wide open, and it is like a window to Heaven. There had been very little humidity; it really had not been that hot during the day. Harry rolled the windows down on the car and we enjoyed the air on a glorious evening.

It seemed as if we had the entire world at our fingertips.

When we pulled into the parking lot in front of the rink, I knew that the manager of the rink had been correct when he told us that this was going to be the event of the summer. Even though the start of the skate-a-thon was still over an hour and a half away, the parking lot had filled to the brim and it overflowed with cars and people. Fancy cars were lined up as far as the eye could see, pretty girls were dressed in their best summer clothes and were wandering around, guys were all dressed out to the max, and folks were cooking hot dogs and hamburgers on grilles in the parking lot. Music was blasting from car speakers and everyone was partying like there was no tomorrow.

We rode around for a while looking for a parking space, with everyone looking at the car, and waving when they saw it was the two of us.

We heard a couple of murmurs through the crowd and overheard a few statements like, "There go those hockey players. I bet they are skating tonight."

We overheard conversations and many other references to our reputations as rough and tumble type guys. Harry was eating it all up. He actually was quite the celebrity, and in his fantastic set of wheels, he was really putting on the show.

"Harry, look at this place, this is unbelievable," I said.

"Yeah, yeah, yeah, it sure is crowded. Paul, please, now I do not want ya thinking about becoming consumed with the Old Lady Syndrome and getting all worried," he encouraged me. "I have this all under control. Do you see Joyce around yet?"

That, I knew, was going to be a tough task through this mass of humanity.

We parked the car, walked to the rink, and made our way through the crowd and into the front door. Harry showed his credentials and since he was a participant, he did not have to pay any entrance fee, but I had to cough up a few dollars for the admission. Luckily, it was a onetime fee, and I received a support token with the charity's logo, so I could come and go all weekend. That was not a concern; Harry said that he was only going around a few times. . ..

Walking into the rink was a scene that I will never forget. It was wall-to-wall people; in fact, it looked like the entire population of northern New Jersey had been crammed into the rink.

The rink was a large building and off to the right side as you walked into the front entrance, was the actual wooden roller rink area, which had a waist-high wall on one side and a large center wall in the middle that divided the oval. In the front of the rink was an entertainment booth, which was the usual position for the disc jockey, the rink announcer, and sometimes, a person playing a large pipe organ that sat within the confines of this area. On the left side, was a large grandstand seating area for persons to sit and watch over the low wall and observe the rink, a large snack bar and dining hall, and a large, all-purpose room, which could be rented for parties or large gatherings. It was a fabulous facility.

The large room had been set aside as a meeting room for this evening's event. Inside the room, the management was now ready to begin a briefing of the skaters who were participating in the actual skate. A roller-rink management official met us in the front lobby, and he instructed Harry to go over to the meeting room, where he will receive all the instructions that he will require, as well as hand in all of his pledge cards. He explained that the pledge cards would require checking by the event officials.

Harry walked over to the doorway to the meeting room and found a person guarding the entrance to the room. He explained to the person controlling this area that I was his assistant for the night. When they saw the box that I was carrying with the large number of cards inside, they quickly waved me in alongside Harry. In the meeting area, were many official looking persons with identification badges hanging around their necks. The titles stamped on the badges varied, but there were titles such as judge, entertainment, skate guard, and security. Some had the name of the charity or the name of a sponsor on the tags. Other person's badges displayed titles such as rink management, press, and local press. These were obviously all the people in charge of running the whole show.

Once more, I could not help but think that we had underestimated the sheer magnitude of the scope of this event, and we had not anticipated just how huge it really was going to be.

Once inside the room, I noticed that the room had many rows of folding chairs set up for general seating. We picked a row, sat down, and looked towards the front of the room, where there was a group of officials standing next to a small podium and a microphone.

Harry's head was on a swivel and all he was doing was

scanning the room while looking for Joyce.

"I do not see her. Do you see her, Paul?"

At the podium in the front of the room a large man in a suit and tie with a tag around his neck declaring his status as "Rink Management," walked up to the microphone, and he started to speak. Harry was talking so much about Joyce, looking around, and not paying attention that I had to tell him to be quiet, so I could hear what the man was saying.

"Shut your trap, Harry, this is important. He is going over the rules for the skating," I said, as I tried to convince Harry to be quiet and pay attention.

"Yeah, yeah, yeah, whatever," Harry said as he made it clear that he was just not that interested in the rules and regulations for the event. On and on, the people in charge of the event went, explaining the rules and regulations in the greatest of minor details. The original speaker and a bunch of other official guys, who were blabbing endlessly in the front of the room, seemed never to run out of rules to convey to us all.

The entire room just sat there, looking a bit confused and bewildered at all the explanations and procedures for the skaters.

As he read from a paper, one of the rink managers droned on endlessly, "Hand in your pledge cards, you will receive a number and a color tag according to your pledge amounts. You have to keep going around the rink in a continuous skate. If you stop for more than a five count, then you are considered stopped, and you will be disqualified. You have to keep your skates moving at all times or we will consider you to be no longer participating. You must go around the rink in the proper direction, you will get a ten-minute break after the first five hours, then after that if you are still roller-skating, you can take one, twenty-minute break, every odd hour, and one fifteen-minute break, to eat and go to the restroom, on the even hours."

The reader took a deep breath, and then to all of the listener's horror, he continued!

"The skate guards will watch on the rink floor and the judges have the final word as to a valid disqualification. You have to wear your number around your neck both front and back at all times, you cannot fall asleep, we have ten judges on duty, a team of paramedics, as well as ten skate guards at all times that will rotate out the entire weekend," and on and on he went.

My head was spinning, trying to absorb all the details. "Harry, this is serious stuff, listen to all these rules!" I said, as I leaned in close to him.

"Don't you worry about all that razz-a-ma-tazz will you, Paul? They are just a bunch of stuffy guys who are running the show." Harry continued, not to be worried in the least.

Just when it seemed like the officials had run out of rules and regulations, they started to speak about some more rules! The large man was still going on about rules. "If you are skating for more than ten hours, you will get one-half hour break on an odd hour to eat one meal."

"Ten hours, Harry!" I yelled in his ear.

"Oh, cut it out, will you? I am in great shape! I can skate for twenty hours. Ya need to stop worrying about what this big blowhard is saying. I am not going to go around that long," Harry answered me as he was getting annoyed at my concern, as well as at the man going on and on in front of the crowd.

While I kept paying attention to the rules and instructions, Harry couldn't care less, because he was anxious to start skating, find Joyce, and get his plan under way. I started to take notes on all the rules to make sure that I knew exactly what was going on.

When the man finally stopped speaking, and he asked if there were any questions, I raised my hand.

When Harry saw my hand reaching up into the air, he

immediately grabbed my arm and pulled it back down.

"Will you quit worrying," he said. "This is all a slam dunk for me! Please do not ask this bozo any questions so he goes on and on some more."

I agreed, "All right Harry, maybe I am taking this coaching role a little too serious," I stammered, lowered my arm, and shook my head to indicate that I had no questions. We all received instructions to line up in the front of the room, hand in our pledge cards, and receive a paper form, to read and to sign. Harry and I got in line and met with one of the officials who looked over Harry's paperwork. He then handed Harry the special form to read over and to sign if he agreed to the content. Harry took the pen, and he was just going to sign it, without even looking it over.

"Harry, did you at least read it over, before you go and sign it?" I asked.

"Nah, nah, nah, what can it say? I am just going to sign the thing and get this show on the road. Stop being an old lady and let me sign it, will ya." Harry barked at me. He signed the form, and handed it back to the official, as I handed the man the box containing the pledge cards.

"Holy smokes," the man said, whistling aloud, while thumbing through all the cards in our box. "You have a lot of pledge cards here," he said, looking up from the box and back to Harry. The man looked back up at Harry again with a funny look on his face.

"Yeah, yeah, yeah," Harry said while nodding his head. "I am really into this and I want to raise a lot of money for the charity."

Of course, I knew otherwise, but he sure fooled the man taking the pledge cards.

"Wait here, son. I have to get one of the special number tags for you." The man instructed Harry, started to walk away, and motioned for him to stand right where he was. We watched the man go over to a table full of other officials and he was showing the other men the box with all the pledges and pointing back to where we were standing. They all were alternating between looking in the box and back at us, and it seemed like they were having a major discussion.

"Man, oh, man, they talk a lot and make a big deal around here," Harry started complaining because he was growing impatient with the entire prelude to the event.

"Harry, look around. *This is* a big deal. There are a lot of people here. Can you imagine how hard this is to organize?" I preached to him in a vain effort to calm him down.

"Well, I just want to get the show on the road here and cut out all of this, mumbo jumbo." Just as Harry finished complaining, the man returned, along with two other officials from the front table area.

"Congratulations!" One of the men with a name tag that had the name of the charity around his neck bellowed out to Harry. He and the other men reached out and took turns shaking Harry's hand. This, of course, Harry was eating up, as he had suddenly become the center of attention. He lost his impatient frown and now was smiling broadly from ear-to-ear.

The other man who was from the rink management then explained, "Young man, you have achieved the gold level tag to wear during the skate-a-thon for reaching the highest category of pledges. There are only a handful of other skaters who have reached the same level here tonight." He handed Harry a gold-colored tag with a neck lanyard and a number on it, and motioned for Harry to place it over his head and wear it with the number displayed in front.

I then remembered that during the instruction session and opening discussion, the management had explained the color of the number tag that the skaters would be wearing during the event, indicating the pledge level that the individual had achieved. They had shown everyone a chart with the colors and ranges, and I remembered that the gold color was the highest level you could reach. To reach this level, you had to have received over two hundred pledges. Harry had reached the highest level by spreading his flim-flam sales pitch throughout the old neighborhood. He was amazing!

The rink manager went on to add, "While you skate you will be in the upper category of raising money for the charity. Fantastic job, son!" All the men shook their heads in agreement and stood around smiling.

"It is nice to see a young man who is so actively concerned about his communities' well-being and so involved with charities!" The man from the charity said enthusiastically.

Oh, brother, I thought . . . if they only really knew the truth. Harry then proceeded to lay it on thick about how concerned he was, and how his only commitment was to help the downtrodden, and on and on. He even told the one man there he was thinking of joining the Charity Mission's Corps!

As soon as the discussion finished, and the men stopped worshiping Harry, and had left the room, Harry turned back into his normal womanizing mode. He turned his attention back to looking for Joyce and he was back to spinning and turning frantically while scanning the crowd for her.

"Come on. It is time to ditch these old blowhards. Let's get over to the side of the rink and get ready to skate. She has to be here somewhere."

Harry elbowed me in the side and motioned for us to work our way through the crowd. It was time to head over to the side of the rink and get in position for the beginning of the skating.

Chapter Five

Skate-a-Thon!

The scene in the rink was now wild, and the crowd was growing larger by the moment. It was getting warm inside the rink as the air conditioning strained under the load of all the people inside. Once more, I felt that we had severely underestimated the magnitude of this event. While we stood on the side of the rink, waiting for the beginning of the skating, and we checked the crowd for Joyce, you could not help but to sense the excitement of the moment.

The head of the charity was standing in the entertainment booth in front of the rink, exaggerating the importance of the event and praising the charity. He was encouraging all the skaters to skate as long as they could, in order to raise as much money as they were able to for the cause. They showed on the projection screen over the rink, the obligatory short film video produced by the charity. It included all the heart-wrenching scenes of despair and flowery music, to tug at your heartstrings and wallet, and force you as you sobbed and bawled your eyeballs out, to hand over your last thin dime to the cause.

On and on they went, with speeches and backslapping, as the officials thanked each other and the rink management for this grand event. Even the owner of the roller rink showed up to receive some type of phony medal to wear on his jacket, awarded to him by the charity for his generous use of the rink. All the while, I could only think of how much dough he was making on the whole thing! All of this hubbub wore thin, and Harry was now beside himself with his impatience.

"Yeah, yeah, yeah, please can these guys now shut up and let's get out on the rink. How many more jerks can they thank? I think they must have run out of people here in New Jersey and went over to New York City to find some more guys to bring in here and tell everyone how wonderful they all are!" Harry was becoming loud and obnoxious and people around us were motioning for him to be quiet and listen. Harry did briefly stop talking when he saw that the local TV and radio news networks were here. The cameras were rolling in to cover the event, along with news crews and support staff to interview the people running the show.

All of a sudden, Harry thought that he might have a chance at being a celebrity and showing off even more.

"Hey look, Paul! Channel 17 from the city is here and the eyeball news team! I bet they will want to interview me since I have one of these gold tags!" Harry now perked up as he saw an opportunity for more self-promotion.

The news crews were snapping pictures, camera operators were dashing around filming the scene, and fancily dressed reporters were interviewing the very important people on the side of the rink. It was an exciting scene for sure.

Finally, the speeches thankfully ended, and the podium and the microphone handed over to the disc jockey for the evening. Another man who appeared to be a professional emcee joined the disc jockey in the booth. It appeared that between the two of them, they would now be in charge of the start of the big event.

We recognized the disc jockey as being the famous Disco Dan. He was the resident celebrity disc jockey at nearly all the ice and roller rinks and other venues in New Jersey. He was, in our circles, about as famous a celebrity as we ever got close enough to, in which we could say we actually knew him.

Disco Dan had a thick, black beard, with black hair teased up in a hairstyle that went almost to the ceiling, and he wore thick, soda bottle glasses with huge lenses that covered most of his face. His glasses were typical for the era; they also, in addition to the large lenses, had 1970s style, heavy black frames. He was, however, a fantastic disc jockey, with great musical knowledge, and a loud, booming, frantic voice. He was a master showman. The show was now about to begin, and Disco Dan was now turning it all up into high gear. The bright overhead lights of the rink dimmed down, and the multicolor entertainment mood lights turned on and began blinking off and on with the rhythm of the soft bass notes that Dan had thumping out of the rink's sound system. The charity promotion blabbermouths were finally ushered out of the booth and off the front stage.

Once they had left and were out of the booths, Dan started some music with a louder bass note at a low tempo that was thumping softly in the background. The disco balls started spinning around above the rink, and the crowd was working up into a frenzy. Flash bulbs from cameras went off all over the rink and the pace was now building to a cataclysmic anticipation of the kickoff.

The skaters were now all lining up along the entrance ramps to the wooden roller floor on the low wall and they were hugging each other. Friends and family along the side of the rink joined to acknowledge the skaters as they all wished each other good luck. Harry and I stood there on the side of the rink next to one another, and we were all in awe at the intensity of the moment.

"Well, it looks like it is time," Harry said to me and he reached down, opened up his skating bag, and pulled out his special skates. He popped off his sneakers, threw them in the bag, and pulled on his skates. I did not have fancy skates; whenever I skated. I just rented the house skates from the skate rental at the rink. Harry had more money than what I ever could dream of having at this stage of my life, and as a result, he had purchased custom built and fitted skates with super deluxe, high-speed, roller bearings and all kinds of comfort features. They were state-of-the art of course, and were a deep, black color trimmed with fancy blue pinstripes and laces.

"Here. Hold my bag, Paul," Harry said, and he handed over his skater's bag to me for safekeeping.

The emcee tapped the microphone, grabbed it, and let out a long loud, "Hellooooo and welcome to the skate-a-thon!" He was dressed in a black tuxedo, had a neatly trimmed beard, mustache, and long, slicked back, blonde hair tied into a ponytail behind his head.

"This is going to be the event of the summer as we raise money for this great cause! We have all kinds of music and entertainment by the famous Disco Dan. Our snack bar is open, the grandstands are full, and the dance floor, next to the rink, is rocking for folks who are not skating, but want to dance. We have it all, and we are almost ready to go!"

The crowd was all clapping and cheering now, and I looked down at my watch. It was just a few minutes to eight o'clock. We were down to the wire and still no sign of Joyce. I began to wonder if all of this effort was for nothing, and Joyce was not going to show after all. Well, at least, I would not have to pony up the money that I pledged to her for skating.

We watched as a large group of skaters jumped on the roller rink, and started to go around slowly, while carefully scanning the crowd, as they all were rolling along. They had portable, two-way radios on their belts and wore headset-type, earpieces, and jackets labeled, "skate guards" and "security." Four men climbed in high stools along the low sidewall where they could view the rink very easily. These four men all wore nametags, printed with the word "judge" in large block letters. This was a well-planned and serious event!

Clearly, there would be no tolerance or patience tonight for any cheaters, troublemakers, and folks looking to bend the rules.

"Where is she, Paul?" Harry was now clearly worried and upset as we looked frantically around the rink, and it looked like the start was just minutes away. In truth, the place was just one solid mass of humanity and looking for Joyce, or any other single person, seemed like an impossible task.

"You mean I went through all these shenanigans and she is not going to show?"

"I don't know, Harry," I answered, shaking my head. This was 1976, and there were no cell phones to use that you could quickly be able to call someone up. The line for the pay telephone was fifty-two-thousand miles long. Therefore, the idea of me running over there and calling Joyce up quickly, was out of the question. I was afraid we would just have to wait it out at this point and see if Joyce would show up. The emcee asked all the skaters to enter the rink. Slowly, what seemed like an endless line of the participants funneled through the ramps and made their way onto the roller floor.

"Keep an eye out for her, remember you are my coach, my right-hand man Paul, and I need you!" Harry yelled as he made his way to the rink, and I watched him step out onto the wooden floor.

The intensity was tremendous and Disco Dan was now playing the music louder. The lights were blinking furiously and the bass notes were thumping, and shaking the rink.

"You can count on me!" I yelled back to Harry. He gave me a little wave, and he disappeared into and amongst the hundreds of other skaters.

All eyes in the rink were on the emcee and he was now looking at his watch, while holding a blank-shooting starter pistol in the air over his head. He was counting down as if he was part of the rocket launch team. Disco Dan and his partner intentionally built up the drama and anticipation for a maximum of intensity to the atmosphere, and it now had worked the crowd into a frenzy. It actually was quite an amazing scene, and the drama was powerful.

"FIVE, FOUR, THREE, TWO, ONE!" He screamed in the microphone and fired off the pistol.

I watched as a solid mass of skaters slowly moved and rolled around the rink. It was ridiculous because it was so overly crowded with skaters; they could all just barely fit on the wooden floor. All a skater could do was barely shuffle their skates along, while you tried to find your speed and pattern and keep from falling down, or banging into a fellow skater right next to you. These first laps around the rink were really a test of survival and some strategic maneuvering of the skaters. It was elbow-to-elbow with skaters, jostling and moving in a slow roll as they worked and shuffled into position. I had never seen anything like it.

The nearest analogy that I can think of to describe this scene was that it was like the crowd filing out of the New York Bugs' baseball stadium, making their way to the exits, after a baseball game ends.

"BRRRING, DO DOODLE DO!"

The opening cords of the famous song, "Spin Around and About" by No Way, rang out over the speakers.

Disco Dan made every effort to impress the crowd, and he was going to start this skate off with a favorite song of all the skaters. The song, "Spin Around and About" was indeed self-explanatory in the meaning for folks who were endlessly propelling themselves around and around a wooden roller rink. It was the perfect song to start the skaters off on the charitable mission; well, all but one skater was on a charitable mission!

"BRRRING, DO DODDLE, DO."

No Way's guitarist played one of the most famous

opening guitar riffs in rock history over the rink's sound system. The famous guitar intro then ended and broke the song wide open, and the crowd went wild. What a scene, and what a night this was going to be!

Disco Dan and the emcee had successfully worked the crowd into wild madness, and kicked off the start of the event in an exciting and turbulent manner. The skate guards were on duty, working hard to keep the skaters in line and organized. All you needed, with this mass of humanity going around, was for one person to trip up and the skaters will fall like a wall of bricks. You would then have a domino effect, with hundreds of folks tumbling and falling over one another. So far, the first couple of rounds around the rink were slow but uneventful, and while there were a few stumbles, most everyone was staying upright.

The music was blasting, and the guitar was thumping along. The crowd had moved into the grandstands, along the wall and to other locations, as everyone began to choose an individual spot to watch the rink and the skaters. After that dramatic start and all the anticipation, the event had finally started and everything was now settling in.

I breathed a little sigh of relief and found an empty spot along the low wall to stand and begin my quest to scan the crowd to find Joyce.

Just as I started to daydream, and it all seemed like it was going to become a little calmer and normal, I was suddenly aware of someone waving at me from the rink and mouthing, "Hello Paul," over the noise and music to me.

Looking up, focusing in among the other skaters, and coming out of a fog, I realized that it was Joyce! She was coming around the corner and closing in on the low wall where I was, and she was trying hard to get my attention. I started to wave back when I noticed to my sheer and utter horror that she was with a guy!

Oh, no! She is with another guy!

The guy had her by the arm and they were skating together, hand-in-hand!

They were all smiles and happiness, as it seemed like they were the perfect little happy roller-skating couple. I, on the other hand, had to push my eyeballs back into my head, and play it straight as quickly as I could for the sake of my buddy, Harry. I could not let Joyce or her newfound beau; think that I was upset that she was here with a new boyfriend.

In all of my wildest dreams by far, this was the most horrible scenario that could ever have happened. Playing it cool, I shifted gears and gave a smile and a casual wave, as if there was really nothing going on.

Okay, here we go, ho hum, just another boring, typical evening at the roller rink skate-a-thon.

Boy, I sure was a crummy actor, I thought.

As soon as they safely passed, I slumped over in defeat and hung on the wall. How can I ever tell Harry what is going on? My mind was reeling in shock and my knees were knocking. As I stood there, thinking of all kinds of alternative scenarios, I noticed that the two of them were already coming around for another pass.

They must have had little rockets on their skates to make it around that quickly, or I was thinking a lot longer than I had realized. I waved feebly back to Joyce and her escort, and made a very poor attempt to smile back as she rolled up closer to me this time around. It even became worse when I saw that her date for the night was very handsome. In fact, it looked like he belonged on the cover of a movie star magazine. He had long, flowing, golden hair, he was all dressed out in fancy clothes, and he had expensive skates on, similar to the type that Harry wore. This fancy guy was like a perfect male model to escort his woman around the rink.

As the fancy guy circled in and past me, my eyes almost popped out of my head when I saw that he also had the gold number tag hanging around his neck!

He is a big shot, charity fundraiser guy too! This was almost unimaginable. I could hardly believe how after all of this that Harry's devious plan was going south really, quick.

How could this happen to us? All of these unimaginable, unexpected scenarios are playing out right before my eyes. I could not even dream up something like this. It was like a soap opera coming to life.

I always prided myself on being a problem solver. Hanging around Harry all of these years sure helped to force me into that role. I stood, thought, and decided to face the facts as I stood there on the sideline.

Calm down, Paul, and think. This is not so bad; I tried hard to convince myself. Let's see what the plan should be. A plan, based upon only the clear facts. Hmmm, Joyce is here, but she has a new, fancy boyfriend. Harry worked as hard as he could to impress Joyce, and went out and got fifty million pledges, new fancy skates, smooth-talked half of northern New Jersey, and he thought he had a foolproof plan in place. The new, fancy boyfriend looks like a Hollywood movie star; he has fifty million pledges and new skates too! He also had Joyce hanging on his arm and Harry did not!

Therefore, Harry's intricate plan to win back Joyce's love is suddenly under a major attack. I sighed and faced the fact that we were doomed.

I recovered from my fruitless planning and now; I started to scan the rink for Harry. Perhaps the best plan, I thought, would be to catch Harry, and tell him of the situation, before he ran into Joyce himself. I was trying to ease the blow of the situation and divert a potential catastrophe where Harry confronted the fancy guy and started to pummel him into submission right in the middle of the rink.

I spotted Harry in and among a million other skaters

and motioned wildly for him to come over to the wall to speak with me. Sensing that my frantic motions indicated that it was Joyce-related, he held up a finger to indicate to me that he needed some time to find a hole in the skaters to work his way over to me.

Now, to make it from the inside of the roller rink edge where Harry was skating, to the low wall along the outside, was very similar to trying to work your way from the hammer lane on the New Jersey Turnpike, all the way over to the right side to take exit 16W, after the big football game gets out. It was no easy task, even for an expert skater like Harry, as he worked and weaved his way through the crowd to try to work close to the low wall where I was standing.

On the next pass, Harry worked his way close; all the while, the judges were keeping a very discerning eye on this evolving situation where a skater might potentially stop along the wall to engage in a conversation. The judges, skate guards, and security, were watching like hawks for anyone who stopped skating for more than a half second and was no longer skating, so they could disqualify them from the event! I think the power and fancy jackets had gone to their heads! Once money gets involved in things, then all kinds of things get crazy.

The skaters had only been going around for about ten minutes, and already, there were some disqualifications of a few daydreamers as well as a handful of rule violators. The disqualified contestants went away shocked and disappointed when they learned they could no longer skate in the event. When one or two folks tumbled down and stayed down on the rink for too long, the very intense team of hyperactive guards and judges also immediately disqualified them. I guess those skaters did not listen as closely as I did to the rules and regulations.

Harry worked his way over to the low wall and I managed to catch up to him. I moved along the wall, going around people who were hanging out there, watching the skating. I also carefully moved around the judges sitting on their thrones next to the wall while they were keeping a close watch for rule violators.

The first thing I said to Harry, as I ran alongside him was, "Please do not stop, keep moving, keep skating."

The judges and skate guards circled in, ready to blow their whistles to signal a disqualification, while intently watching Harry and his skates to make sure they did not stop for even a second.

"These detective guys take this seriously. Ya think these jokers would be on our side!" Harry frowned and complained, while he cast an evil eye at the guard focused on his feet and skates.

"I tried to tell you that, but you would not listen." I answered, running alongside him as he cruised down the wall.

"Yeah, yeah, yeah. Forget those ding-dongs. Cut to the chase man, what do you have for me? Is she here?"

"She is here, Harry. But I know she has not seen you yet and you have not seen her . . . that is for sure." I answered him as quickly as I could as he glided in along the low wall. All the time, I am very aware of the fact that I am running out of wall space alongside the rink. Suddenly, I am out of the wall. Harry cannot stop, and we have run out of real estate.

Harry frantically waved back for me to meet him up at the other end of the wall when he returned for the next pass around the rink. After two or three of these comical passes, where I kept running alongside the wall, and asking people to excuse me to talk to Harry, all I have managed to convey to him were short, incomplete conversations.

All the time the hovering, annoying, skate guards were sadistically drooling to catch the famous show-off Harry, not skating and disqualify him. I still had not been able to bring myself to tell Harry the whole truth about Joyce and her new fancy boyfriend.

On about the fourth pass, people sitting and leaning along the wall, were now really becoming annoyed, as I asked them, please to move once again.

"Do you really have to talk with this guy every time he comes by?" An angry man yelled at me as I chugged along one more time trying to talk with Harry.

"I am very sorry sir, this will be the last time, I promise," I said as the man picked his hot dog and soda off the wall one more time and moved away for me to converse with Harry.

Harry swooped in close to the wall with the skate guards in tow and he was clearly annoyed. "Come on, man, tell me where the hell she is! Look, we only have ten feet more of the friggin' wall left!"

I looked up and saw that we were once again running out of the wall and the turn was coming up. I figured that now was as good a time as any to tell him about the horrible situation. Therefore, I just laid it all out there as fast as I possibly could.

"Harry, yes, Joyce is here. She is skating with another guy, and the guy is really big and handsome with fancy skates like yours, and you will not believe it, but he has a gold-colored number tag too!"

The turn was coming up . . . and boom! I ran into the end wall.

Harry flipped his cork.

"WHAT? I HAVE BEEN REPLACED! HOW THE HELL DID THIS HAPPEN? WHAT THE HELL IS THIS BULLSHIT?" Harry was screaming obscenities and yelling, and his arms were waving up over his head.

I watched as he made the turn and sped up, disappearing among all the masses of other skaters who were all joyfully rolling along raising money for their favorite charity in the entire world. I put my head down and rested for a few seconds.

I was sweating terribly from running up and down the wall, and I wished that we had never gotten involved with this completely crazy scheme. It seemed that for once in his life, someone had snookered the world-famous Harry and that Joyce had pulled the rug out from under him. I only hoped that on the other side of the high center wall of the rink, in the area that I could not see, Harry had not found the fancy guy, and that he was not, pummeling him into a little wreckage of a human being. In an effort to calm the perturbed crowd, I reassured all the folks along the wall that I was finished interrupting them, thanked them for cooperating, and retreated to a spot along the edge of the wall to hide and see what the next move for Harry would be.

This role of being a bench coach to Harry, and his revolving door of emotions, and women, sure was a difficult job.

Chapter Six

Let the Competition Begin!

This scene was entirely too stressful for me, so I retreated to the low wall, and worked my way to the far end to blend in and stay away from any further controversy. I just stood there watching as the skaters went around and around endlessly. The music was blasting and thumping, and Disco Dan was in fine form. He effortlessly had moved from rock-and-roll, to disco, and even to a little rhythm and blues sound, and he appealed to the masses like the expert musicologist that he was.

Just as I had settled in, and was very content to just stand there and try to enjoy the event, along the low wall came Joyce and the fancy guy, skating close to where I was standing. She had spotted me and she was closing in while waving at me to come closer to the wall. I moved up a bit, but there was no way I would tempt fate and interfere with any more spectators who settled in along the wall.

Joyce must have made the connection, which was that I was not here just to watch her skate and support her efforts because she yelled to me, "I cannot stop skating, but I need to ask you something!"

"Believe me, I know the drill!" I answered, not wanting to revisit that adventure.

"Is Harry here?" Joyce asked.

"Yes, Harry is here. He is actually out there somewhere skating!" I yelled as Joyce and the fancy guy made the turn and faded back into the rink. The fancy guy looked at me. He scowled a little, and Joyce got a little smile on her face.

Ah, ha, I thought . . . a little spark rekindled! Suddenly, a faint glimmer of hope appeared on what had been, until now, an otherwise bleak and sad love horizon.

This was really turning into an interesting event. One hour went by, and then two hours went by, and slowly a few skaters dropped out by the wayside. The casual skaters, who only had committed to skating for a few hours to raise a little money, were now packing it in for the night, and the rink surface had started to open up. At around eleven o'clock, there was now a little freer skating room out there and the rink surface no longer looked like Paterson Square on New Year's Eve. I could see Harry moving around now very easily, as well as Joyce and the fancy guy. I had a chance to move over to the low wall as many of the spectators had now left, and I caught Harry for a conversation.

"How much longer are you going to go around, Harry?" I asked, remembering that he had originally told me he would go around for a few hours, impress Joyce, and it would be all over. Besides, I had to go to work in the morning, and it was already past eleven. I rode with Harry; therefore, I did not have a vehicle of my own to get home in.

"How much longer? Are you kidding me?" Harry screamed back at me while skating slowly. "I cannot quit as long as this guy is moving in on my woman and he is still out here going around! He is not only working hard here to beat me for Joyce's heart, but he is also skating to beat me out here on the rink!"

I realized that Harry was correct, and he now became locked into a serious competition in more ways than one. It was now Harry versus the fancy guy, and I knew Harry well enough to know that he was going to dig in hard, and do his absolute best to bring it on as hard as he could. I hoped the fancy guy knew whom he was dealing with here.

Harry passed by and rolled by me with a little more speed. As he rolled by, he shared that Joyce had waved to him and they had spoken. He relayed that Joyce was thrilled that he was there, raising the money for the charity. She asked how he was, and she was very nice to him. Harry, of course, played it like it was all about the charity and he was very much committed to the "cause."

Joyce had him right where she wanted him at this point. It was obvious that his spirits had improved considerably as he realized that he did have a chance here for redemption. Joyce had very slickly manipulated the entire situation into a very intriguing competition between the two guys.

It was now past midnight, and the rink, as well as the grandstands had emptied out big time, as the event started to turn towards the hard-core skaters and fundraisers who remained out there, rather than an entertainment event. A lot of the excitement of the grand start of the event had now faded away, and Disco Dan had toned the music down into more relaxing music selections, allowing the skaters a chance to relax and conserve energy.

Harry now had more room to maneuver out there and he now turned on his big moves. Like the pure showman that he was, he danced, spun around, whirled, twirled his way around the rink, and attracted "oohs" and "aahhhs" from the crowd, as they admired his performance. This was the moment he had waited for, as he now was putting on a show and far outclassing the fancy guy! The fancy guy was a solid skater, but there was no way he could keep up with the moves and strength of Harry.

Harry danced on one skate, he flipped around backwards with his hands on his hips, he sang aloud to the music, and he expertly wove between the other skaters, while the crowd marveled at his amazing skating abilities!

Harry's confidence was building now, and as he passed by the wall, he told me, "I have this fancy guy right where I want him now. This is a piece of cake, Paul. I can easily take this guy out, and I just need to keep skating. There is no way that he can keep up with me! Look at him, he is struggling, and sucking air already. What a wimp!"

Since I was actually the bench coach, I then thought about it and kicked into my role. I told Harry to keep it cool. Even though I knew Harry was in tiptop shape, I emphasized that the fancy guy may be pacing himself. My hockey training and experience had kicked in, and I knew that you should never underestimate your opponent.

Harry needed to preserve his energy, just in case the fancy guy managed to hang in there. Harry shrugged it off, and he dismissed him as being inferior in his physical ability as well as his endurance. I was not so sure. We had underestimated many things so far, and I was not about to dismiss the fancy guy just yet. My concern was also growing as it was really getting late for a young man who had to be at work the next day.

Since I had paid attention to the rules and regulations, I knew the first twenty-minute break was coming up at one in the morning. I was looking forward to having a real conversation with Harry as opposed to our running alongside and over the wall discussions that we had been having.

Sure enough, at a few minutes before one o'clock, the emcee approached the podium and explained that the first break was coming up.

"I will shoot off the gun and all the skaters . . . please, make your way to the rink exit ramps. The judges will check off your numbers as you leave the rink and we can all take a twenty-minute break. Please pay attention, because you need to be back on the rink surface and ready to skate when the twenty minutes are up, but I will give you a five-minute warning, so you can all get in position. If you are late getting back out on the rink, then you will be disqualified, but please remember that you have all done a fantastic job and you have skated for five straight hours already!"

Oh, my, they never relax around here! More serious rules and regulations! He counted down and shot off his gun much in the same way that he had when he started the event.

I met Harry at the ramp and gave him a pat on the back for a job well done. Harry was fresh, and all fired up with enthusiasm. He headed for a restroom break, and I waited for him to return. Harry came over to me and sat down on the grandstand seat. I could tell he was ready for a serious conversation.

"Look, Paul, I know. I told you that I was just going to go around for a little bit and win back Joyce, and we could split. But, as you can see, this fancy guy has changed the rules of the game. You should see the evil eye he gives me out there, and the way he grabs Joyce's backside when he knows that I am looking. He buries his hand in her backside and squeezes it on purpose . . . right in front of me! This guy is not giving up yet, so I am in it for the long haul. I have to hang in there, as long as he is skating. You know, I have to hang in there for me to impress Joyce. I refuse to let him win . . . just because it is getting a little late."

I was listening intently to Harry now because I knew that he was indeed correct in his assessment of the situation. He could not give in now.

"I know you understand. What is the latest you can hang in here?"

I would do anything to help Harry, so I said, "Look, I understand. I know that I need to get some sleep before work, but I will hang in here as long as I can, or maybe, I can hitch a ride with someone else. I think it is way too late for any buses and my old man would kill me if I called him to ask for a ride."

Harry stood up and stretched his legs a little while,

telling me, "Yeah, yeah, yeah, don't call your old man. Look, if you really need to leave, just wave me over to the low wall, and I will give you the keys to the Sonicmobile, and you can get out of here."

Wow, the keys to the Sonicmobile! It was indeed the first time that Harry ever suggested that I would be able to drive the Sonicmobile!

"Really, Harry, you would do that for me, but how will you get home when you stop skating?"

"I am not quitting, Paul!" Harry nearly blasted me off my seat when he heard the mere suggestion of quitting.

"I understand, but you really cannot imagine that you can hang in there all night into the morning, Harry. Or can you?"

Harry sat down next to me, and he grew quiet for a minute or two. He wiped his face with the towel from his bag and looked at me.

"That's all changed now, as long as he is out there, Paul. I can always call my sister or my old man, and they will come by and pick me up. After work, we can meet back up. Park the Sonicmobile in front of my house and stick the keys through the mail slot on the front door. You can walk home. It is only a few blocks."

It was a good plan. I stood up just as the emcee gave a five-minute warning call over the sound system. Harry also stood up, and we both nodded in agreement at our plan.

I gave Harry a hard handshake and said, "It sounds like a plan, Harry. I know you will take this guy out."

Harry headed back out to the rink, and he got into position for the restart signal. I stood next to the low wall to watch.

Just then, I realized that Joyce was standing along the wall, a short distance away from me. She had her skates off, she was back in her street shoes, and it seemed like she was finished for the night. I have to admit one of my first thoughts was that my wallet was relieved that she had stopped skating!

I then turned my attention back to the situation at hand. My eyes scanned the rink and sure enough, there was the fancy guy going around! He was not quitting, and Joyce was waving and blowing kisses to him over the wall while he waved back. To be honest, the exuberant, over the top, public display of affection was a little too much to handle. He had a gleam in his eye, and I could tell that the fancy guy was digging down deep to compete with Harry to win Joyce's love, as well as out-last him on the rink.

Joyce came over to me, and said with a little coy smile, and a slight bit of doubt in her voice, "I see that Harry is back out there and he is continuing to skate."

Time to defend the home net there, Paul.

"Sure, he is, Joyce. Harry is in fantastic shape, and he wants to raise a lot of money for this charity," I answered, while exuding a positive spin and defending my buddy, when I knew that Joyce was already wise to the real reason that all of this was going on.

Joyce smiled as she clearly enjoyed being the center of all of this competition. "Well, John, you did notice John, didn't you, Paul?"

I nodded while trying hard to show that I was not impressed.

"John is really, really, into this, and *he too* is going to raise a lot of money for the charity and the cause."

It was a plot, and Joyce had pitted the two young men against each other, in a lock out, drag out, competition to win her heart. Joyce wished me a goodnight and explained that she had to go to work at nine in the morning today and that her mother was picking her up. I bid her good evening and settled into the grandstand.

I then focused on working hard to stay awake.

Disco Dan had packed it all in for the night, as well as the emcee, and a rink manager now assumed the rink announcement duties.

The music shifted over to soft, canned, generic recorded music, and every once in a while, a canned promotional announcement for the charity would play. The number of skaters remaining reduced to a little less than half of the original crowd. The judges shifted out, as well as the skate guards and the security persons. It was really getting a little bit boring watching them all go around endlessly. I hung in there until the next restroom break. The breaks now became more frequent, and I explained to Harry that I just had to get out of the rink.

We shook hands, and I patted him on the back. "Don't worry Harry, hang in there, you are going to beat him."

"Oh, I know that," Harry said confidently. "Here are the keys to the Sonicmobile, Paul. I really appreciate all of your help. Give me a call when you get out of work, and we will see what our plans will be for the night."

I took the keys and watched as he headed back out to the rink and the skating mission restarted once more.

I walked out into the moist, cool night and it felt good to get some fresh air. Starting the Sonicmobile's engine, I watched as all the fantastic array of gauges on the dashboard came to life. The big needle on the tachometer bounced as the big engine roared.

I sighed a little. The excitement of driving this finely tuned machine now became dampened, as I could not help but think how tonight had changed around so dramatically.

I wondered how long it would be until Harry and the fancy guy packed it in.

Chapter Seven

It Becomes Serious

I drove home, and I parked the Sonicmobile directly in front of Harry's house and dropped the keys into the door slot. By the time I got home and climbed into bed; it seemed like I was asleep for ten minutes before the alarm was going off for me to get out of bed and head to work. I was tired at work, but since I only had to work until two in the afternoon, I just muddled through the best that I could. Thankfully, it had turned out to be a very good workday, and all of our jobs went smooth. I actually had forgotten about Harry and the skate-a-thon, until I looked at the clock and saw that it was close to quitting time.

My curiosity had now peaked, and I now wondered how it all had turned out. I left off work at two o'clock and drove home, took a shower and grabbed a bite to eat. My mother asked about Harry, I explained about last night, and how he had decided to continue. Not wanting to burst my mother's bubble as to the real motives of Harry, I omitted the part about Joyce and her newly found suitor.

My mother was concerned, and all she said was that she hoped he was not overdoing it, and that he knew when to quit. I said that he would be fine, but now I really needed to check and see how it all turned out. I grabbed the telephone and dialed up Harry's number. I was confident that Harry would answer and give me the details of how he had easily beaten John, and it was all over.

Instead, I was quite surprised when Harry's father answered the telephone.

"Mr. Redmond, hey this is, Paul . . . is Harry around?"

"No, Paul, he is not. Harry is still over at the roller rink. He called early this morning and explained that he is still skating around for the charity."

Mr. Redmond had no previous inclination into the real reason that Harry was there, so I just played it cool and kept my mouth shut.

I was shocked, and the best I could manage to say was, "Wow, I thought he would have been done by now."

"Yes, Paul. It was my hope that he would be done quickly too." Mr. Redmond explained, "I have a feeling that this thing is going to cost us all a fortune!"

I did not want to tell my old man that fact.

I thanked Mr. Redmond and told him that I would head over to the rink and check on Harry. Mr. Redmond asked me to call when I could and keep him posted, which I promised I would do, and we hung up. I told my mother about the situation, and she seemed a little more concerned than she was before, and advised me that I had better go check on my friend. I jumped in my van and headed for the roller rink.

As I rode over towards the rink, I could not help but think about how this had all changed from the original mission. It was amazing to think that Harry would still be skating at this point.

I arrived at the rink, parked my van, and ran into the front door. The scene inside the rink was like something from the old Twilight World television show. All the excitement, all the spectators, and all the noise and activity of the previous night was gone. There was some of that soft organ, roller rink, type music playing over the sound system and it was really, really quiet.

Skaters rolled around slowly, most of them skating silently alone, their heads down, some of them barely even moving along. I scanned the rink surface quickly for Harry or John, but I did not see them right away. After a quick gaze around the roller rink, I guessed that there might have been about a hundred or so people still skating around. It was very hard to tell the numbers; however, I could tell that it sure was a lot less than when I left at three in the morning. I glanced at the clock over the rink and saw that it was just about five in the afternoon.

I then spotted Harry, as he appeared from behind the center wall and he looked pretty good. He was moving a little faster than I had expected him to be moving for a guy that had been skating for over twenty hours.

Sure enough, a few strides behind him, followed John, both of them locked into mortal combat now, still going head-to-head! John was moving along, but he did not look as fresh or as alert as Harry did. Nonetheless, he was still hanging in there. I could not help but think I was right, that this was not going to be as easy as what Harry had originally thought.

Harry spotted me. He smiled, waved, and gave me an enthusiastic thumb up signal. I waved back and took a seat in the grandstand to watch and wait for the next break.

The break came, and Harry slowly made his way up to where I sat in the stands.

"Hey, Harry," I said as I patted him on the back.

He sat next to me and sighed. In one of the great understatements of a situation that I had ever experienced, Harry piped up and proclaimed, "This is turning out to be a little rougher than I thought it would be, Paul. This guy will not quit. I am getting a little tired here, but I cannot quit. It is beyond that now. I am in it way too deep now and he is still out there. Did you bring the Sonicmobile?" Harry grabbed his towel back out of his equipment bag and wiped his face down. He looked a little worse for the wear, but overall, I was impressed that he actually was still functioning at all.

"No, I brought my van. I really was surprised that you are still skating, to be honest with you," I answered, while handing Harry some water from his little bag of supplies.

Harry took a long drink and nodded as he swallowed the water.

"He is fading. I can tell he is hurting and his feet are killing him. The bad news is they will be starting all of this all back up again and they will be bringing back Disco Dan and all that razz-a-ma-tazz!"

"Oh, geez. Harry, this is getting serious now. It is a good thing that you are in good shape, or you would be hurting, just like John is right now."

Harry mumbled back at me and conveyed something about freshening up his water for him for the next break. I nodded my head as we heard the announcement for the skaters to gather back out on the rink, and he waved and made his way back out to start rolling around once more. His determination was admirable and his competitive juices had diminished, but they still were flowing.

After refilling his water bottle with fresh water and some ice, I sat there watching and wondering, and to be very honest, I was finding it hard to stay awake myself after working all day and not really sleeping very much either. It was pretty boring with only the occasional commercial promotion for the charity, breaking the pattern of the death dirge, organ music and the skaters rolling around.

An hour or two later, the lull of the late afternoon started to break. I noticed some more activity in the entertainment booth, and I spotted Disco Dan and the same emcee from last night, setting up to begin the evening's festivities.

It all seemed to be starting back up, as it did for the first night kick off, with the local news channel bringing in equipment and the camera crews and reporters filtering in. The spectators were now increasing in numbers; it looked like the rink was filling up with more event managers and general admission persons. Disco Dan was back on the air, the emcee guy was back on the microphone, the music was back to the loud, exciting, dance and rock mix, and before you knew it, it was once more, a full-blown party atmosphere.

The only difference was that the number of skaters who were remaining was only a minuscule amount from the original group, which had initially flooded the roller rink at the start.

The television and radio crews would conduct interviews with the skaters during the breaks, and Harry maneuvered to try to get close to being on the air, but the crew did not select Harry for an interview. The charity folks would take over the microphone on occasion, and one of them mentioned that Harry and John, as well as one or two other remaining skaters, were gold-pledge skaters.

The crowd and the speaker acknowledged the outstanding efforts that they were making by continuing to skate, with a loud round of applause and some cheers. The television crews would zoom in on the skaters going around the rink, so I knew Harry must have been on the air in some way, shape, or form, even if it was from a distance.

I used the pay phone to call Mr. Redmond and my parents, and told them to watch the evening news so they could see if Harry was on. This was big stuff for sure, and it was getting exciting.

Harry's sisters Linda and Patty came by, as well as Jeff and his girlfriend stopped to wish Harry good luck, and to cheer him on. It was some sight to see, these gutsy skaters still managing to tread on, despite the hours and the toll it was taking on each of them.

Sure enough, around eight at night, along wandered Joyce. I spotted her standing alongside the low wall, smiling from ear-to-ear, waving to John, and cheering him on. On a break, she hugged John and gave him a little kiss; it was all just more ammo to send Harry into a frenzy and wind him up even more. Harry was now working as hard as he possibly could. You could see that he was sweating heavily at this point; he was tired as well as really nervous. He was no longer that neat, trimmed up, cool guy. Harry was a mess.

Harry was reaching down deep into the pits of his stomach for the strength and courage to keep skating. The things that men would do to recapture the love of a young woman were really a great lesson for me to learn.

"How are you holding up physically, Harry?" I asked him on one of the breaks.

"I am all right, but I am sick of the food here. Can you please run out and get me a burger, some black coffee, or something different? I just need . . . something."

I understood and headed out to buy him some food, which he ate on his next break. I brought him some water, a burger, some tangerines, and a banana for energy and nutrition, and some black coffee. I could tell that even the big, strong Harry was now wearing down, and he was starting to hurt as badly as the others did. The food seemed to perk him up a little bit, and he managed to skate a few dances and some tricks here and there, but for the most part, he conserved his energy, and stuck to a more conservative type of roller-skating.

There was no question that this was now inflicting a heavy toll on poor Harry and many of the other skaters. Disco Dan seemed to sense this, and he kept it in a lower key than he had the night before. He sensed the worn-out condition of the skaters now, and Disco Dan knew they did not need to expend any more energy than necessary.

The clock ticked towards eleven o'clock at night, and the atmosphere throughout the rink turned very serious, as Harry and a significantly reduced number of skaters continued to roll along. You could sense the shift of the mood, the change in the energy levels from an entertainment event, to what the main purpose actually was. . ..

On a break, I checked on Harry, and although he was

now suffering, he remained steadfast.

"What are you going to do, Harry? People in our neighborhood are starting to take second mortgages on their homes, in order to pay off your pledges."

He shook his head, and he remained stubborn. There was not one ounce of quitting in his heart.

"As long as this jerk is out there, I am not going to pack it in. I am going to fight for my gal."

I understood that it was now too serious for either of these combatants to give in; it was way beyond that right now. We were now down to about fifty or so skaters, and you could tell that most of them were serious athletes, all conditioned to maintain such a grueling test of stamina.

Joyce came over by me, and she praised John and his efforts, and dropped hints at how impressed she was that Harry was still out there. She also seemed to know that Harry was fighting for her, and I sensed a change in her demeanor toward Harry. Joyce had realized that he knew he had hurt her badly and was working as hard as he could to win her back. I knew right then and there that she still cared very deeply for Harry. This was going to be some interesting situation as to how it was all going to turn out.

Disco Dan and the emcee packed it all in again around one in the morning. The announcing and operation of the skating now switched back over to the rink manager. He played the quiet, canned music, just as he had on the opening night. All the spectators that remained seemed to be family members and friends, and only the hard-core folks were now hanging in there.

Tonight, was now a lot more tense and serious, as the atmosphere had shifted from a party to a profound appreciation of the tremendous commitment these skaters were making in an effort to raise money for the charity. Skaters were dropping often now, and when they did, a team of representatives from the charity, families, rink managers, friends, and occasional news reporters greeted and congratulated them warmly for their fabulous efforts.

They gave the skaters who quit now small ribbons and medals for the extra efforts. Some even required medical treatments, for the pain and suffering that skating for over thirty hours straight inflicted upon a body.

One man's feet swelled up so badly that they had to cut the skates off him. This was some serious stuff going on, as you could see the efforts put forth, not to recapture the heart of a teenage gal, but to raise money for the cause. These remaining skaters believed in the hope that the charity extended to the people who needed it so badly.

It was becoming heart wrenching to see these ordinary people putting forth superhuman efforts like this, and it brought tears to your eyes. I was hanging in there, watching my best buddy, for lack of any other description—suffering big time to keep going around. I could see that John was now in some serious pain. Joyce had gone home after giving John a hug and a big kiss, and she actually came over, thanked Harry, and wished him luck too.

That was a huge boost to his spirits, and he remained steadfast in his resolve to hang tough. It was now about two in the morning and I was exhausted, but I was determined to hang in there and support my best friend.

On the next break, I preached my case to Harry.

"You can quit, Harry. Look what you have accomplished. Joyce is really impressed. I know she cares more for you than she does for John. I just know she does, it is all going to be all right, Harry."

Harry would not budge, though, and I encouraged him as best I could.

He was one stubborn, tough guy. In fact, he was a lot tougher than I could ever have imagined.

"I have to get some shut eye, but please, if you quit, just call my house. I will tell my old man to answer the telephone at any hour and we will come and get you."

"Thanks Paul, but I am not quitting!" Harry rolled his way back out there. He was being held up now by sheer guts and determination. I shook my head and sighed because I now was genuinely concerned for his health and well-being.

The judges had not let up on the rules one bit though, and Harry was back out there rolling around when they called for the break to be over.

I was just going to leave when I heard a small cry from the crowd and I turned to the rink to see what had happened.

John . . . had gone down!

He hit the wooden surface of the rink hard. He rolled around and he was staying down, and not getting up. Skate guards and security ran to assist him, and he looked as if he was in bad shape.

Harry rushed over to him, and although Harry could not stop, he offered his support. Harry shouted encouragement out in his direction and patted him on the back as he passed by. The rink team carried John off to a standing ovation of the remaining folks and the waiting team of paramedics. The rink announcer made a very nice announcement praising his efforts as a gold-pledge skater.

Even though he was the enemy, I clapped and cheered too, as he had been a worthy opponent and his efforts were truly remarkable.

Harry had won! He had beaten John!

It was quite the moment, and I held a tremendous amount of admiration for what John had accomplished for skating over thirty hours. Harry and the remaining skaters cheered and clapped too, in sincere appreciation of John's efforts.

It was an amazing scene!

John had been a tough opponent, and I now hoped that all of this could end, and we could all finally go home.

Chapter Eight

What It Was Really All About

I did not leave after John dropped out, but I went back to wait for the next break to speak with Harry. When it came, he slowly climbed up into the grandstands and sat next to me. He lay back on the seats; he let out a long sigh, and I could see how this was taking an incredible toll on him.

"It is over, Harry. You beat him, you won, let's pack this all in, and get the hell outta here."

I put my arm around him and he slowly sat up and said, "Yeah, yeah, yeah, I won, I beat him. He was a lot tougher than I thought. You were right, Paul, when you said that we should not underestimate him. He was quite a guy." Harry was sitting there exhausted, covered in sweat, and he was thinking about it all.

"Come on. Let's go, Harry," I said. I started to tug at his arm now as he sat there, in order to lead him away from the rink and to coax him into leaving.

Harry very slowly stood up; you could see the pain he was now feeling from the way that he held his body as he tried his best to stand upright. He tugged at his back, flexed it, and then looked at me.

"No, Paul, it is a lot more than that now. These people from the charity, well, they need the money. I have come this far, so I am going to finish this. I cannot let them down. It is not about Joyce or John, or anything else any longer. It is very different. It is about being a man and doing the right thing."

Harry looked at me intently.

"Don't you see, Paul? When we started this skating mission, there were tons of people out here. You could not even move out on the rink."

I nodded my head in acknowledgement and respect for the skaters who had started the mission. Harry continued flexing his back and he continued to speak in a serious tone.

"Now, it is just a handful of skaters who are left, and that includes me! We are all that is left of all those piles of people from the start. It is up to us now, to carry the torch for those hundreds of skaters who also believed, but have had to quit. They had to quit, because they physically could not do what the last few of us who remain, have been able to do. They did not quit because they did not believe in the cause or the hope that they had to make people's lives better . . . they quit . . . only because they just could not skate any longer."

Harry was standing up looking at me, and his eyes were weary, but intense.

"God gave me the ability to hold up here under this challenge and still skate, unlike the others, who do not have my abilities. I now know and believe in helping and doing what is right to make a difference in people's lives. Those of us who are still skating need to continue on, as long as we physically can, it is up to us now."

Harry sat back down, and he was wiping the sweat off his head and brow with a towel. He looked down at his skates, and then back up at me, and he started to speak very quietly.

"You know, I haven't always treated people with respect, and I have been a little selfish at times. Life is not always about running around being a hotshot, having a good time at the expense of others. I was thinking, after I saw John go down, and I knew that I could quit, of that saying your old man told us years ago, when we were having that bacon and eggs breakfast together."

I laughed and answered, "The one where he taught us the difference between the chicken and the pig as it refers to bacon and eggs."

"Yeah, yeah, yeah, remember your old man taught us that the chicken made a contribution to your breakfast, but the pig made a commitment."

Harry stood back up and continued.

"I have to make a stand and grow up sooner or later, and I think now is as good a time as any, to make a commitment and stand for something in my life, other than just having good times. I need to finish this, Paul. I need to finish it for all those people that need me to finish it. For once in my life, I need to do something for others and not just for myself."

I understood, and I did not know if he was speaking of changing his ways, or if he was speaking of helping the charity, but either way, I understood. I now wished I had signed up to skate too, as it was really about so much more than winning back a young woman's love.

Right there, it turned for Harry. He had become a serious man, who was now fighting for a cause and meaning in his life. It was no longer about fancy skates, having a lot of money, impressing young women, or fancy cars and loud music.

It was about a cause and a purpose.

Remarkably, it had all come back around to be all about the true cause, which was the charity.

He looked back at me and smiled. He had that look in his eye.

I had seen that look when we were on the hockey rink, after I had made a big save to hold the lead for our team in a close game. He would come by and tap my goal pads, and I knew that he was going to go all out, and do whatever it would take to join me in preserving the win.

He had that same look right now. The eye of the tiger.

Defeat for Harry M. Redmond Jr. was just not an option now.

I hugged him and the rink manager called out for the weary skaters to head back to the rink. Some skaters were receiving first aid, some had ice packs on their knees and legs, and they provided the skaters with as much respite as they possibly could give to them. It was about as serious as it could be for these remaining skaters who chose to go back out and continue.

As Harry made his way back, I called out to him. "I will be back as soon as I can. Call me if you need me!"

Harry waved back, and I watched as he rolled his way back out onto the rink. I would guess there to be only about twenty skaters left, they were a sad, worn out bunch. It was almost four thirty in the morning and it had long gone past the point of being brutal.

I left the rink at five o'clock and drove home, all the time during the ride, I was thinking of what Harry had said; about this being about so much more than just a ploy to win back his true love's heart. My old man met me at the front door, and when I told him that Harry was continuing to skate, he was amazed.

"Dad, he is still going around! He will not quit. It is almost as if he needs to do this to make up for things that he has done that were not right or good. It is amazing."

My father shook his head. "I saw it on the television and we saw Harry, he did not look so good, it must be beyond the point of being rough. You better call his old man."

Despite the hour, I did dial the Redmond's home. Mr. Redmond answered, and I gave him the run-down of what was going on. He thanked me, and reported that if he was still skating at daybreak, then the entire family was planning to meet up at the rink to cheer him on. Right now, everyone was just trying to get some sleep. I felt I needed to share a little of the background of what actually started this, and I gave him the condensed version of the entire story.

"Wow! Now, it is not about Joyce, but it really is about the charity," Mr. Redmond said, amazed at the situation. I told him not to worry; Harry was a tough hockey player who was in prime, physical shape, and that alone, along with his courage, was keeping him going. I promised him that I would sleep a little and get back there as soon as I could, and we hung up.

I went to bed and tried hard to fall asleep. In my heart, I did not think there was any way that Harry could physically keep going. I was exhausted from the weekend, and my lack of sleep, and I had not even skated! I fully expected the phone to ring or that I would find Harry asleep on the grandstands when I returned to the rink.

The call never came, at least to our telephone it never came.

Sleep did not come very easily, and I was up by eight in the morning. I ate quickly and called Mr. Redmond to see if they had heard from Harry since we last had spoken.

Mr. Redmond told me that he had not heard a word, so I promised to call them as soon as I made it to the rink. My parents also were concerned, and I told them I would give them an update as soon as I arrived at the rink. My heart was pounding and thoughts raced through my mind as I jumped in the van and drove as fast as I could out to the roller rink.

When I arrived, the first thing I noticed was that there were only a handful of cars left in the parking lot. It really looked abandoned, or to be honest, like they closed the roller rink.

I ran to the front door, fully convinced that I was going to find my best buddy sound asleep somewhere. When I walked in the front entrance and walked over to the low wall, it was like one of those scenes that you play in your mind a million times over and over as long as you live. I looked out on the rink and scanned the surface for skaters.

There was some very low organ music playing and two skate guards going around very slowly. I was confused as to why there were skate guards, but there were no skaters that I could see, so I turned and began to look for Harry in the stands.

Suddenly, by the center dividing wall, I saw two skaters just barely moving along, but still skating!

Two skaters, only two skaters!

One was a middle-aged man, just barely moving . . . almost like a dead man skating on his feet. The other skater I could not pick up yet, as I had only caught a quick glimpse of him before they went behind the wall.

Around the corner, the other skater emerged, and sure enough, it was Harry! He was still going around! He looked like death warmed over, and he was a mere shadow of himself, just rolling and then gliding whenever he could. He spotted me, forced a smile, and waved. I waved back, and the emotions were overwhelming. I began to get teary eyed at the sight of my best buddy out there and the incredible sacrifice that he was putting forth. The emotions overwhelmed me and I just started to clap aloud and cheer. I could not help it, but it was all that I could think of to do, just stand there and clap my hands in respect of these two remarkable men and the superhuman effort that they were putting forth.

The small remaining crowd of persons in the rink heard me clapping and saw the tears rolling down my cheeks. When they realized what was happening, they all stopped in their tracks and joined me in clapping, until the entire rink filled with clapping and cheers for the remaining two skaters.

I called the Redmond's house and my parents and gave them the amazing report that Harry was still skating. They all told me that they were on the way over to the rink as fast as they could arrive there. I went back to the grandstand, found a seat, and just watched as these two men fought all the odds and continued on their mission.

When the break came, I ran and joined Harry and shook his hand and told him how proud of him that I was. He was in about as bad a shape as any person that I had ever seen who was not in an intensive care unit in the hospital! Harry forced a smile. But the pain was obvious at this point, and he could not hide it anymore.

"Man, Paul . . . geez, this is brutal! I had no idea how rough this was going to be." We barely had any time to speak, and it was already time to get back out there. Off the two remaining men went to continue this brutal torture for a cause. As the end of the skate-a-thon grew closer, the crowd started to grow within the rink. I think that the organizers of the event were shocked that they still had two skaters going around the rink almost forty hours later. It seemed like no one had really ever imagined in his or her wildest dreams that someone could actually hang in there that long.

They seemed to have had only speeches and promotional activities planned in order to pat each other on the back for the wrap up of the event. Hastily, they now had to reorganize the schedule to focus on these two remaining warriors out on the rink.

The reporters and news crews came back, all the so-called important folks were back, and the reporters were providing play-by-play of this marvelous story of the two remaining skaters.

The other skater who was out there with Harry was not a high pledge guy, but he was still going around.

He was suffering big time.

On a break, the reporters grabbed Harry and the other man and they interviewed them quickly, but out of respect for their conditions, they let them go rather fast. I made sure that the reporters understood that they needed water and the restrooms, and they understood the situation.

The crowd was now building and Harry's family and

my parents arrived to cheer Harry on. I was standing there next to my folks when I saw Joyce come rushing in. She saw me and immediately ran up next to me.

"I saw it on the television! I had to come as quickly as I could. I cannot believe that he is still out there!"

She gave me a hug, a kiss on the cheek, she thanked me, and then greeted the Redmond family and my parents. We then all turned our attention to cheering on the two skaters. I was afraid to ask Joyce how John was. All I could think of was that he was lying in a hospital bed somewhere!

As the final time and turns approached, the crowd was working into madness, cheering, and urging Harry and his skating partner to continue to trudge on. It was like the last few seconds of a football game, as the crowd erupted into cheers and loud screams whenever the skaters glided by the front of the grandstand. The other skater was hurting badly, and Harry was doing all he could to prop him up and encourage him on. It was looking bad, like the other guy was going to collapse and not make it.

The rink emcee had returned for the grand finale and he was working the crowd and cheering the skaters on over the sound system.

What a scene it was! The skate guards placed a special ribbon across a finish line as the emcee counted down the time and the last lap.

Harry grabbed his skating buddy, and they held their arms up together as they crossed the line in unison, breaking the ribbon at the same time! It was a heart-wrenching scene, and people were cheering and flooding the rink to congratulate the skaters.

Now, there were film crews rolling, and the reporters were reporting, "live from the scene," while the entire scene turned into madness! The flash bulbs were going off right and left. Paramedics rushed out onto the rink to grab Harry and the other man, who had collapsed in a heap of weariness and emotions shortly after breaking the ribbon. I made my way onto the rink to find Harry and pushed through the crowd that was now rushing onto the rink surface.

I watched as Harry gently picked his fallen comrade off the wooden surface, turned him, and steadied him on his weary legs.

Harry looked at him and asked, "What is your name? Please tell me your name!" The older man looked back at Harry and smiled as best he could.

He barely managed to answer. "Ryan, my name, is Douglas Ryan. You?"

Harry smiled at him, picked up his hand, and gently shook it.

"Nice to meet you, Douglas Ryan, I am Harry M. Redmond Jr."

"God bless you, Harry M. Redmond Jr., you were the inspiration I needed to keep going. My wife died from this disease, which we are supporting. I had to do this for her. Thank you."

The two men embraced, with tears rolling down each of their cheeks. Mr. Ryan could not stand. The medics brought a stretcher out and took Mr. Ryan off, as Harry wished him well. Harry then skated over to us. Reporters, the charity sponsors, the rink managers, and all kinds of other people, who were shoving microphones in his face and taking pictures, were rushing over and surrounding him.

The Redmond family and my parents followed my lead as we dove into the fray and when we reached him, we all congratulated him, and we all hugged him together. He was like the war hero returning home from battle.

Then it happened as we all watched Joyce run over and grab Harry. They embraced and kissed as the many cameras rolled and tears rolled down her cheeks.

Joyce and Harry reunited, and all was well once more.

Harry was pumping his fists and arms in the air and

shouting out, "We did it! We did it!"

It was an unbelievable scene.

We carried Harry over onto a bench, and the medics brought a bucket of ice, and started to check him out. We pulled off his skates, and his feet ballooned up as if they had air inflated into them. We plunked them down into the ice bucket to try to take the swelling down. Reporters crammed around all of us. They were asking questions, and rudely sticking microphones in Harry's face, while I tried hard to keep them away. Finally, they heeded the warning when the medics, my old man, and I pushed the reporters away, and the medics stuck an intravenous flow in Harry's arm to pump him up with some fluids.

To add to the excitement, the emcee was in the entertainment booth reporting about the extraordinary amount of money raised by the event, and the charity folks were once more standing up on the stage and speaking from the podium, thanking everyone.

I cannot remember how much money that Harry individually had raised, but it was a huge amount. Despite how poor our neighborhood was, no one complained when it was time actually to donate the money either!

Joyce was hanging on him, hugging him, and she could not stop crying. Harry sat there with the drip in his arm, and his swollen feet in the ice bucket surrounded by his family, friends, and girlfriend.

He looked awful. He had not shaved in days. His eyes were sunken deep in his head, and I am sure he had lost a few pounds.

He looked up at me and extended his hand out and I took it.

He said, "You know, it got to a point where it was so much more than what we had originally set out to do, Paul." Joyce knew, of course, what his initial goal was; she just smiled at him and studied his face.

"I know, Harry. I know. It became the same for

everyone."

It had started out to be a self-centered mission for a completely different purpose, but it turned out to be an amazing effort that brought joy, memories, hope, and happiness to many other people.

I could not tell you how proud of my best friend that I was on that day. The pride in knowing what he had accomplished was almost beyond comprehension. He was a hero in my eyes as well as many other folks on that day so long ago.

No matter what Harry chose to do in the future, or which path of life he was going to follow, he could always look back on this event and weekend and say that he stood for a cause. That in any person's life is something that is very real and something to be proud of forever. If each one of us could say that about our own lives, then this world would really be such a better place.

Joyce and Harry stayed an item for many years before they finally drifted apart for a reason that I could not really remember. Harry was like the man that the singer was singing about as, "His gal got lost along the way."

We would go on in our lives together to have many more adventures involving young women and lost loves, but those stories I am better off leaving for another set of words down the road, maybe, to tell someday in the future.

Nevertheless, this story was really about how an ordinary teenager became a man over a weekend. For the love of a gal and through his own guts, courage, and determination, he contributed so much to so many people. He made a difference in people's lives, provided a ray of hope for those that needed it and worked for a cause, which he felt was just and right.

You do not hear about these types of fundraisers anymore, or for that matter, simple places that provided entertainment like roller rinks. All have seemed to have faded away from our landscape altogether.

The good times, wholesome fun, exercise, and memories that they brought to us make this hard for me to understand why they would not be popular anymore.

Perhaps it is old fashioned and considered humdrum in today's modern world. Indeed, for us, and a whole load of other folks who were at that rink over that summer weekend, it provided good times and treasured memories, in which we forever etched in our minds.

I think that was part of the magic of this era of the 1970s. It was a time when simple things and events provided joy, and they did not cost a lot of money, or were very complicated.

Oftentimes in our lives, it is the simple things that mean so very much.

Sometimes when my doorbell rings, and a little girl asks me to buy some cookies, or I throw a dollar in the pot of the bell ringer at Christmas, I cannot help but remember that weekend so long ago, and the pain that was suffered and the effort that my best friend extended for a cause that he believed in.

I am then reminded how there are folks that for whatever reason, turn from ordinary people into heroes. They choose to make commitments to make other people's lives better.

I think when it is all said and done that is what it is really all about.

THE END

Epilogue

If you take the time in your life to sit and think about all you have done, where you have been, whom you knew, and where it is all going, then you will be amazed at your own adventures.

You see, I believe that simple adventures in life are the best ones to experience. The quiet times, the funny times, the adventurous times, the wonderful people you meet or speak with over the years of your life . . . all contribute to make you the person whom you actually are.

Life is not always going to be funny or easy, in fact, the majority of the time it will not be. However, the adventures of your own life can be just the same as the adventures of Harry and Paul. You can change the names, and fill in your own names in place of Harry and Paul, maybe change the settings or the time, but everyone can experience the same things such as simple joy, hope, and life to the fullest. You just need to look around with open eyes and a joyful heart.

The best part is that you do not have to spend a bank account full of money to do it!

I make myself a promise every day, always to remember and thank in my heart all the people who have added joy, hope, and happiness to my life.

It makes each day better. It really does.

I also know that in the world of Harry and Paul, there will be another adventure right around the corner. There always will be, you see Harry and Paul adventures never really end. The years may pass, but they go on forever, as long as there are memories, dreams to dream, fun-loving people who enjoy life and care for one another in special ways, stories to tell, roads to travel, music to hear, dances to dance, and love to give.

They go on and on until the end of all time.

ABOUT THE AUTHOR

If you ask Paul John Hausleben, he will tell you that he is not an author, he is just a storyteller. His mission is to continue to write and tell stories to warm your heart, make you laugh, and sometimes make you cry, just a little. Most of all, he deals in memories, and helps you to remember the good times of your own life, and the special people who touched you along the way. Paul was born and raised in Paterson, and then nearby Haledon, New Jersey, and began writing at an early age. He revisited a writing career later in his life, and he now is the author of a number of novels, compilations, short stories and audio and video works. Most of his work, touches upon nostalgic remembrances of simpler times, and tells the stories of heartfelt, humorous, and special human relationships. Other than writing, among many careers both paid and unpaid, he is a former semi-professional hockey goaltender, a music fan and music reviewer, an avid sports fan, photographer and amateur radio operator. He now resides in Somewhere, U.S.A., but his heart always remains along Belmont Avenue in good old Paterson, and Haledon, New Jersey.

Titles by the same author that you also may enjoy

The Night Always Comes, Another story from the Adventures of Harry and Paul.

Reunion, A sequel to the Night Always Comes and Another story from the Adventures of Harry and Paul

The Autumn Collection

The Christmas Tree and Other Christmas Stories. Tales for a Christmas Evening

The Miracle Tree, Another story from the Adventures of Harry and Paul

Heaven's Gain

As well as many others

Coming soon?

You may contact us via email at ctte27@gmail.com

www.ingramcontent.com/pod-product-compliance
Lightning Source LLC
LaVergne TN
LVHW020711110826
845149LV00012B/2210

9780988633605